Sarah Mallory grew up in the West Country, England, telling stories. She moved to Yorkshire ith her young family, but after nearly thirty years .iving in a farmhouse on the Pennines she has ᴜw moved to live by the sea in Scotland. Sarah is an award-winning novelist, with more than twenty books published by Mills & Boon Historical. She ¹oves to hear from readers, and you can reach her ia her website at: sarahmallory.com.

Also by Sarah Mallory

His Countess for a Week
The Mysterious Miss Fairchild
Cinderella and the Scarred Viscount
The Duke's Family for Christmas
The Night She Met the Duke
The Major and the Scandalous Widow

Lairds of Ardvarrick miniseries

Forbidden to the Highland Laird
Rescued by Her Highland Soldier
The Laird's Runaway Wife

Discover more at millsandboon.co.uk.

SNOWBOUND WITH THE BROODING LORD

Sarah Mallory

MILLS & BOON

First published in Great Britain 2023
by Mills & Boon, an imprint of HarperCollins*Publishers* Ltd,
1 London Bridge Street, London, SE1 9GF

www.harpercollins.co.uk

HarperCollins*Publishers*, Macken House, 39/40 Mayor Street Upper, Dublin 1, D01 C9W8, Ireland

Snowbound with the Brooding Lord © 2023 Sarah Mallory

ISBN: 978-0-263-30546-3

11/23

To my family, for a wonderfully memorable year!

Chapter One

London, June 1810

It had been the most wonderful June day. Sabrina had visited the tea gardens with her friends, admiring the beautiful flowers and being admired in return by numerous gentlemen. And now she was going to Almack's! This was not her first visit, but tonight the little fizz of excitement was stronger than ever. In the family house on Russell Square she sat down at her dressing table, but it was very difficult to keep still while Jane put the final touches to her hair. She was fixing rosebuds amongst the curls, their orange blush perfectly matching her new muslin gown.

'Sabrina. Sabrina, are you ready yet?'

Mama swept into the bedroom in a cloud of raspberry gauze and cream silk. 'The carriage will be here any moment, my love, you must hurry.'

'I am nearly ready, Mama.' Sabrina smiled and met

her mother's eyes in the looking glass while her maid tweaked the final few curls into place.

'There, I have done, Lady Kydd.' Jane stepped back and regarded her charge with a satisfied smile.

Sabrina jumped up and gave a little twirl. 'Well, Mama, will I do?'

'Yes indeed, love, you look beautiful.'

'Thank you!'

Sabrina blushed, grateful for the compliment, although privately, she considered her fair hair and green eyes a trifle insipid. She would much prefer to be a dark-eyed beauty, like her friend Helen, who was now betrothed to the eldest son of the Earl of Tarleton.

'I know dark, curling hair is by far more fashionable,' remarked Mama, as if reading her mind, 'but you have a good figure and pleasing manners and you must make the most of yourself, if we are to find you a husband.'

Sabrina protested, laughing. 'Surely there is plenty of time for *that*.'

'Perhaps, but Papa's funds will not stretch to another season such as this, my love.'

Mama was looking troubled and Sabrina could not bear that.

'We do not *need* another season!' she said, running across to hug her mother. 'Much as I enjoy all the balls and routs, we managed very well in London last year without them. We had friends and parties enough, did we not?'

'Yes, of course.' Mama brightened and patted her cheek. 'And I am sure we shall do equally well next year. Quickly now, Sabrina, we must say goodnight to Papa before we leave.'

Obediently, Sabrina followed her mother downstairs to the little study, where they found Sir Anthony working at his desk. He looked up as they came in and removed his spectacles as he smiled at them.

'Well, well. My two lovely ladies. And both in new gowns, I see.'

'Oh, tush, sir, would you have us go out in rags?' exclaimed Mama. 'What do you think of your daughter? Is she not beautiful?'

Papa got up from his chair and came across to Sabrina. He took her hands and fell silent as he studied her for a moment.

'Exquisite,' he said at last, a faint tremor in his voice. 'I have never seen you looking better, my love. I am sure the young men will be falling over themselves to dance with you tonight.'

She squeezed his fingers. 'I wish you were coming with us, Papa.'

'Bless you, child, but Almack's is not a place for me, much as I love to watch you dance. I have work to do here, but I shall wait up for you, and you can tell me all about it when you return.'

She stretched up to kiss his cheek before skipping out to the waiting carriage. Her spirits were already buzzing with anticipation at the evening ahead. She knew Almack's was known as the Marriage Mart and she was aware that Mama had strained every sinew to obtain vouchers to enter those hallowed halls for the sole purpose of finding a suitable husband for her only daughter.

Thankfully, her previous visits had been a success. There was no shortage of partners and Sabrina had taken great pleasure in standing up with every one of them. It was no hardship, because she loved to dance, but as she followed her mother into the ballroom, this time she found herself hoping to see one man in particular.

There were several fair-haired gentlemen present, but not one of them was the Adonis she was looking for. The charming, handsome, eligible bachelor, who was notorious for breaking hearts. They were all either too tall or too short, too old or too young to be him; too narrow shouldered or pot-bellied. She was disappointed, but it would not do to show it. A stammering young gentleman came up to beg for the pleasure of standing up with her and Sabrina accepted with her sunniest smile.

* * *

Then he was there. It was nearing eleven o'clock and as Sabrina's partner escorted her off the floor she spotted his tall, athletic figure standing beside Mama.

She could not stop her happiness bursting out into a smile.

'Sabrina, my dear, here is Lord John Callater come to dance with you,' declared Mama as she came up to them. She sounded triumphant, because she, too, knew that Lord John rarely came to Almack's.

'Miss Kydd.' He bowed over her hand with exquisite grace.

'My lord.'

He held out his arm to her, and she placed her fingers upon the woollen sleeve, a little shiver of pleasure running through her when she felt the strong muscle beneath fine material.

'You came,' she murmured as he led her away to join the set that was forming.

'You wanted me to come and I said I would do so. I am not one to let down a friend.'

'*Are* we friends, Lord John?' she asked, peeping up at him.

'I'd like to think so.' Those blue eyes glinted down at her. 'And is it not time you called me Jack, as my other friends do?'

She knew she must not beam back at him and yet,

inside, her heart was singing. It continued to sing louder with every glance, every touch of the hands. She had never felt like this before.

The two country dances were all too short, but afterwards he begged to be allowed to take her into supper.

'Such as it is,' he remarked, eyeing the thinly sliced bread and plain cake through his quizzing glass.

Sabrina chuckled but she said primly, 'One does not come here for the refreshments, my lord.'

'True.' He looked around him. 'I wish we could forego the supper and find a quiet corner where we could talk, but that would give rise to all sorts of gossip and speculation.'

Sabrina nodded. She was well aware of Lord John Callater's reputation as a charming flirt. Mama had warned her of it after their first meeting, a few weeks earlier, but so far his behaviour towards her had been exemplary. He had not singled her out by any word or gesture; anyone watching would think them nothing but friendly acquaintances, but Sabrina felt sure it was so much more than that. It was not merely her fancy. She heard it in the tone of his voice, read it in his glinting smile. She felt a connection whenever he was near. It warmed her, made her feel…cherished, although she was afraid to hope it meant anything more than friendship.

Lord John Callater might cause her to lie awake at night reliving their all too brief encounters; he might haunt her dreams, but she knew better than to think it might mean anything more serious to such a worldly-wise gentleman.

When their meagre supper was finished, they went back to the ballroom, where Sabrina spotted her next partner standing beside Mama. She pointed this out to Lord John, who nodded.

'I will take you over to them.'

She was strangely dissatisfied with this answer. She would have liked him to whisk her away in the opposite direction. She wanted him to carry her off to some secluded corner where they might flirt outrageously. A little thrill ran through her. He might even kiss her…

'Tell me,' he said suddenly, breaking into her thoughts, 'Will you be at home tomorrow?'

'Why, yes.'

'And your father?'

She laughed, puzzled. 'I believe so.'

They had reached Mama now and stopped. Lord John took her hand and bowed over it.

'Until tomorrow then.' His wicked smile flashed. He whispered, 'Sabrina Fair.'

And with that he was gone.

Questions buzzed around in Sabrina's head for the

rest of the evening. What could it mean? Why did he ask if Papa would be at home? Surely…she felt suddenly dizzy with the thought of it…surely that could only mean one thing. Lord John Callater was going to propose.

Sabrina danced and laughed her way through the final hours at Almack's, then rode home to Russell Square in a rosy haze, reliving every moment she had spent with Lord John. Jack. An extra glow of happiness ran through her at the thought of calling him that.

When they reached the house, she wanted to slip off to her room, to climb into bed and go over it all again, but her mother said that Papa would be waiting for them. They went to the drawing room, where they found her father sitting by the hearth, an empty brandy glass at his elbow. He was staring into the fire and Sabrina skipped across and dropped a light kiss on his head.

'We have had the most wonderful evening!' she exclaimed, sitting down onto the footstool beside him. 'Oh, Papa, if only you had been there to see for yourself!'

It was as if he had not heard her. He looked over her head at Mama, his eyes staring out from a face suddenly grown pale and haggard. Lady Kydd gave a little cry of dismay.

'Oh, my dear sir, what is it, are you ill?'

Sabrina took his hands in her own. 'What is it, Papa, what has happened?'

He looked down at her then, such anguish in his eyes that her blood ran cold.

'Sabrina.' His voice cracked. 'Oh, my dear child. We are ruined.'

Chapter Two

London, October 1816

By the time Lord John Callater arrived at Tarleton House, the Masquerade Ball was well underway. He nodded at two gentlemen who were just leaving, exchanged a smile with a lady he passed on the stairs and paused for a word with his host before strolling into the ballroom. A waltz was in progress and he stood for a moment, raising his quizzing glass to survey the colourful scene.

Unmasking would be at twelve. But for now everyone wore either a full mask or at the very least a strip of satin across their eyes, as he did. A few black dominoes were in evidence, but most of the guests had chosen to come in costume, and any number of Harlequins, sailors and chimney sweepers were dancing with shepherdesses, Roman ladies or orange sellers. There was even Queen Elizabeth trying to dance in an ungainly farthingale...

'Jack!'

The familiar voice caused him to turn. An imposing Roman emperor was approaching, accompanied by a tall lady shrouded in Egyptian robes. Jack grinned.

'Hail Caesar!' He turned to the lady and raised her hand to his lips. 'Good evening, Pru. Or should I say Cleopatra? How did you manage to persuade Garrick to dress up?'

The Duchess of Hartland tucked her hand into his arm and turned to smile at her husband. 'Oh, he is much less curmudgeonly, these days, Jack.'

'Married life must agree with him then!'

'Damned insolence!' Garrick scowled, but the effect was marred somewhat by the twinkle in his green eyes. 'You, I see, have come as Byron's Corsair.'

'I made an effort,' Jack replied mildly.

'I did not expect to see you here,' remarked Pru. 'I thought you were visiting friends in the north.'

'I was, but I arrived in town yesterday. There is some business that I need to discuss with my lawyers. Concerning my Norfolk estate.'

'Lingwood Priory?'

'That's it. I need to make some adjustments to the tenancy agreements, lowering rents and deferring payments for those who are struggling the most.'

Garrick nodded. 'Aye, there's a deal of unrest in the country about the high cost of everything at the moment.'

'I know it! Many of my people are concerned I will turn them out if they cannot afford to pay. And it is not just the farmers. With the price of everything going up so much, the rest of my tenants are worried, too. I have assured them no one will be evicted unless there is good cause. I can stand the loss, for now at least.'

'We are doing the same,' replied Garrick. 'But dissent is growing. Cobbett is at work again with his pamphlets and newspapers, stirring up trouble. Not so much at Hartland, but certainly here in town there are clear signs of discontent.'

'One cannot blame the poorer people,' reasoned Pru. 'Low wages and high prices…it is a terrible position for them.' She sighed, then shook off her melancholy thoughts and smiled at Jack. 'But this is dismal talk for an evening such as this! Tell me how you fared at the Doncaster races.'

'He did very well, I hear,' remarked the Duke.

'Yes, I did. There was a promising filly called the Duchess. After being groomsman at your wedding, how could I do anything but put a wager on her?' He grinned at Pru. 'You are my lucky charm.'

He kissed her cheek, which caused the Duke to growl impatiently.

'Enough of this flummery! You are too dashed charming by half, sirrah!'

'Jealous, Garr?' Jack murmured.

'Pray do not tease him,' implored Pru. 'I had enough trouble persuading him to come here tonight.'

'And you owe it to me not to flirt with my friends!' retorted her husband. He held out his hand to her. 'Now, madam, are you going to dance with me or not?'

'Of course, my love, but we have a little time yet.' She took the outstretched hand but turned back to Jack, saying, 'You are coming to Hartland next month for our November ball, are you not?'

'Of course. It is already agreed. And I want to see my godson. He is what, eighteen, nineteen months old now?'

'Yes, and already he is a bundle of mischief,' replied Garrick, pride in his firstborn evident in his voice.

'We are going into Devonshire at the end of the week,' said Pru. 'Come and join us as soon as you wish, Jack. You know you are always a welcome guest at Hartland.'

'Am I?' He raised an enquiring brow at his old friend, who grinned at him.

'Damn your eyes, Jack, of course you are!'

'You aren't afraid I will steal away your duchess?'

Pru laughed merrily at that.

'Even you, Jack, with all your fabled charm could never do that,' she said, giving her husband such a glowing look that even Jack felt the affection flowing between them. The Duke kissed her before turning back for one final word to his friend.

'I'd say join us at supper after the unmasking, Jack, but doubtless there will be a host of beauties vying for your attention, as always!'

With that, he bore his wife away, leaving Jack smiling after them. Pru and Garrick had been married almost two years but it was clear to him they were still very much in love. He was struck with a sudden wistfulness at the thought of Garrick's new-found contentment and it surprised him.

He was very happy with his bachelor lifestyle and he had funds enough to make it unnecessary for him to marry a fortune, so why would he not be content? As heir to the Marquess of Doune he knew he must marry at some time, but he enjoyed his freedom and had no plans to change the situation for years yet.

It was at that moment that Jack's eyes fell upon a dainty, sylphlike figure dancing with a Falstaff. From the symbols embroidered on her white gown he guessed she was dressed as Diana, goddess of the hunt and the moon. The thin muslin draped over her body showed off her excellent figure as she glided effortlessly over the floor, every movement graceful, fluid. A white velvet mask covered most of her face but he observed the thick, honey-coloured hair coiled up around her head, the dainty chin, the gleaming smile that lit up the room and felt the hairs rise on the back of his neck.

He had not seen her for six years but he was in no doubt of her identity. Then she had been Miss Sabrina Kydd. Now she was Lady Massyngham, the wealthy and notorious Wicked Widow.

Sabrina kept her smile in place as she skipped and twirled through the last few bars of the country dance. It was not easy. Falstaff had sweaty hands, a predatory smile, and although he was masked, she detected a lascivious gleam in his eyes. He was one of the few guests here who had guessed her identity and, like everyone else in town, he believed every-thing he had heard about her. And why should he not? Sabrina had never made any effort to deny all the rumours about her.

The gossip had begun when she had married Rogue Massyngham and it had not stopped when he died. It had been further fuelled when it was discovered that her late husband had settled a vast fortune upon her.

Society had been outraged when she had returned to town barely six months after Sir Roderick's demise. The scandals attached to her name continued to keep the gossipmongers busy, but Sabrina paid them no heed. Her wealth and popularity gave her entrée to the houses of all but the highest sticklers, and she continued to enjoy herself in the ballrooms and salons of the ton.

As soon as the music ended, Sabrina thanked Falstaff prettily enough but made her excuses to leave him. He let her go with a good grace, as she knew he would: after all, she had had plenty of practice at rejecting ballroom Lotharios and knew just how to do it without causing offence.

It was early and she knew there would be several more dances before supper, but for once the idea did not please her. She was feeling out of spirits, even a little bored with the masquerade. She should not have come; there were very few of her usual circle of friends here but it would not do to leave just yet. Lady Massyngham was famous for her partying and she must do her duty. She must laugh and chatter and stand up for every set until her dancing shoes were quite worn through. That was what Society expected of her.

These rather depressing thoughts were interrupted

when a Barbary pirate stepped out in front of her and bowed low.

'The Goddess Diana is without a partner, I see. Will you honour me with your hand for the next two dances?'

Sabrina froze. She knew that voice. Even after all these years that deep, seductive tone had the power to unnerve her. Her heart was thudding painfully and she waved her fan slowly, taking a moment to calm herself before raising her eyes to look up at the man standing in front of her. He wore a mask of black silk but it only covered his eyes. There was no mistaking the lean cheeks and square jaw, or the sensuous mouth with the fine laughter lines etched at each side. If she needed more confirmation, it was provided by the curling fair hair she could see beneath the edges of his scarlet turban. Lord John Callater. The most charming bachelor in town, according to many ladies of her acquaintance. A man she had not spoken with since her marriage.

Her throat went dry. Suddenly she was nineteen again, a blush spreading across her cheeks and her pulse racing from being so close to this charming, handsome man. She remembered it so clearly, that first meeting. It was the beginning of her only official Season, attending any number of balls where she knew barely a soul. She had been desperate to dance and one evening Lord John Callater had appeared, and he had obliged. More than that, he had wholly entranced her.

He persuaded their hostess to present him and bowed over her hand as if she had been a princess. He had stood up with her for two country dances, holding her fingers in a warm grasp and guiding her through the movements, smiling, talking. Winning her heart. She had known a few short months of happiness before her world had been turned upside down.

'So, will you dance the next with me, Sweet Diana?'

She blinked and shook her mind free of the past. The Barbary pirate was holding out his hand to her. It was difficult to see his eyes through the slits of his mask but his lips had curved into a teasing smile. Could it be that he had not recognised her? Sabrina's frantic heartbeat slowed a little. That must be it. Her hair was dressed in the Grecian style and almost all of her face was concealed. She was nothing more than a pretty stranger that Lord John Callater would like to add to his conquests.

Well, why not? she thought. After all this time, what harm could one dance do? She smiled and gave him her hand.

'With pleasure, sir!'

He led her onto the dance floor, where everyone was chattering, but Sabrina could think of nothing to say as she stood opposite her partner, waiting for the dance to begin. However, as soon as he took her hand and wrapped his fingers around hers, all the old feelings came flooding back. Her thoughts flew to the last time they had danced together. As if it had happened only yesterday.

Her head was filled with jewel-bright images of the crowded ballroom. How happy she had been when Jack led her out to join the set, bursting with pride to have the most handsome man in the room as her partner. She remembered the way her heart sang when he bowed over her hand and looked up at her, a glinting smile in his eyes as he said, 'Until tomorrow.'

Only that tomorrow never came…

Sabrina pushed away the painful memories. The dance was starting and she needed to concentrate on the steps, and she reminded herself to smile as she skipped and twirled. Meeting Jack Callater again had brought back all the old heartache but she must not let him see that. If he had not recognised her, then it was far better to pretend they were strangers. It was not so far from the truth, she told herself. They were both much changed by the past six years. She was certainly not the innocent girl she had been the last time she had stood up with him.

Never had a dance seemed so long. Sabrina kept her smile in place, but she was painfully aware of her partner, every touch of his hand when he led her down the set, the brush of their shoulders as they crossed in a figure eight. The masks added an extra frisson of excitement to the evening and around them, couples were openly flirting on the dance floor. Thankfully her partner did not attempt anything of that nature, although she knew he was watching her. She could feel his eyes on her. Nothing unusual in that, she told herself. She was accustomed to men being unable to keep their eyes off her, but somehow Jack's watchfulness made her uneasy.

When the music ended, she made her curtsy and begged that he excuse her.

'You will not stay for the second dance?' He followed her off the floor.

'Alas, sir, I must not. I am almost swooning with fatigue.'

'You would not desert me so soon, cruel Diana.'

She laughed up at him. 'Even a goddess must rest sometimes.'

He caught her hand. 'A pirate would not allow you to escape him thus.'

'Ah, then Diana would slay him with an arrow from her bow!'

She gave him what she hoped was a roguish smile and slipped away into the crowd.

She had disappeared, and Jack felt as if she truly had slain him. Not with an arrow, but that final, sparkling look. He shook his head, trying to clear it. Her eyes had dazzled him, shining out from behind the velvet mask. He had known many beautiful women in his thirty-one years, but only one had ever affected him like this. Only one had ever caused him a moment's heartache.

The disguise enhanced the coquettish nature of the laughing glance she had thrown at him. It was a look that would inflame any man, and he knew that he had now experienced for himself the allure of the Wicked Widow. The girl he had met all those years ago had not known that trick! Or had she? He had thought Sabrina Kydd an innocent, but perhaps it was merely that he had not known her long enough.

The hard, uncomfortable knot tightened in his stomach. She certainly did not remember him. There had been no sign of recognition in her tonight. Over the heads of the crowd he caught sight of the Goddess Diana moving towards the big double doors. He thought of going after her, but dismissed the idea almost immediately. He should never have gone near her tonight. Dancing had only brought back things— feelings—that were best forgotten.

It was still early. He could go to his club and divert himself with cards until the early hours. Or he could return to Albany and drink himself into oblivion. Neither appealed. Jack Callater was known for his good manners. He was not one to quit a party while there were ladies wanting to dance. He buried the unwelcome memories, squared his shoulders and went off in search of a dance partner.

Lady Tarleton had set aside one room for the sole use of the ladies that evening and Sabrina quickly made her way there. Thankfully, it was empty and she dropped down onto one of the sofas. She could not stop shivering and she crossed her arms, trying to warm herself, to dispel the icy chill inside. The Wicked Widow was never out of sorts. She was always happy and smiling, guaranteed to add lustre to any gathering.

Not tonight. Tonight all she wanted to do was to scurry away and hide. She thought miserably that she had been hiding for the past six years. Avoiding any meeting with Jack Callater. Thankfully, their social circles were very different, and it was not difficult to choose entertainments where there was little chance of seeing him. She had thought that after all this time, if by chance they should meet, it would be as indifferent acquaintances. How wrong she had been. The last thing she had felt tonight when he took her hand was indifferent.

Gradually her nerves settled. Sabrina told herself it was the shock of the meeting that had overset her. It could not be anything else. She had not acted well by him. In truth, she had behaved abominably! However, it was done now and far too late for regrets. She had made a very comfortable life for herself, filling her days with outings and entertainments and diversions. She would not allow anyone to upset that. Jack Callater belonged to her past. He had no place in her present or her future.

She went over to a looking glass, pulling off her mask to study her reflection. Heavens, she looked pale! A group of ladies entered, all laughing and chattering. Some of them glanced at Sabrina as they passed, but no one stopped. She turned back to the mirror and pinched her cheeks to put back a little colour. She should stay at least until supper but no later. She would leave as soon as it was announced. Her absence would be remarked, she had no doubt of that, but her critics would conclude she had slipped away early with her latest conquest. A hollow laugh rang in her head. If only they knew the truth! Fixing her mask back in place, she shook out her skirts and went back down the stairs.

The ballroom was more crowded than ever; the noise and heat buffeted Sabrina as she entered. She scanned the assembly, looking for the distinctive figure of the Barbary pirate, but there was no sign of him and she began to relax a little. A gentleman in a garish frock coat and black periwig claimed her as his partner, and soon she was back on the dance floor, performing a lively reel that left her no time to think of anything else. A jig followed and Sabrina whirled and skipped about the floor, losing herself in the well-known steps and familiar music.

By the time the dance ended, she was feeling much better. Her smiles came easily, and she was able to flirt gently with the bewigged gentleman as he escorted her from the floor until at last she dismissed him and he strutted off happily, having enjoyed a half hour's dalliance with a beautiful woman.

Chuckling, she turned away, only to find herself once more confronted by the exotic costume of the Barbary pirate. She stifled her momentary alarm. He had no idea who she was; she had no need to panic. This was masquerade, after all. A pretence.

'We meet again, Diana.' His mouth curved upwards, sensual, seductive. 'I have come to claim my second dance.'

A moment's hesitation to gather herself, to beat down the little curl of desire that was unfurling inside, then she smiled back at him.

'I think not.' She gave a little laugh to take the sting from her refusal, then a few words of flattery. 'One dance with the Corsair is quite dangerous enough.'

'But I insist.'

She shook her head.

'Alas, I do not dance again tonight,' she said firmly. 'I am sure you can find yourself another partner.'

'But you are my choice.' He leaned closer and said quietly, 'I *know* you, Lady Massyngham.'

All her assurance fled and she took an involuntary step back. Heart pounding, she raised her eyes to his face. There was no warmth in his smile and through the slits of the mask his eyes glittered like ice.

Run away, Sabrina. Turn and run. Now!

She said, trying to sound confident, 'I think you are mistaken, sir.'

'Am I?' He put out his hand. 'Dance with me.'

It was a command, and she was unable to find the words to refuse. She could feel the danger; it swirled about them, thick and tangible. It clogged her brain, sapped her willpower. She did not resist as he escorted her to the dance floor. The strains of the waltz began and he led her around in a brief promenade. Sabrina breathed deep and slow, trying to regain her composure. All was not lost. She had admitted nothing. She could still bluff this out.

'How long has it been,' he asked her. 'Six years?'

Six years, five months...

'La, sir!' From somewhere she summoned a smile and feigned a look of surprise. 'Can it be we have met before?'

He laughed as he pulled her into his hold for the *pirouette*.

'You have had so many lovers I daresay you have forgotten.'

His careless response flayed her, but she was well practiced at concealing her pain. She tossed her head and laughed back at him.

'I daresay I have.'

She kept her chin up and continued to look at him, as the waltz demanded. But not quite *into* his eyes. She could not bring herself to do that.

He had always been an excellent dancer, although the waltz had not been in vogue when they had first met. Heavens, how would she have fared back then, dancing so close to this man? Every touch, every look brought the memories flooding back. The good memories, not the hurt and loneliness she had suffered for so long. She was nineteen again and carefree. *Happy.*

The music began to work its magic and, as Sabrina concentrated on the dance, she found she was no longer pretending to enjoy herself. She did not need to avoid his eyes, and her smiles came naturally as they flew over the floor for the last flurry of movements. His hands were on her body, holding her firm, their steps perfectly in tune, as if they had danced the waltz together many times. As if they knew each other intimately.

When the music ended, Sabrina was grateful for his arm as they walked off the floor. She felt dizzy, disorientated. She wanted to slip away and hide; she needed time to make sense of what had just happened.

A sudden fanfare of trumpets echoed around the ballroom.

'Ah, the signal that we can remove our disguises,' remarked her escort. 'Perhaps you will allow me—'

He reached out to pull at the strings of her mask, and she put up her hand to block him.

'Not yet!'

'What is this?' He paused. 'A sudden display of modesty, Sabrina Fair?'

Her knees nearly buckled. No one else had ever called her that. It was impossible for her to deny she knew him now. She managed a careless shrug.

'I am here *incognito.*'

'Ah, an intruder then. Should I tell Lord Tarleton and have you ejected?'

There was an edge to his words. Sabrina could not be certain that he was merely teasing.

'Oh, I have an invitation,' she told him, trying desperately to sound playful. 'Of course I have. I am a friend of Lady Harby.'

'The wife of Tarleton's heir?'

Her head went up at the insinuation that she was not worthy to be friends with anyone so respectable.

'We have been friends since our schooldays.'

'But naturally the lady would not want anyone to know her association with the Wicked Widow.'

His contempt stung but she said nothing. The Tarletons had been very kind and assured Sabrina there was no need for such secrecy, but she preferred not to reveal her presence at the masquerade. Some of the guests had recognised her, a few more might guess, but others would be scandalised if they knew they were brushing shoulders with the Wicked Widow.

'If you insist on keeping your mask, we should return to the dance floor.'

Sabrina shook her head. 'I will dance no more tonight.'

'Then let us go down to supper. We can talk over old times.'

He was standing very close, and there was a steely

look in the eyes that glittered out from the slits in his mask. Sabrina knew he would not let her escape him. She could not risk a public struggle and inclined her head.

'Very well.'

He pulled her hand onto his sleeve and guided her downstairs to the dining room, where the food had been set out on long tables. Dishes were piled high with tempting food and colourful exotic fruits, but Sabrina had no appetite. The elation of the dance had faded, leaving her a little despondent.

Noting her reluctance, her escort led her away from the buffet.

'It has been a long time, madam, since we last danced together.'

She was silent, still unsure how to respond to him. What did he want with her? Covertly she studied him. His face looked leaner, the lines about his mouth etched a little deeper. Signs of dissipation, perhaps, if the rumours of his rakish existence were true.

'I should give you my condolences upon the death of your husband,' he said. 'Although—only six months in mourning—you were hardly the grieving widow.'

'It would have been hypocritical of me to pretend I cared.'

'Then why did you marry him?'

She hesitated. 'It was…expedient.'

He had led her to a small table in one of the secluded alcoves of the supper room, and they were both silent as a footman held the chair for her. Another servant hurried forwards to fill their wine glasses.

'You admit, then, you did not love him.'

'No, I did not love him.'

He sat back, his lip curling in a sneer. 'You married him because he was rich and powerful.'

'Yes.'

Tell him what happened. Explain.

But that was not possible. It was far too late for explanations.

Sabrina had endured much during the past six years, but most painful of all had been the way Jack had snubbed her after her engagement to Sir Roderick Massyngham. She remembered it only too well; she had been shopping with Mama in New Bond Street and seen Jack walking towards them. He had ignored her, looking through Sabrina as if they were strangers. Perhaps she deserved it, after the way she had treated him, only a few weeks earlier.

She had not seen him again after that. Sir Roderick had insisted upon marrying her without delay and had whisked her off to Massyngham, where she had remained, save for visits to her husband's friends and the occasional trip to London, until Massyngham's death two years ago. Coming out of mourning six months later, Sabrina had taken up residence in town, but she had kept away from any gatherings where she might meet Lord John Callater. It was not difficult; her acquaintances were mainly those of her late husband, very different from Jack's circle of friends. But although she could avoid Jack, it was impossible not to hear news of him.

Sabrina's hasty marriage to a man more than twice her age had caused a stir at the time, but even today the flirtations of Lord John Callater were the talk of the town. Rich, handsome and charming, it was no wonder the ladies vied for his attention. It was rumoured he treated his mistresses well, but at least one was known to have sunk into a decline when he ended their liaison.

Lord John was rich, thanks to his late godfather, who left him Lingwood Priory, a prosperous estate in Norfolk as well as a small fortune. He was sociable and an excellent dancer, appreciated by hostesses because of his willingness to stand up with the most unpromising of debutantes. He was also extremely eligible, being the eldest son of the Marquess of Doune, but despite all these attributes, Sabrina knew that wise parents warned their daughters against him. He was happy to engage a lady in a mild flirtation, but to expect anything more from this man was to risk heartbreak or even ruin. Had not Mama said as much to her, all those years ago?

He was gazing down into his wine glass, apparently unperturbed by her silence.

She asked suddenly, 'Why have you never married?'

Jack looked up, his brow rising. 'Why should I? I can have everything I want without being leg-shackled.'

The inference brought a fiery blush to her cheeks.

'A clinging wife would be the very devil.' He went on, adding after a slight pause, 'You appear to be enjoying your, er, independence, madam.'

She detected disdain in his voice and took refuge behind the façade she had cultivated over the years to protect herself.

'I am indeed.' A flutter of the fan was called for, a little chuckle of amusement. As if she had not a care in the world. 'Widowhood, plus a very substantial jointure, provides me with the freedom to do as I wish.'

'And you are taking full advantage of it.'

'Of course.' She managed a small, carefree laugh. 'That is why they call me the Wicked Widow.'

That slow, sensuous smile curled his mouth again.

'Perhaps we should put that to the test.'

* * *

Confound it, man, what are you doing?

Not by a flicker of an eyelid did Jack show how shocked he was by his own words. This was not what he had intended at all. He had meant only to dance with Sabrina and then take her into supper. To treat her with friendly indifference and demonstrate that he was no longer in thrall to her. What a mistake! He admitted to himself now that the sight of her dancing with other men had been too much to bear, especially after that earlier refusal. He had been unable to resist trying again.

Like a moth to a flame.

And to ask her to waltz, of all things, how could he have been such a fool? To hold her so close, her breast brushing his waistcoat and his arm about her waist as she looked up at him, her lips parted so invitingly. They had not been halfway through the dance before he was lost. Old desires flared and the attraction hit him again like a battering ram. He could not deny that he wanted her.

Jack had been five-and-twenty when he had first met her. Looking back now, he realised he had been foolishly naïve, despite his growing reputation as a rakehell. Sabrina had enchanted him. She was vivacious and witty, they shared the same sense of the ridiculous, but her humour was never at the cost of others. He had thought her kind. Honest and true.

How mistaken he had been about her. He remembered now how innocent she had appeared. The shy looks she had given him and the maidenly blush that adorned her cheek when he spoke to her. He had completely lost his heart, and she had led him to believe she felt the same. But in the end she had sold herself for an old man's gold.

He looked again at the beautiful woman sitting opposite. Half her face was obscured by the velvet mask but even in repose, those red lips were tempting. Full of promise. This was his chance to be done with the foolish passion that had lain dormant for so many years. He could finally sate his youthful desires and put them to rest. If she was as dissolute as rumour said, then what had either of them to lose? Jack pushed himself to his feet and held out his hand to her.

'What shall it be, the ballroom or the bedchamber?'

Chapter Three

Sabrina's smile never faltered. She was accustomed to men flirting with her, but very few were quite so blunt. He might court other ladies charmingly, but he had clearly decided she required no such finesse. Deep inside, her emotions were in turmoil. Anger swirled around like a boiling cauldron, rage at him for his effrontery, even more at herself for caring.

She ignored his outstretched hand and rose, taking a moment to shake out her skirts as she blinked back the angry tears that stung her eyes. She had only herself to blame; she played this game too well.

When she was sure she was in command of herself, Sabrina shook her head.

'It will be neither, sir. It is time for me to leave. Alone,' she added quickly, lest he should suggest he go with her.

'So soon? The night is yet young. Stay and dance with me.'

Another little shake of her head. To be held in his arms and look up into those eyes that had once gazed at her so warmly was more than she could bear.

'Goodnight, Lord John.'

She gave him what she hoped was an enigmatic smile and moved towards the door. He followed, falling into step beside her as they emerged into the pillared hall.

'You have an assignation, perhaps,' he suggested.

'Perhaps.' Peeping up at him, she saw his jaw tighten. *Good*, she thought. *Let him suffer a little!* Then she relented and added, 'Or mayhap I am merely fatigued.'

He caught her arm. 'Which is it, my lady?'

She panicked at his touch and shook him off angrily.

'That is none of your business!'

She turned away to speak to a lackey, who went off to summon her carriage. Then she sent a maid running for her cloak. She was done with this pretence. She no longer wanted to play games with Jack; it was far too dangerous.

At that moment several ladies and gentlemen swept down the stairs like a flock of noisy and colourful birds. As the group made their way towards the main door, Sabrina recognised several acquaintances amongst them and she stepped back into the shadowy space between the pillars and the wall. She was too overwrought to be drawn into their conversation, nor did she want to be seen with Lord John Callater. Since her marriage she had never shied away from scandal, some would say she relished the gossip, but for some inexplicable reason she was reluctant to have Jack's name linked with the widow of the debauched, lecherous Sir Roderick Massyngham.

When Sabrina moved back, Jack followed, unwilling to let her go so easily. The maid returned and he took the velvet wrap from her and placed it around Sabrina's shoulders. He could feel the delicate bones beneath his fingers, and when he breathed in her familiar perfume he was swamped by a rush of bittersweet memories. And raw, overpowering jealousy.

'Are you going to meet your lover, madam?' he whispered in her ear. When she did not answer, his hands tightened. 'Tell me!'

'A lady does not divulge her secrets.'

'A lady!' Angrily he turned her around to face him. 'You stopped being a lady the day you sold yourself in marriage to that ageing *roué*!'

She gasped in outrage. Her head snapped back and she tried to slap him, but he caught her wrist. She raised her other hand and he grasped that too, twisting her arms behind her back so that she was held against him, breast to breast.

'They say the Wicked Widow's bed is never empty,' he muttered, his lip curling in disdain.

'Then it must be true.' She flung the words at him, her eyes darting fire through the slits of her mask. 'You would do well to stay away from her!'

'Oh, I will,' he muttered. Her breasts were pushing against him with each deep, angry breath, and the last shreds of his restraint snapped. 'After this!'

He tore off her mask even as his head came down, and he captured her mouth with his own in a hard, demanding kiss. She froze, but only for a moment, then she was responding, leaning into him, returning his kiss with a hungry passion that left him reeling.

His arms tightened. She was everything he had dreamed of and more. The half-forgotten scent of her, a mix of soap and summer flowers that inflamed his senses far more than any heavy perfume. Her tongue tangled with his in an erotic dance that had his body hardening.

He wanted to cover her face with kisses, to trail them down her neck and run his hands over the silky skin beneath the flimsy gown. He wanted to hear her cry out in pleasure…

'Lady Massyngham's carriage!'

The doorman's sonorous call echoed around the

hall, recalling Jack to his surroundings. He raised his head, gasping for breath as Sabrina tore herself out of his grasp. She gave him one final, savage glare before turning on her heel and hurrying towards the door, throwing up her hood as she went.

More people were coming down the stairs and Jack recognised the Duke and Duchess of Hartland. Confound it, the last people he wanted to see were such good friends! He remained in the shadows, hoping they would not notice him, but they turned back towards the supper room, and he knew he had been spotted.

'Jack!' Garrick hailed him cheerfully. 'I am just taking Pru into supper. The dancing has not yet recommenced. Come and join us!'

'No. Thank you. I have just come from there.' Jack ripped off his mask and stretched his mouth into a smile. It was a struggle to concentrate with his thoughts still on that kiss and the blood pounding through his body.

'We are a little late coming down,' said Garrick, adding with a laugh, 'I hope you haven't eaten everything—'

The Duchess interrupted him, her voice full of concern.

'Is something wrong, Jack?' She stepped forward and put her hand on his arm. 'Are you unwell?'

Trust Pru to notice, he thought, giving himself a mental shake. Kind, generous Prudence who was alive to everyone's troubles. Not for the world could he explain what had occurred. Not when he didn't quite understand it himself.

'No, nothing like that,' he said, trying to speak lightly. 'Too much wine, I fear. And these pirate's robes are damned uncomfortable. I shall go home.'

'So early?' Garrick's brows went up. 'That will surprise your man, to see you back before dawn!'

'Aye, won't it just?'

Jack managed what he hoped was a creditable grin and a cheery wave as he took leave of his friends. Outside, the chilly October darkness wrapped about him and he set off in the direction of Piccadilly. A walk was just what he needed to clear his head.

Meeting Sabrina again had brought back all the hurt and anger he had felt six years ago. Within a few short months of meeting the lively, pretty Miss Kydd, he had fallen headlong into love with her. Jack had behaved impeccably. He had done nothing more than kiss her hand, but it had made no difference. He knew it was love. He had never felt such a deep and ardent passion for anyone. And he had been convinced Sabrina felt the same. Every look, every gesture confirmed it. And yet she had rejected him for Rogue Massyngham, a man old enough to be her father.

'But as rich as Croesus, damn him!'

He had not realised he had spoken aloud until a gentleman walking in the opposite direction stopped and demanded angrily what he meant by it. Jack quickly begged pardon and walked on, raging inwardly. A chance meeting with the Wicked Widow had brought it all back to him but he could not, *would not*, allow Sabrina to destroy his happiness again.

The short carriage journey from Tarleton House to Brook Street was not long enough to calm Sabrina. She was still trembling when she reached the privacy of the bedchamber, where her maid was waiting. Jane took one look at her mistress and threw up her hands.

'Heavens, ma'am, you look chilled to the bone!'

She put one arm about Sabrina and led her to a chair beside the fire before slipping away to fetch a cup of hot chocolate. Sabrina barely noticed. She sat hunched in the chair, staring into the fire and rocking herself back and forth until her maid returned.

'Oh, bless us and save us, you are as white as a sheet,' muttered Jane, setting down the cup and hurrying across the room. She bent and put her arms about Sabrina, rocking her gently back and forth as she crooned. 'There, there, my poor lamb.'

The kindness of the older woman was too much to bear. Sabrina burst into tears.

'That's right, dearie, you have a good cry. Jane will look after you. You are safe now, my sweeting.'

The maid continued to murmur softly as hard sobs wracked Sabrina. The tears continued to fall and it was a good ten minutes before she could control her weeping. She gently pushed herself free from Jane and sat up, hunting for her handkerchief.

'I beg your pardon, Jane,' she sniffed, wiping her cheeks. 'I am not normally such a watering pot.'

'I know, dearie, which is why I want to know just what has upset you.' She drew up a chair and sat down facing her mistress. 'Come along now, Miss Sabrina. I knows you inside out, so you tell me all about it. When you came in, you looked as if you'd seen a ghost.'

'Oh, Jane, I think I did.'

Sabrina wiped her eyes. Jane Nidd had looked after her in the nursery before progressing to become her maid when she left the schoolroom and accompanying Sabrina as lady's maid when she wed Sir Roderick Massyngham. There was very little about her mistress that she did not know. She had been her only confidante during those long, unhappy years of marriage, and now the temptation to unburden herself was too strong to resist.

'Not a ghost exactly,' she said now. 'Someone I knew once. Before I was married.'

'Ah.' Jane sat back, her shrewd eyes on Sabrina's face. 'A gentleman you were sweet on, was it?'

'Yes.' Sabrina dragged her handkerchief back and forth between her fingers. 'I did not tell you—I did not tell anyone—but I think, I believe he was about to propose to me when Papa received the...the offer from Sir Roderick. I had encouraged him, you see. I had made it clear that I would w-welcome his addresses.'

'That's as may be, Miss Sabrina, but you were not then one-and-twenty. It could not have gone ahead without your parents' approval,' argued Jane. 'And after...' She stopped and drew a breath, then she closed her lips for a moment, as if to prevent herself saying something she should not. Then, 'You would have had to refuse him.'

'Yes.' More tears fell and Sabrina was obliged to wipe them away. 'But I didn't even tell him. I pretended I was not at home instead of speaking to him. I should have explained, told him why I c-could not marry him.'

'How could you, ma'am? The whole thing had to be hushed up.' The maid sniffed. 'Your father would have turned *me* off, too, only he was afraid I would blab what I knew.'

'And I would not let you go. I needed you to come with me when I married,' added Sabrina, giving her a watery smile. 'You were my only comfort, Jane. You still are.'

'Thank you, my lady.' They sat in silence for a few moments, then Jane took Sabrina's hands and peered up into her face. 'Now, is there anything more you want to tell me, my lady?'

'No.' Sabrina shook her head. 'I had not been expecting to see him. It was the shock of it that upset me, but I am well now, I promise you. And I will not allow it to happen again.'

'Very well, ma'am. Let's get you into your bed, and then I will take away your chocolate and warm it up again.'

'No need, Jane. Thank you, but I do not want it.'

'It will help you to sleep.'

But Sabrina was adamant. She assured Jane she did not need anything to help her sleep. What she did not say was that, despite all her tears and unhappiness, she *wanted* to stay awake. Once her maid had gone, she slipped from her bed and drew back the curtains so that she could look out at the stars while she thought about what had happened tonight at Tarleton House. She wanted to go back over every shocking, frightening, *precious* moment that she had spent with Lord John Callater.

When Sabrina awoke, the distress of the previous night had melted away and the October sun creeping over the horizon and into her room promised a fine day. It had been unnerving to meet Jack Callater again and to discover he was every bit as attractive as she remembered. More so, because six years ago he had been charmingly correct and had done no more than salute her hand. That had been enough to win her heart, and yet, innocent as she was, she had known there was so much more to come. Sabrina no longer considered herself innocent, and yet she had not expected to be so moved by last night's encounter. The searing kiss they shared had rocked her to her very core.

She had been quite unprepared for the way her body had responded, the powerful instinct that made her press her body to him and kiss him back in a way she had never kissed anyone before. Even here, alone in the security of her own room, her body tingled with the memory of the feelings that kiss had evoked. She felt so very alive, as if she had suddenly been wakened from a deep slumber. What shocked her most was that she wanted to do it again, to throw herself into Jack's arms and give herself up to him completely.

Could she do it? Sabrina stared out at the lightening sky. Six years ago she had been quite inexperienced in the ways of the world, but she had loved Jack Callater with every fibre of her being. It had broken her heart to accept Sir Roderick Massyngham's proposal. Afterwards she had deliberately kept away from Jack, because it was impossible to reveal to him the true reason she was marrying Sir Roderick, but she could not bring herself to lie. Nor could she bear to witness the pain she would cause him. Since then, she had often wondered just how much he had suffered from her actions. Lord John Callater's name was always appearing in the society pages, and one could not ignore the gossip about his numerous affairs.

He had been very angry with her last night, and of course he had every right to be since she had as good as jilted him. And yet, although that final kiss had begun in anger, Sabrina was very sure that it had stirred old passions for them both. She had stayed awake for hours, going over every word, every look, and with the morning sun came the first tiny rays of hope. Perhaps, just perhaps it might be possible to win back his affection.

By the time Sabrina had finished her solitary breakfast, she had come to a decision. She went into the morning room and opened the drawer of her little writing desk, where she kept her correspondence. Her parents had moved from London very shortly after Sabrina had married and now lived in Devonshire, in the parish of Hartland and close to the residence of the Duke and Duchess of Hartland. It was only after they were settled there that Sabrina discovered Jack was a good friend of the Duke. Once she learned that he was a regular guest there, Sabrina was very careful to arrange her own visits to her parents for occasions when she could be sure Jack would not be in Devon.

She pulled out the most recent letter from her mother and quickly read it until she reached the lines she was looking for:

We have now received our invitation to the November Ball at Hartland Hall. It includes you, Sabrina, and the Duchess has written expressly to say how welcome you would be. She considers you to be friends now.

Friends! Sabrina smiled a little at that. There was no doubt that in Devonshire she and the Duchess enjoyed each other's company, but here in town Sabrina was careful to keep her distance. It would not do for the Duke's new bride to be seen in the company of the Wicked Widow.

Sabrina refolded the letter slowly. She had replied already, giving her apologies, but now things had changed. She drew a fresh sheet of paper towards her and picked up her pen.

Chapter Four

The short November day was drawing to a close as Jack's elegant travelling chaise pulled up at the south front of Hartland Hall. Lamps were already glowing from most of the windows, and he was glad to see Garrick coming out of the stone porch to greet him.

'Welcome back to Hartland, Jack. Good journey?'

'Yes, it was, but you are a dashed long way from civilisation!' he retorted, grasping the Duke's outstretched hand. He turned to greet Pru, who had come out to join them. He kissed her cheek. 'And how is my favourite duchess?'

'Relieved to see you safely arrived before dark.'

'Aye, and I hope my baggage coach arrives soon. I do not want to sit down to dinner with you in all my dirt.'

'But you have your portmanteau with you,' Garrick pointed out.

'I do, but I need Weald here if I am to dress properly.'

'Fustian,' growled the Duke. 'You can manage very well without your man.'

Pru laughed. 'Of course he can. Stop teasing us, Jack. You wish everyone to think you are something of a fop, but we know it is very far from the truth. And in any case, we do not stand upon ceremony when you are here. You may come down to dinner in your nightgown and banyan, if you wish.' She took his arm and urged him towards the house. 'Come in now, and take wine with us.'

Jack accompanied his friends into the house. Hartland Hall had started out as an old manor house and still retained many of its original features, but they passed through the original screens passage and into the great hall with its minstrels' gallery before moving on to the drawing room in the newer west wing, where a cheerful fire burned in the hearth.

'I was surprised when you said you were coming here so soon,' remarked Garrick as they made themselves comfortable. 'The ball is still two weeks off.'

'Can it be that you are tiring of town life?' Pru teased him, 'or are you escaping some romantic entanglement?'

Jack started. The Duchess's question was far too close to the truth for his comfort. However, one look at her innocent smile reassured him that she knew nothing of his encounter with the Wicked Widow.

It was four weeks since the Tarleton House masquerade and he had not seen Sabrina again. He was kept busy attending to his business affairs, and if he did venture out it was to card parties or gatherings where he was sure the notorious Lady Massyngham would not be welcome. Yet somehow, just knowing she was in town was too distracting, so he had packed up and set off for Hartland. Not that he was about to admit that to anyone.

'I wanted to spend time with my best friends,' he said. 'I mean to stay at least a month, having seen too little of you in town.'

'We were not there for long,' said Garrick.

'That is my fault,' added Pru. 'I was anxious to return here and see Baby John.'

'Ah, my godson,' said Jack. 'How is he?'

'Growing apace,' said Garrick proudly. 'He is walking now, as you shall see for yourself. Nurse always brings him down to the drawing room before dinner, to say goodnight.'

'Not for long, I assure you,' put in Pru quickly. 'Tired young children are not the best company and certainly of very little interest to single gentlemen! Garrick, however, is proving himself a very good father. He spends some time every day with the baby, but I think he will like little John even more when he is older, and he can teach him to ride and play cricket.'

'Aye, I will,' affirmed Garrick. 'You will be shocked, my friend, but I am very much enjoying the quiet country life with my family.'

Jack observed the loving look that passed between the Duke and Duchess, and he was aware of a sudden and unexpected feeling of envy. Not that he wanted to spend his days with Pru, lovely as she was. No, his ideal partner would be someone far more spirited. A gold-haired goddess, perhaps. He thought of Sabrina dressed as Diana in a diaphanous white gown that clung to her every curve. Angrily he tore his thoughts away from that image. The Wicked Widow was no goddess, and in no way his ideal partner. He had come here to forget her.

'I do not think it shocking at all, Garr,' he said quietly. 'In fact, I am rather envious of your happiness.'

'By Gad, Jack, that's the first time I have ever heard you speak thus!' declared Garrick, regarding him in some surprise. 'Can it be that you are thinking of settling down at last?'

Jack hastily denied it, adding with a laugh, 'You know I am a confirmed bachelor.'

'Truly?' said Pru. 'Have you never met *any* woman you wanted to marry?'

'No.' Jack lied without a blink. 'Never.'

He was glad now that Garrick had been out of the country when he had committed the gross folly of falling in love with Sabrina Kydd. If not, Jack would have been sure to confide in his oldest friend. And thank heaven his courtship had been carried out with perfect propriety. He had told no one he intended to propose, and thus there was no one who knew of his true feelings.

Except, perhaps Sabrina herself, and she had proved herself quite heartless.

'Well, perhaps you will meet your match at our ball,' said the Duchess comfortably.

Jack was saved from replying by the entrance of a footman to announce that Tom Weald had arrived with the baggage coach and he escaped further questioning by going off to change.

The last days of autumn blazed over the Devonshire countryside and Jack was determined to enjoy himself. He drove out with the Duke and Duchess, spent full days shooting with Garrick or riding over the estate with him, seeing all the improvements he had initiated. In the evenings the three of them met for a quiet dinner followed by a few hours of cards or music before retiring well before midnight. Pru might apologise for the lack of entertainment, but it was a balm to Jack's spirits to be able to relax with his friends, and he said, quite truthfully, that he did not miss London at all.

The day of the ball was very different. Not only had the weather turned noticeably colder, but from the moment Jack left his room he found the house bustling with noise and activity. Pru was quite distracted with all the last-minute arrangements. When she suggested the two men should spend the day out of doors, saying that all she required of them was to be back in time for dinner, they were only too pleased to oblige.

The weather was icy cold but it was a dry, clear day, and they took the opportunity to ride along the coast to Appledore, where Garrick was keen to visit the shipbuilders and see for himself the progress on the yacht he had commissioned. They returned at sunset and in plenty of time to bathe and change into their evening clothes before going downstairs to meet the guests who had been invited to stay at the Hall overnight and those invited for dinner.

Jack had enjoyed the day and would have preferred to spend the evening quietly closeted with his hosts rather than attend a party, but he knew his duty. He dressed with his usual care in his newest coat of blue superfine, white waistcoat and black pantaloons before making his way to the drawing room, where he was determined to please and be pleased by the company gathered for dinner. The Duke and Duchess were already present, and Pru immediately took his arm to draw him further into the room.

'We are quite a small party, you see,' she told him, when all the introductions had been made. 'There will be only fourteen of us sitting down to dinner. Everyone else will be arriving later, for the ball itself.'

Fourteen? Jack frowned. He had not thought it was that many. He glanced around him, then said, 'I can only count eleven.'

'Ah, well, there are three more to come. A neighbouring family, at least one of whom you will have met in town.' She broke off as the door opened. 'Here they are now!'

Along with the rest of the company, Jack turned, the welcoming smile on his face freezing when he saw who was standing in the doorway.

Hope had been building within Sabrina since she left London, but it evaporated like the morning mists when she followed her parents into the room and saw the look on Jack's face. She knew him too well to miss the tightening of his jaw and the fleeting shadow that crossed his features before he concealed his displeasure behind a charming smile. She had dressed very carefully for this occasion, leaving off the eye-catching creations she wore in town and choosing a pale green satin slip with an overdress of white lace. The bodice of holly green satin had a modest neckline, which, along with the sleeves and hem of the gown, was decorated with scallops of white lace. The ensemble was completed by white gloves and shoes and a single string of fine pearls around her throat. When she had looked in the glass earlier, she had seen nothing in her appearance that could offend the sternest critic.

Sabrina always dressed far more soberly when she was at Hartland, and she had hoped her modest appearance might appeal to Jack and remind him of the young lady he had known all those years ago. She wanted him to see that she was not the flighty Wicked Widow she appeared to be in town. One look at his cold, unsmiling face told her she had not succeeded, and her heart sank. She wished desperately that she had stayed in London, but there was no avoiding the meeting now. The Duchess was dragging Jack closer, intent upon introducing him to Mama and Papa.

'Unnecessary, Your Grace, we are already acquainted with Lord John,' said her father, giving Jack a friendly nod.

'Oh, of course, Sir Anthony.' The Duchess smiled. 'I was forgetting you will have met at last year's ball.'

Sabrina's hands tightened about her fan, wondering how the conversation would proceed.

'Oh, our acquaintance goes back far beyond that,' declared Papa. 'We met in London, when we were living in Russell Square, although it was several years ago now.'

'Yes, it was,' replied Jack politely. He followed the words with an elegant bow to Sabrina. 'It was the year of your daughter's wedding.'

She made the mistake of looking into his eyes, and the full force of his rage hit her like a whiplash.

She was shocked and dismayed to think of him, harbouring such anger for all these years, but she concealed it well, only the merest flicker of her eyelashes acknowledging the searing disappointment. But Sabrina did not dwell on her own discomfort. The mention of her wedding had put her mother on edge, and Lady Kydd replied now, her voice unnaturally bright.

'Yes, we left London soon after. We have not been back since.'

'Never felt the desire to travel again,' put in Papa, with a laugh that sounded false, at least to Sabrina. 'We are very happily settled in the country now.'

'I am delighted to hear it.'

Jack's polite if slightly bored response led Sabrina

to hope that he might now move on, but her torment was not yet over, for he turned and addressed her.

'However, I am surprised, Lady Massyngham, that you have never mentioned to me your connection with Hartland.'

The years Sabrina had spent disguising her true feelings now came to her aid, and she was able to reply with apparent ease.

'Why, my lord, you and I meet so rarely in town, the opportunity has never arisen.' Then, with a glittering smile, she excused herself and moved off.

Jack made a conscious effort not to watch Sabrina as she walked away. Instead he kept his attention fixed on exchanging pleasantries with her parents. They were older than he remembered, and Sir Anthony in particular looked thin and worn down, despite his assurance that he was very well. Jack remembered him as a genial, outgoing gentleman, but now he seemed quiet. Shrunken, somehow. Jack wondered if he had been ill, and he put the question to Garrick later.

'It's possible, I cannot really say.' Garrick shrugged. 'He and Lady Kydd moved here from London a few years before my father died, and they live very quietly. I am barely acquainted with them. You could ask Pru. She knows them better than I.'

'No, I shall not trouble her. It is not that important.'

The Duke moved on to speak to his guests, and Jack put the matter from his mind. He had no interest now in Sabrina or her family. Or so he told himself. Yet when he saw Sabrina standing alone in the large bay window, the siren call was too strong to ignore. She was looking down into her wine glass, lost in thought, her beautiful mouth drooping a little, and he walked across to join her.

'Do you visit your parents frequently, Lady Massyngham?'

He had caught her unawares. She started, and he noted the effort she made to arrange her features into a smile.

'Not as often as I should, I fear.'

'What made them choose this area?' She looked at a loss how to answer, and he went on, 'I would have thought it very remote for one accustomed to the hustle and bustle of London.'

'It was my mother's wish.'

'She has connections in Devon, perhaps?'

'N-no. She visited the coast here, as a girl, I believe. But more importantly the property was available, and they were able to move in immediately.'

'Almost before the ink was dry on your marriage settlement.' Her eyes flew to his face, but he could not resist continuing, goading her, 'It was rumoured Massyngham paid most handsomely for his bride.'

She bristled at that. 'One should not always believe rumours, my lord. My father was perfectly capable of purchasing their house in Hartland for himself.'

Surely it was not his imagination that Sabrina was looking discomposed? Good. Why should he be the only one put out by this chance meeting?

He said, 'But to give up a lucrative government post to move here…'

'My father took that position in the hope of doing some good,' she told him, a little sternly. 'He gave it up because Mama no longer wished to live in town, once…'

'Once you had made your brilliant alliance?'

'Quite. Excuse me—'

She went to move away and he stepped in front of her.

'I understand this is the first time you have attended the November Ball at Hartland, my lady. What made you decide to come this year?'

He waited, but she said nothing and he leaned closer. 'I hope you are not planning to set your cap at the Duke. You will not succeed there, you know.'

She glared at him, two spots of angry colour staining her cheeks, and her bosom swelled with indignation.

'How dare you!'

'Easily, my lady. Your name has been linked with so many noblemen.'

'Mere tittle-tattle.'

'Really?' His lip curled. 'It is well known your husband connived at your...liaisons. And since his death...well.' He spread his hands. 'Your soubriquet is the Wicked Widow, is it not?'

He knew he was insulting her. He saw the flash of anger in her eyes and gave a cold little smile.

'Yes, you would like to hit me, would you not, Sabrina Fair? But you tried that at Tarleton House, you will recall.'

He knew he was upsetting her; part of him felt ashamed at such unchivalrous behaviour. It was unworthy of a gentleman, but to see her here, looking so damned beautiful, reminding him of the disappointment he had suffered, he wanted to hurt her. He wanted to punish her for the pain that her rejection had caused him. He thought this time she would respond, fly up at him, but instead, she gave a little shrug.

'Yes, I do remember,' she replied coolly. 'What followed was most...disappointing.'

And with a toss of her head she walked away from him.

The hour before dinner was a trial for Sabrina. She regretted the impulse that had made her come all the way from London, chasing a dream that should have died years ago. Jack Callater had no wish to renew their acquaintance, and with good reason. Six years ago she had encouraged his advances and then dropped him without a word. If there was one thing she had learned during the intervening years, it was how much men hated to be ignored. It hurt their pride, where they were most vulnerable.

She had thought tonight she could show him she was not the giddy, pleasure-loving and scandalous widow everyone thought her, but her modest dress had made no difference at all. And his suggestion that she would try to flirt with the Duke of Hartland proved just how little he thought of her.

The man was despicable, and a hypocrite, too. How dare he criticise her behaviour, when he openly acknowledged his own mistresses? He was well known for being a flirt and a dandy. A frippery fellow, no better than the infamous Mr Brummel, whose fashions he imitated, and who had been obliged to flee the country earlier in the year. Jack Callater deserved nothing but her contempt.

She was tempted to plead a headache and go home, but how could she, without causing comment? It would ruin the evening for her parents, and besides that, Pru had always been kind to her, so she must stay and do her duty. She ignored Lord John Callater and talked, laughed and chattered with the other guests until dinner was announced. Only then did she discover, to her chagrin, that she was to sit beside Jack at the table.

Sabrina had quite lost her appetite. She only picked at her food, selecting tiny amounts from the dishes around her. She understood why her hostess had arranged it so. Pru knew she and Jack were acquainted, although thank heaven she had no knowledge of their history. She should have foreseen that good, kind, Prudence might try to bring her and the Duke's best friend together, but foolishly Sabrina had been so caught up in her own concerns that the idea had not occurred to her.

This could not have happened if she had informed the Duchess that she and Jack had once been close, but Sabrina had told no one of that early romance, and it had seemed unnecessary to confide in Pru, since Sabrina had always timed visits to Devon for those occasions when it was impossible for Jack to be at Hartland. That had been easy enough; a close study of the society pages informed her of Lord John Callater's movements. In London, her meetings with the Duke and Duchess were rare, and there had been no opportunity since arriving in Devonshire for Sabrina to talk to Pru about such a delicate subject, even if they had been close friends. She stared miserably at her plate, thinking once again what a fool she was to have come.

'Allow me to help you to a little chicken, ma'am,' said Jack, interrupting these dismal reflections.

She was about to refuse, then thought better of it. She did not want him to think he had caused her a moment's discomfort.

'Thank you, my lord.'

'The Duchess speaks very fondly of you,' he remarked. 'I had no idea you were such good friends.'.

'We are not,' she replied, surprised. 'That is, we meet when I come into Devonshire, which is rarely, but in town we move in very different circles.'

'Naturally,' he drawled. 'You would not wish to embarrass Pru, I am sure.'

Sabrina blushed with anger and mortification, although he spoke no more than the truth. It had suited her to adopt the role of a disreputable widow with a host of admirers, and it would be useless to deny it now. And yet...

'The Duchess is very generous,' she replied. 'She is aware of my...reputation but pays no heed to the gossip.' She dared to look at him then. She said earnestly, 'And it *is* only gossip, my lord.'

Looking into those green eyes, Jack caught a glimpse of the young and vulnerable Sabrina he had once known. He wanted to believe her, but how could he? Everyone knew she had married Sir Roderick

Massyngham for his wealth, and it was no secret that she had been present at his notorious parties. If only half the rumours were true, the man had been as licentious as the legendary Sir Francis Dashwood almost a century earlier.

He shrugged. 'If you say so, madam.'

Sabrina said nothing but Jack knew he had hurt her. It was evident from her little moue of disappointment. He should be pleased; he had been trying to punish her, but somehow the idea of making her unhappy did not sit well with him.

What does she expect of me? he thought angrily. *She rejected me in favour of a dissolute old man. I will give her no sympathy now!*

She hunched one white shoulder and turned away, affording him a perfect view of her exquisite profile and elegant back. As if she was not perfectly aware of her charms! He felt his anger growing. Beneath that beautiful exterior, she had the soul of a courtesan.

Jack divided his attention between his dinner and the lady sitting on the other side. He was determined to pay no more heed to Sabrina, but he found it impossible to ignore her. He was painfully aware of her talking in a very animated fashion with the man sitting beside her. She even joined in with conversations across the table, laughing and joking as if she had not a care in the world. *Well, let her enjoy her-*

self, he thought grimly. It was nothing to him. She was not his concern.

He pushed his food about his plate and let his mind wander back to his first meeting with Sabrina Kydd, six years ago. She had been wearing green then, he remembered. To be precise, she had been wearing a gossamer thin muslin gown decorated with green acanthus leaves and a green ribbon threaded through those glorious honey gold locks. It had been an unforgettable moment at one of the many very forgettable balls of the London Season.

Chapter Five

London, June 1810

Hostesses adored Lord John Callater because of his charming manners and Jack was too soft-hearted to refuse to dance with any of the debutantes presented to him. However, even he sometimes grew tired of the social round. One particular evening, having been invited to dine with his hosts, he was heartily bored even before the meal was over, and he slipped away for a few moments' respite before he could be called upon to join the first of the dances.

Thankfully, on that occasion he was well acquainted with his hosts and knew that there was a small garden tucked away at the back of the house. He made his way there, preparing to enjoy the peace and quiet of a balmy summer's evening.

He was surprised, on stepping outside, to see a young lady dancing on the lawn. She did not notice him, and Jack moved into the shadow provided by the garden wall to watch her as she skipped gracefully about the garden. She had a dainty figure and luxuriant hair the colour of dark honey. The way the evening sun glinted on her curls reminded him of an old song about a lady with amber-dropping hair.

He could not resist reciting a line: '"Brightest Lady look on me!"'

'Oh!' She stopped dancing and turned, surprise and a hint of apprehension in her look.

He said, by way of explanation, 'It's from a song, by John Milton.'

'I know.'

She smiled, as if reassured by his words. As she walked towards him, he saw that her eyes were a rich, emerald green.

She went on, 'Sabrina Fair. It was a favourite of my mother's and she named me after it.'

'Very apt, then, because your hair really is the colour of amber.'

'Thank you.'

Jack was intrigued. She was dressed as a debutante, but looked to be a little older than most. Perhaps nineteen or twenty. She seemed quite self-assured, too, not at all discomposed to be alone in the garden with a strange gentleman.

'Why are you not in the ballroom?' he asked her.

'Because I do so love to dance, and I did not want to sit without a partner and watch everyone else enjoying themselves.'

'But someone might have asked you to stand up with them, if you had remained in the room.'

'Oh, no.'

She replied with surprising candour, and that made him smile.

He said, 'You cannot know that.'

'But I do.' She smiled back at him. 'First, all the rich young ladies are asked, the heiresses and those with excellent lineage. Then, if there are any gentlemen left who wish to dance, they ask the pretty ones.'

'Then you would surely be asked.'

'La, thank you, sir!'

She curtsied and peeped up at him, her green eyes twinkling with laughter. Jack was entranced.

'Will you tell me your name?'

'I have told you. It is Sabrina.'

'No, who *are* you, who are your parents?'

She regarded him for a moment, as if making up her mind.

'I am the only daughter of Sir Anthony and Lady Kydd, of Russell Square.'

'And are you here with them tonight, Miss Kydd?'

'Yes…why do you wish to know?'

'Because I must achieve an introduction before

I can dance with you. I am Lord John Callater, by the way.'

She was laughing now. 'And are you a good dancer, Lord John Callater?'

'I am a *very* good dancer.' He grinned. 'Now, off you go back to the ballroom and I will follow shortly!'

Jack allowed himself two dances with Sabrina, but afterwards he did not approach her again that evening, fearing the gossips would brand her his latest flirt. However, it was not difficult for him to discover all the parties and balls where Miss Kydd was likely to be present. He attended every one of them, always making sure he danced with several ladies as well as Sabrina. Occasionally he would escort her to supper, but he was careful to do nothing that could give rise to the sort of speculation ruinous to a young lady's career.

He found himself one of a small group of admirers all vying for Miss Kydd's favours, but although he was sure Sabrina's affections were engaged, Jack refrained from pressing his suit until he was certain of his own feelings. It was unnerving. No woman had ever caused him so much heart-searching. He was unsure, off balance, and he found that slightly terrifying.

Afraid of making a misstep, Jack was more circumspect in this courtship than he had ever been before, but when he found himself breaking his habits and entering the hallowed portals of Almack's just to dance with Sabrina, he realised how serious things had become. He knew then it was time to ask her to marry him.

The following day he made his way to Russell Square only to be told that Miss Kydd was not at home. A slight setback, but Jack was sanguine. It was Lady Barnard's ball that evening and Sabrina was sure to be there. He would talk to her then and make a more formal request for an interview with her father.

He duly arrived at Barnard House and did his duty by any number of ladies while he waited for Lady Kydd and her daughter to arrive, but by midnight it was clear they were not coming. He returned to Albany, still unaware that anything was amiss.

It was the next morning that he picked up the *Morning Chronicle* and read the news of Sabrina's betrothal to the notorious Sir Roderick Massyngham.

Devon, November 1816

Jack pushed the food around idly on his plate as he thought back to those dark days. Thank God he had been circumspect in his courtship. There was no one to witness his disappointment, although that word hardly expressed his feelings when he learned that Sabrina was going to marry Rogue Massyngham.

At first he could scarcely believe it. He was desperate to speak with Sabrina, to know why she had accepted a man old enough to be her father, but that proved impossible. The family was accepting no callers and his letters to her were returned unopened. He spent hours in Russell Square, hoping for a glimpse of her and then eventually, when he was riding in Hyde Park one day, he saw her in an open carriage with her fiancé. Jack rode past and caught her eye, but she acknowledged him with the merest nod, as she would any slight acquaintance.

There had been no signs of discomfiture or sorrow in the lady's face. No remorse in the look she gave him, only cold and haughty indifference.

Jack shook off the sombre thoughts and dragged his attention back to the dinner table. It was then he realised that Sabrina was no longer entertaining her neighbours with lively talk. The atmosphere in the room had changed, the general chatter had died away and most people were listening to the conversation going on at the far end of the table, where a portly gentleman was holding forth on the parlous state of the country.

'I expected matters to improve once the war ended,' he grumbled, 'but they ain't. More beggars wandering the streets, unrest in the towns…and there's a tax on everything these days. Even travel hasn't escaped. Why, 'tis said the government owns a wheel of every coach on the road these days!'

'The farmers here are struggling,' declared another gentleman, shaking his head. 'Wheat prices are only half what they were three years ago.'

'Aye,' said a third. 'During the wars when prices were high, many of them ploughed up extra land to keep up with demand. Now they can't sell their wheat, and they can't pay their rents.'

'It is not only the farmers.' Sir Anthony leaned in a little to make his point. 'Labourers and mill workers are suffering too. There is a deal of injustice in England today. It is little wonder people are unhappy.'

Sabrina was sitting very straight in her chair. She seemed nervous, and a fleeting glance showed Jack that she was listening intently to her father.

'But it's the landowners they'll blame,' replied a lady sitting across from him. 'Yet what can we do? We must increase the rents to cover our own rising bills. I vow I am loath to go into Exeter now for fear of the mob!'

'The militia will deal with them, ma'am, never fear,' said the man beside her. 'Riots won't help anyone.'

'But many must be suffering genuine hardship,' added Sir Anthony.

'I am sure they are, sir, but it ain't helped by that scoundrel Cobbett's pamphlets and newspapers. The man positively encourages men to feel ill-used,' retorted the portly gentleman. 'And then there's Orator Hunt, exhorting all and sundry to sign the petitions and march on Parliament.'

Lady Kydd was looking uneasy and she pinched her husband's arm to stop him responding further. The Duke turned the conversation to a more comfortable subject, but Jack was intrigued by the look of apology that Sir Anthony gave his wife as he sat back. As the conversation ebbed and flowed around them, Jack turned to address Sabrina.

'Your father was a minor official in the government at one time, was he not?'

'That was some years ago.' She answered briefly and appeared more interested in choosing another morsel of lamb from the platter in front of her.

'I also recall that he had always been somewhat… radical in his views. I remember him claiming an acquaintance with Henry Hunt.'

'That was a long time ago,' she said quickly. 'He has little interest in politics now.'

'But he is still concerned about the plight of the poor.'

'As anyone with an ounce of compassion should be,' she replied. 'I believe there is some justice in the claims that landowners are to blame for the high rents.'

'Most of us sitting around this table are landowners, ma'am,' he reminded her, but gently.

'Yes, but some work to alleviate the plight of the poorest under their charge. The Duke and Duchess, for example. *They* do not spend their time in hedonistic behaviour funded by the high rents they make from their own people!'

This was too pointed to be ignored and he challenged her.

'Are you talking of me or your late husband?'

She flashed an angry glance at him. 'If the cap fits, sir!'

Jack's jaw tightened with anger. 'It might interest you to know...'

He stopped. He would not explain himself. Let her believe what she wished of him. What a hypocrite she was, he fumed silently. Massyngham's wealth quite threw his own modest estates into the shade. It was the reason she had married him. And if reports were true, Sir Roderick had provided most generously for her in his will. She had no need to curtail her own extravagant lifestyle!

The great hall had been cleared for dancing and transformed into a ballroom. Candles glittered from the chandeliers and wall sconces, and the fire that had been burning for days provided a comfortable warmth for the guests as they milled around the ancient hall, waiting for the musicians in the minstrels' gallery to strike up.

Pru had asked Jack to lead out a sprightly dowager viscountess for the first dance, and he obliged with his usual good grace. After that he stood up with any number of young ladies, but although he was smiling and charming to them all, his attention was elsewhere.

Sabrina filled his thoughts. Despite his conviction that he no longer cared, he could not be comfortable. There was a brittleness to her demeanour that suggested she was not as happy as she made out. He might tell himself he did not care, but it gnawed at him, and although he did not allow his eyes to follow the lady around the room, he was constantly aware of her.

He noted how the candlelight sparkled in her honey-eyed curls, the graceful way she flew across the floor when she was dancing. The delightful smile that never wavered. She stood up with no man for more than one dance and made no attempt to flirt with any of her partners. That surprised him, but he guessed it was out of respect for her hostess. Sabrina would not wish to offend a duchess. Aye, Lady Massyngham was a cunning female and no mistake! He was well rid of her, and should be thanking fortune he had escaped her clutches.

And yet, no matter how hard he tried, Jack could not ignore the siren call of the beautiful temptress.

Sabrina had been dancing for hours. She wished she could go home but that was impossible. Mama and Papa were clearly enjoying themselves, and she would not curtail their pleasure. They lived very quietly in Hartland, but she knew it had been a great wrench for them to leave London with all its entertainments. Mama had greatly enjoyed the parties and plays, and then there were the various societies, where her father had been such an active member.

The thought of Papa made her sigh. He was such a caring man, and it must be very difficult for him not to air his views. There had been a few difficult moments this evening, not only at the dinner table, when Mama had been obliged to remind him not to draw attention to himself, but in the drawing room beforehand. Sabrina had been standing with her parents and a small group of their acquaintances when the talk had first turned to the state of the country.

'These are hard times, and no mistake, but riots won't solve anything,' opined one gentleman, frowning and shaking his head. 'All this violence and machine breaking. It is my belief that the poor are being stirred up by lawbreakers. Dear me, I do not know where it will all end.'

'On the gallows,' declared another. 'And as for stirring up trouble, that devil Cobbett is one of the worst culprits. He is demanding change and encouraging the poor to riot! Damme, he should be locked up again. Him and all his supporters…'

The men had continued to animadvert on the dire situation, and Sabrina could only be thankful that her father did not say anything. In the past he would have fired up in response and espoused the cause of parliamentary reform, but he had remained silent, although he shook his head and looked uncomfortable. Poor Papa, how difficult it must be for him not to express his liberal views.

Once the ball had started, however, her father had become much more cheerful, and Sabrina was pleased to see him and Mama standing at one side, watching the dancers and chatting so happily with their neighbours. No matter how wretched she felt, she could not drag them away from Hartland Hall before the ball had finished.

As the music ended, Sabrina thanked her partner and moved off to wait for the next. She maintained a cheerful demeanour, even though she would very much prefer to sit in a corner and weep. She had come to Hartland hoping to win back Jack's regard. Or at the very least, perhaps to regain his friendship, that easy camaraderie that she had felt with him during the first weeks of their acquaintance, but he had openly scorned her at dinner and had not come near her since.

You were foolish even to consider a reconciliation, she told herself crossly. *The past is gone and it is best to leave well alone!*

'Lady Massyngham.'

For an instant Sabrina thought she had conjured up that deep voice at her shoulder. A little thrill ran down her spine, and her heart was thudding so hard against her ribs it was almost painful. She swung around to find Jack standing before her, tall and imposing in his dark coat. She kept her eyes on the fine detail of his embroidered waistcoat, breathing in the faint trace of spices and musk that hung about him. It made her want to step closer, breathe deeper.

She wanted to touch him so badly it hurt. She had to grip her closed fan with both hands to stop herself reaching out. It was shameful, alarming. Especially since she knew he only wanted to torment her. He had almost provoked a quarrel with her at the dining table. Was that not enough? She would put up with it no longer. She raised her eyes to his face.

'My Lord John.'

'Another set is forming.' He held out his hand to her. 'Shall we join them?'

Of course she would not dance with him. How could he even think it? A snub and a set down was all she would give him.

Three matronly ladies were close by, and Sabrina waited for them to pass before making her refusal. They were all giggling as if they had enjoyed a little too much of their host's good wine, and one of them stopped to tap Jack's shoulder with her fan.

'So, my lord, you have at last plucked up the courage to ask the lady to dance. Good for you, young man!' The woman gave a fat chuckle. 'Oh, no need to look like that, sir. I cut my eye teeth years ago and I have seen the way you were watching her. You have not been able to keep your eyes off the lady all night! Go to it, man, go to it. And you, my lady.' The matron turned her flushed, beaming face towards Sabrina. 'Put the poor fellow out of his misery and stand up with him!'

This forthright intervention made Sabrina quite forget her anger. She was strongly tempted to giggle and, as the matron sailed off to catch up with her friends, she glanced up at Jack. There was a reluctant gleam of amusement in his eyes, too, and they smiled at one another. Miraculously, the tension was gone.

They were momentarily united, and the air around them suddenly felt much warmer.

'Well, ma'am, what can I say after that? *Will* you do me the honour of dancing with me?'

'I fear the lady may come back and scold me royally if I do not!'

She gave him her hand and let him lead her onto the dance floor. Within the silk glove, her skin tingled as his fingers closed around hers. A frisson of pleasure ran through her, quickly suppressed. She must be careful. This was a truce, but she should not read anything more into it than that.

And yet, as they went down the dance together, performing the familiar steps, the years fell away. It was not so much a dance as a courtship carried on in time to the music. They held hands, exchanged smiles. Every glance, every touch was enhanced while the company around them faded into a blur. It was as if they were trapped together in a bubble, and when they were separated by the movement of the dance, she went through the steps mechanically, only coming alive again when she was reunited with her partner.

For Sabrina, the dance seemed to last a lifetime, but when the music finally stopped, she wanted to protest that it was too soon. Jack reached for her hand, and the fire in his eyes sent her spirits soaring to dizzying heights, but only for an instant, until she realised there was no tenderness in his look. Passion, yes. And desire. He wanted her. She had seen that same look in too many men's faces to doubt it. But there was something else, consternation. As if he, too, had been shaken by the emotions stirred up by that one dance. Suddenly being so close to Jack felt very dangerous. Panic gripped her.

You cannot control this, Sabrina. Leave him, now.

'Excuse me.' She pulled her hand free. 'I must go.'

Then, with the merest curtsy, she left him.

Sabrina had no real idea of her direction as she moved this way and that between the guests. She only knew she must get away from Jack's disturbing presence. Everything was noise and bustle. Dancers were changing partners, people were moving on and off the floor. She hoped that, in the confusion of the crowded ballroom, she could slip away unnoticed.

There was a stone archway leading off the great hall, and she hurried towards the shadows beyond. She had just stepped through when she heard Jack's voice close behind her.

'Sabrina, stop.' He caught her arm. 'Where are you going?'

'Home. I need my cloak…'

'You won't find it here.'

Angrily she shook him off and took a hasty step away. She looked about her. They were in a deep alcove, with windows on two sides and a door on the third, but one glance told her it was not an outer door.

'That leads to the library,' said Jack, following her gaze. 'We can go inside, if you wish.'

'No. I will not go anywhere with you!'

She backed away from him and he gave an exasperated sigh.

'Confound it, woman, you are in no state to go back into the ballroom. And to be truthful,' he muttered, 'neither am I!'

Sabrina hesitated, biting her lip, and the next moment she found herself being propelled firmly through the door.

The library was empty, but candles burned around the room and a cheerful fire crackled in the hearth. Even with the door closed, it was possible to hear the faint strains of the music as the orchestra struck up for a Scotch reel. She shook off his hand.

'Thank you, my lord. I can manage now.'

'I doubt it.

'Why have you brought me here?' He was standing between her and the door and she felt trapped.

'You need to compose yourself before you return to the ballroom.'

'I am not going back there. I want to leave.'

'Impossible to do that without going through the great hall,' he pointed out, with infuriating logic. 'Unless you propose to climb out the window.'

That made her want to giggle, which eased her nerves somewhat, and she stopped shaking. Now she needed to gain control of herself. Of the situation.

'And why do you wish to leave?' he continued. 'Are you ill?'

'No.'

'Then what?'

She shook her head. What could she say? It was impossible to explain when she did not understand it herself. She felt she was standing on the edge of a precipice, and she had a fearful dread that the slightest wrong move would send her tumbling to disaster.

'Is it me?' He took a step closer. 'Are you frightened of me?'

'No!' She raised her head at that. 'I am afraid of no man!'

'I'm glad to hear it.'

There was a note of amusement in his voice that stiffened her resolve. How dare he laugh at her! She turned away and went across to the fire to warm her hands.

She said, keeping her back to him, 'I am a little tired.'

'Tired?' He openly laughed at that. 'The Wicked Widow is renowned for dancing through the night.'

'Do not call me that!'

'Why not?'

'Because it is not true. I am not…wicked.'

'A little late to protest your innocence now, Sabrina. Who would believe you?'

She raised her eyes to the mirror above the mantelshelf and stared at her reflection. He was right. She had played into the hands of the gossips. Widowed at four-and-twenty, she had felt suddenly free and far too young to retire from Society. Instead she had chosen a life of gaiety and pleasure, dancing until dawn, picnic breakfasts, theatre visits, rides in the park. But she had resolved not to tie herself down to any one man. Instead she had chosen to have a string of admirers that could be called upon to escort her. Who could blame them if they boasted a little, if they exaggerated their connection to the Wicked Widow?

Jack moved up to stand behind her, but she would not meet his gaze, even in the mirror.

'It is usual to stand up with a gentleman for two dances, you know,' he reminded her.

'Then you will be disappointed.'

'Will I?'

'I do not intend to dance again tonight.'

'No?' His voice was very close, smooth as velvet in her ear. 'You have told me that before.'

Her spine tingled; she could feel the heat from his body on her back and closed her eyes, trying not to give in to the ache of desire growing inside her.

'This time I mean it.'

'Do you?'

His hand stole around her waist. She felt his lips on her bare shoulder, and her head tilted, inviting him to kiss her neck. He obliged with a series of butterfly kisses that made her sigh. Sabrina leaned against him, her eyes closed, her resistance melting under the featherlight touch of his lips. She put her hand on his sleeve, where it rested against her waist, and slid her fingers between his.

His mouth brushed her ear. 'I have waited six years for this, Sabrina Fair.'

'Oh, so have I.' The words were little more than a breath as she reached up to cup his face with her free hand, giving in to the sensual pleasure of his touch. This was where she belonged, she thought dreamily. Safe in Jack's arms.

Safe! With a little cry she opened her eyes and pushed herself away from him. There was nothing *safe* about Jack Callater.

But this is what you wanted, is it not? The words

taunted her and she turned to face him. *You came here to win him back.*

No! The thought of it brought the blood rushing to her cheeks. Not like this. She wanted him to *love* her. Truly, sincerely. As he had done six years ago. As she thought he had done. It occurred to her now that perhaps she had been too young, too naïve then to understand what it was he wanted from her. Perhaps the love of her girlish dreams did not exist. She turned to face him.

Jack stood silent, hands clenched into tight fists as he tried to calm the desire that was raging through his body. By God, how he wanted her! She had been ready to give in, to fall willingly into his arms, but now she was standing and staring at him as if he was the devil incarnate! He braced himself. She was going to rip up at him, to accuse him of trying to seduce her. He shrugged inwardly. It was not so far from the truth.

'I, I beg your pardon.'

What? He felt winded. *Was she apologising to him?*

'I am sorry if I led you to…if I made you think I wanted…'

She was blushing, looking so damned adorable he had to fight the impulse to drag her back into his arms. If this was some cunning ploy to increase his ardour, then it was succeeding only too well! But he knew how to play these games. He schooled his face into a look of understanding.

'Let us blame it on the wine, my lady, and think no more about it.'

'Thank you.' She stood, hesitant, her tongue flickering over her lips. 'I should go.'

'Not until I have had my second dance. You owe me that much.' She looked at him uncertainly, and he smiled. 'Here, or in the ballroom? It is your choice.'

Chapter Six

Sabrina swallowed. Heavens, when he looked at her like that, with his sensuous mouth curving upwards into that wicked smile and the laughter lines deepening around his blue eyes, all she wanted to do was to throw herself back into his arms and call the world well lost. Her insides were dissolving at the very idea of it. She tried to pull her wayward thoughts together. She needed to be sensible. The danger had not lessened; she was still standing on the edge of an abyss.

She reminded herself that she had been in far more dangerous situations than this. All those parties at Massyngham. Many men had propositioned her, and with the full blessing of her husband. Then she had had nothing but her wits to aid her. Here, once she was in the ballroom, there would be plenty of people to protect her from Lord John Callater.

But they cannot protect me from myself.

Sabrina pushed that thought aside. It was not helpful. She steadied her breathing, fought down her panic and summoned a smile.

'In the ballroom.' It was difficult, but she managed a creditably steady voice. 'One last dance.'

'One last dance,' he agreed, holding out his arm. 'Shall we?'

Jack escorted Sabrina back to the great hall, where they took their places on the dance floor. He felt physically battered and bruised by what had just happened. Or rather, by what had *not* just happened. The woman standing beside him was as confusing as the devil. One minute she was in his arms, soft and sighing, the next she was running away from him. And he had no idea if it was all a pretence.

He glanced down at her as they stood waiting for the music to begin. She looked calm enough. She even managed a friendly smile at the young lady watching from the edge of the dance floor. There was no sign of her earlier turmoil, whereas he was still feeling shaken and confused. Enough was enough, he decided. After this one final dance he would waste no more time thinking about the Wicked Widow.

Sabrina stood beside Jack, holding his hands and waiting for the music to start. She wished with all her heart that it could have been anything but a waltz.

She saw the Duchess smiling at them from across the room, and she fought down the feelings of panic. Her head was spinning, her heart beating so hard she feared it would send her off balance. She must not allow that. She had waltzed hundreds of times before, and very successfully, so why should this be any different?

'I can do this,' she muttered to herself. 'I only have to get through this dance and then I can leave. I shall tell Mama I am not feeling well and go home. The carriage can come back for them later, but I will not stay a moment longer.'

She thought it would be easier once they started dancing, and at first it was. They clasped hands, separated, turned, twirled and promenaded in perfect time. Gradually the music and familiar patterns began to soothe her ragged nerves. It was not long before she did not need to concentrate so much on the steps, but that left her wayward mind free to follow its own path, which was to her partner.

Her world narrowed until it was only Jack. The touch of his hand, his arm around her back, his eyes holding her gaze and sending messages she was afraid to believe. But oh, how she wanted to believe them! He was beguiling her with every look, every move, and she was responding, feeling the energy flowing between them. There was no future, no past, only the dance. The music filling her senses. She had never felt so alive. So in love.

As the final notes died away, they stared at one another. Sabrina was dimly aware of the people moving around them, dancers looking for partners, couples making their way to the supper room on the far side of the screens passage. It meant nothing. Jack held her whole attention. When he pulled her hand onto his arm and led her out of the ballroom, she did not resist. They passed through another arched opening, this time one that led to the inner hall, where the highly polished oak staircase wound its way up into the relative darkness of the upper floors.

Fewer candles burned here, and after the brilliance and bustle of the great hall, it was quiet and empty. Jack drew Sabrina into a shadowy corner, and without the slightest hesitation, she moved into his arms. He lowered his head and she felt his lips on hers, gentle, seductive. Arousing.

Jack's pulse leapt as Sabrina responded to his kiss. He knew this was madness. Desire heated his blood and he felt dizzy, light-headed. As if he had been waiting for this moment these past six years. He breathed in the fresh, alluring scent of her as she clung to him, exulted as the luscious curves of her body pressed against him, turning his desire into a fever. He trailed kisses down her throat, felt the quickened pulse beneath his lips. She breathed his name softly, and he raised his head to look at her. She leaned back against his shoulder, her green eyes glowing with an inner fire as she gazed up at him.

'What now?' he whispered, his breathing hard, ragged.

'Take me to bed, Jack.'

He hesitated, thinking he had misheard her. She smiled and cupped his cheek with one hand.

'Take me to bed, my love.'

Jack closed his eyes, and something half groan, half growl escaped him.

He swept her up into his arms and Sabrina slipped her hands about his neck. She clung to him, her face resting against his shoulder as he carried her up the stairs and through the dim passages to his bedchamber. His heart was singing, he felt giddy with elation. It took precious moments to open the door to his room, but once inside he kicked it shut behind them. There was just enough light in the glowing embers of the fire for Jack to see his way to the bed.

He carefully laid his precious burden on the covers, but she clung on, dragging him down with her. Her kiss was eager, passionate, and Jack responded, tongues tangling, hands exploring. They began to undress one another, kissing and caressing the newly exposed flesh. It was as much as Jack could do not to tear at the fastenings, but at last they were almost naked.

Sabrina's stockings were still in place, but much as he wanted to slow down, she was pulling him closer, and he gave in to the urgent desire coursing through his body. It was a swift, wondrous, *joyous* coupling that left them both exhausted. With a sigh, Jack gathered her to him.

This was not what he had intended. It had all been too quick. Too rushed. He had wanted to take it slowly, to kiss and caress every inch of her until she was crying with the sheer joy of it. He was not an inexperienced lover, but having her in his bed, her silky skin pressed against his body, he had been overwhelmed, unable to hold himself back and pleasure her as she deserved. Confound it, she would think him a damned novice in the bedroom!

Sabrina sighed and snuggled into him, already asleep. His arms tightened. No matter, he thought, kissing her hair. It was the first time, but it wouldn't be the last. They would do this again. And again and again. There was no knowing the heights they could achieve. Together. He smiled to himself as he closed his eyes and drifted off to sleep.

I have come home!
Sabrina felt a warm glow spreading through her.

When she had woken and found herself in Jack's arms, in his bed, she had a sense of the most profound happiness. There was also regret for the wasted years, but now, at last, she thought it would be possible to forget the past with all its pain and sadness.

A clock somewhere chimed the hour and beside her, Jack stirred.

'It grows late,' he murmured. 'We should return to the ballroom, sweetheart, before we are missed.'

'Yes.' She sighed, dragging her thoughts back to the present. 'I wish I could stay here with you until the sun comes up, but it will be time to leave soon.' Her new-found happiness bubbled up in a laugh. 'What a pity I am not a house guest. These things are always so much easier if one is staying.'

The words reminded Jack that she must be experienced in these things. Not that it mattered.

'I suppose they must be.' He kissed her before rolling away. 'I will help you dress.'

He moved off to light the candles on the mantelshelf while Sabrina slipped off the bed. The fire had died to a sullen glow, and the room would soon be growing chill. He pulled on his pantaloons and picked up his shirt before going back to Sabrina. She was already wearing her chemise and was busy sorting the rest of her clothes into some sort of order.

'Shall I help you with your stays?' he asked, throwing his shirt over his head.

Before it could fall, she put her hands against his skin, her fingers tracing the contours of his chest, her touch arousing him as quickly as before. By heaven, she knew just how to please a man!

Sabrina had never explored a healthy, strong body in this way before. Her husband had been an old man and in failing health even when he had married her, and his was the only other male body she had ever seen naked. She wanted to tell Jack how new all this was to her, but she was afraid he would laugh at her inexperience. Instead, she slid her arms around him.

'Let me enjoy you a little longer,' she murmured, pressing her cheek against the soft linen of his shirt where it had fallen between them. It smelled of soap and sandalwood, and she breathed in deeply, storing up the memory.

A laugh rumbled in Jack's chest.

'Unless you want me to drag you back into bed this minute, you had best put on some clothes!'

She chuckled. 'Tempting.'

He caught her face between his hands and kissed her before gently releasing himself from her embrace. 'Away with you, baggage! Now, let us get you dressed.'

She held the stays in place and turned away from him, relishing the intimacy of this moment. Her skin tingled as she felt his fingers at her back, tightening the laces. There was so much she wanted to tell him, but now she felt shy, tongue-tied.

'Thank you for tonight,' she said at last. 'For what you—we—did. It was…wonderful.'

She smiled to herself at the inadequacy of her words and barely noticed the slight hesitation before he responded.

'Was it now?'

'Yes, truly.' She winced a little as he tugged hard at the laces. 'I have never known such happiness in a man's bed before.'

With her stays secure, she looked around to give him a quick, shy smile before pulling on her gown. Was this what it was like to be in love? To feel such joy, such pleasure in a man's caresses? She was about to ask Jack but he spoke before she could frame the words.

'You will need help with the buttons, I suppose.'

'Yes, if you please.' She turned away again, still glowing from the wondrous union they had shared. She could feel his fingers between her shoulder blades, brushing the skin close to the top of her gown. She said, 'Now that we are friends again, I hope we can—'

'Friends? I think not.' He laughed. 'Do not imagine a quick tumble on the covers makes any difference to us, madam.'

Sabrina frowned, confused by his cold tone. He went on.

'In fact, it only proves to me that you are as wanton as your sobriquet. There.' His fingers fastened the last button and he gave her a little push away from him. 'I believe that is all you will require from me. You will find a comb and a looking glass on the washstand. I will leave you to tidy your hair before you come downstairs.'

And with that, he walked out of the room.

It was all Jack could do not to slam the bedchamber door behind him. How could he have been so crass as to fall for her wiles on the dance floor? He should have known better. And Sabrina—did the jade think him so naïve that he would fall for her lies about his performance in the bedroom? It had been pitifully rushed. He had taken her with all the speed and finesse of a callow youth, and she expected him to believe her when she said it was *wonderful*? Bah! She must have bedded a dozen lovers who performed better than that.

He ran quickly down the stairs, the music from the ballroom growing louder as he descended. He glanced into the dark corner where he had pulled her into his arms. By heaven, he had been so close to declaring himself tonight. When she had lain with him between the sheets, so eager for his kisses, he had been within an inch of admitting that he had never stopped loving her.

That was not his only intended folly. He had made up his mind that before they returned to the ballroom he would ask Sabrina to marry him. What better place to announce his betrothal than here, in the house of his best friends? A chill ran through him and he shuddered. Thank heavens he had come to his senses in time!

The musicians were playing another lively tune, and from the ballroom came the sounds of laughter and merriment. Jack stopped under the arch, allowing his eyes to adjust to the glare of the light from the chandeliers. She had broken his heart once; he was damned if he was going to let it happen again. He straightened his shoulders, summoned up a smile and stepped back into the crowded room.

Sabrina stood, immobile and alone in the silent bedchamber. This was not what she had envisioned. This was not what she had understood from Jack's glowing looks, the tender way he had put her down on the bed. True, their lovemaking had been swift, but it had also been passionate, and for her it was the culmination of a dream she had kept locked deep in her heart for so many years.

A quick tumble on the covers, Jack had called it. She crossed her arms, feeling a sudden chill. Perhaps that was all it had been for him; she was too inexperienced to know. She had hoped to regain his regard, but all she had done was to earn his contempt.

Tears stung her eyes and she quickly blinked them back. She had been carried away with the passion of the moment and thought he had felt it, too. She had believed that even after all this time, there was a chance he might still love her, but she was wrong. Perhaps she had always been wrong, and he had never loved her. That was far more likely, was it not? Her memories were those of a young and very innocent debutante. Six years ago, Lord John Callater had already been a man of the town. In all probability he had only been amusing himself at her expense. It did not explain his anger, but then, men never liked to lose. She had been the one to end their courtship, such as it was. She had wounded his pride.

Sabrina went over to the washstand and looked in the mirror. The countenance staring back at her was pale, even in the warm glow of candlelight, and her hair, that had been so modestly drawn back in a simple knot, had come loose from its pins. Wispy tendrils framed her face and ragged curls hung about her shoulders.

You are as wanton as your sobriquet.

Jack's words stung, but she refused to cry. She had survived far worse than this, even though it did not feel like that just now. She picked up the comb and set to work tidying her hair. One could not rekindle a cold fire and she had been foolish to try.

No one observing Lady Massyngham when she re-entered the great hall some half an hour later would have thought anything amiss. Indeed, the lady appeared to be in the best of spirits. She danced tirelessly for the remainder of the evening, chattering and laughing until the final notes of the very last dance faded away, when she flirted gently with her partner as he escorted her across to join Sir Anthony and Lady Kydd at the side of the room.

Jack saw it all. Despite his best efforts, he could not ignore the lady. His eyes were drawn to her time and again. He knew any attempt to retire before the very end of the ball would draw questions from his hosts, so he stayed and did his duty on the dance floor with any number of matrons. His fabled charm was so ingrained that it was little effort for him, although he would have preferred to be anywhere but in the same room as Sabrina, even, occasionally, in the same set on the dance floor.

He survived it tolerably well, but by the time the last of the guests had left or retired and he was alone in the drawing room with his hosts, his nerves were wound so tight that a chance remark from the duchess caused him to give a bark of hollow laughter.

'You were *pleased* to see Lady Massyngham at Hartland, Pru?'

'Why yes, of course.'

'Even though she is the subject of so much scandal?'

'Is she so very bad?' countered the Duchess. 'We see little of her in town, but I have met Sabrina several times when she is in Devon, and although she has a lively wit, I have never observed anything flirtatious in her nature.'

'Because you are too good, too kind, to look for it!' he retorted.

'I, on the other hand, am neither too good nor too kind, but I have to agree with Pru,' replied the Duke, handing Jack a glass of wine before sitting down next to his wife. 'I have never seen any sign of flirtatious or untoward behaviour when she is in Devon.'

'But you cannot deny her reputation.'

'No, Jack, I don't deny it.' Garrick shrugged. 'Mayhap she was corrupted by her late husband. Massyngham was notorious for his debauchery, and it caused a great scandal when he married a girl less than half his age.'

'And how do you know that, my love?' the Duchess enquired. 'You were out of the country at that time.'

'Anyone might know of it,' said Jack, bitterly. 'Their marriage was the talk of the town. As are all the widow's exploits.'

'That does not mean it is all true,' argued the Duchess.

'But she has never denied any of it. And it is well known that she was happy enough playing hostess at her husband's parties,' said Jack, his lip curling. 'If only half the rumours are to be believed, she took as many lovers as her husband!'

'Pru pays little heed to rumours, thank heaven,' said the Duke, taking his wife's hand and raising it to his lips.

She smiled up at him, then said, seriously, 'Even if the gossip about her marriage is true, it is possible the lady has changed now that she is a widow. Oh, I know she spends her time on frivolous pursuits like dancing, and everyone in town agrees she is very entertaining, but I have always thought Sabrina—' her brow furrowed '—*un peu triste.*'

'It is *ennui* rather than *tristesse*, Duchess,' drawled

Jack. 'Her life has been one long round of balls and parties. And lovers!'

She gave him a considering look and he laughed quickly. Not for the world would he have anyone guess his own association with the Wicked Widow.

'I know, Pru, you are about to say I am not so very different.'

'It does seem a little hard to criticise the lady for behaving very much as you do,' she remarked.

Jack was tempted to say it was different for men, but he did not really believe that, and he knew Pru would not allow it. He waved a hand, trying to justify himself.

'I enjoy London Society, I admit, and I have had my share of lovers, but I draw the line at such wanton dissipation. Why, Massyngham was not dead six months before she left off her widow's weeds and returned to town!'

'You do not like her,' observed the Duchess.

'It is not a case of liking or otherwise,' he replied, prevaricating as much as he dared. 'We move in very different circles.' Then the outright lie: 'I hardly know her.'

'Well, I understand Sabrina is staying with the Kydds until Christmas, and as they are our neighbours, you are sure to meet her on several occasions,' Pru replied comfortably. 'I think you might be pleasantly surprised in the lady once you become better acquainted.'

Garrick came over to refill Jack's glass.

'I do not know them well, but the Kydds seem a very agreeable couple,' he remarked. 'No one really knows why they chose to settle here. They do not appear to have any friends or family in the area.'

'I believe that gave rise to no little speculation at the time,' put in Pru, adding judiciously, 'But we know nothing of what happened, save that they left London quite suddenly and retired to Hartland.'

'Then let me enlighten you,' said Jack drily. 'Sir Anthony had a minor role in the government until his daughter's brilliant marriage. The marriage settlement provided him with the funds to retire and take up the life of a country gentleman.'

'Can that be true?' Pru looked at him, amazed. 'The Kydds live so quietly. They never flaunt their wealth. He is always such a quiet, mild-mannered man. In fact, tonight's discussions about the hardship in the country was the most animated I have seen him.'

Jack frowned a little. 'I remember thinking he might be a radical when I met him in town.' He added hastily, 'Not that I knew him at all well.'

'Perhaps his rich and powerful son-in-law put paid to his radical tendencies,' suggested Garrick.

'Or his fortune-hunting daughter did not wish to see her chances of a good match ruined just because of her father's conscience!'

The Duchess shook her head at him. 'You are very hard on Lady Massyngham, Jack.'

'With good cause. She is a heartless woman, intent only upon her own pleasure.'

'Do you think so?' Pru frowned. 'I have always felt a little sorry for her.'

'That is doubtless what she wishes you to be!'

The Duchess was looking concerned, and Jack decided not to say any more on the subject. He drank the last of his wine and rose.

'It grows late and I should retire. Goodnight Pru, my dear.'

He bent to kiss her cheek, nodded to the Duke and went up to bed, praying that Sabrina's scent on the sheets would not ruin his slumbers.

Chapter Seven

Sabrina's pillow was wet with tears. Angrily she sat up and turned it over.

'Damn you, Jack Callater!'

Shocked to find herself uttering aloud such an unladylike phrase, she hunted for her handkerchief and blew her nose before settling down again. He had dashed her hopes most cruelly, and she would not waste any more time on the odious man. Resolutely she turned her thoughts back to her parents. She was worried about Papa. He was looking quite frail, and there was a wistfulness about him that tore at her heart.

She went back over the conversation she had with him, shortly after her arrival in Devon. Mama was engaged elsewhere, and she and Papa were sitting together in the morning room when he asked her for news from London. She shook her head.

'I know only what I read in the papers, Papa, the same as you.'

Her reply drew a sigh from him.

'Your Mama made you promise not to tell me what is going on there, did she not?'

He took her silence as an affirmative and nodded. 'I swore an oath to her that I would cease all connection with those wanting political reform, and I will not go back on that. The only thing I regret is that I am no longer in touch with my old friend Henry Hunt. I admit the rest of them were far more extreme in their thoughts and actions, and your mama was right to insist that I give up their society. We never speak of these things here, although one cannot escape the reports in the newspapers. I know there are endless petitions and meetings that achieve nothing, which makes me wonder where it will all end. I am so out of touch here in Devon.'

'Do you miss London very much, Papa?'

He looked so sad that her heart went out to him.

He said, 'I do, my love, but it is my punishment and I must not repine. My injudicious actions have caused too much harm. It cost you very dear, Sabrina, far more than your mother or I had to bear. I will never forgive myself for that.'

'Oh, Papa…'

'No, love, do not attempt to deny it. You told me

you were very willing to marry Sir Roderick, but it broke my heart to agree to it.' He dropped his head in his hands. 'If only I had not been such a coward! I should have let the scoundrel hand those damning letters to the authorities and taken my punishment. Even being imprisoned could not have been more painful than seeing you trapped in such an unhappy situation.'

Sabrina flew out of her chair and fell on her knees beside him.

'But it would not have been only you, Papa,' she said, putting a hand on his shoulder. 'It would have been Mama and me, also. We would have all have been ruined. Destitute.' His distress made her try to comfort him and she added in a lighter tone, 'And it has not worked out so badly, has it?'

He raised his head and looked at her, his face haggard.

'We are none of us impoverished, I grant you that, but how can I be comfortable knowing the misery I put you through? Your mother is very good. She has never once reproached me, but I know she feels it as keenly as I. We should never have let you marry that *monster*!'

'It was my choice,' said Sabrina, blinking away her tears and making her voice cheerful. 'And it was not so very bad. I survived, and now I am a widow with an independent fortune that no one can take away from me.' She hesitated. 'You might return to town now, I think. If you wished.'

'It is not what *I* wish. Your mother will not countenance the idea.' He shook his head. 'Here we live quietly, without the distractions of the world, but if we returned to the capital she knows I should not be able to sit by while this government ignores the plight of so many. She would never forgive me if I involved myself in politics again.' He gave another long sigh. 'But I do miss those meetings we had. Do you remember, love? Dr Watson would come with his son, James. They were so eager to change the world! Cobbett, too, when he was in town. And Hunt, such a persuasive speaker!'

'I remember. I would sit in the corner and listen to the lively discussions! It was very exciting.'

'Yes, yes.' Her father nodded, the old fire returning to his eyes. 'We talked of ending poverty and hardship in the country. Radical ideas such as giving all men the vote.' The fire died and he sighed again. 'It nearly cost me everything I hold most dear.'

'But the cause was just, Papa, even if the time was not yet right for change.'

'But will the time ever be right?' he asked her. 'Will we ever effect a peaceful transition to a fairer world?'

Mama had come back in then, and they had moved on to less controversial subjects, but now, lying in her bed, Sabrina considered her father's words again.

A just cause, she thought sleepily. Perhaps that was where she should direct her energies. In her efforts to do more for others, perhaps she might at least find some contentment.

A sleepless night convinced Jack that his situation at Hartland was intolerable. Merely dancing with Sabrina had sent him out of his mind with desire. She bewitched him; one look from her sea-green eyes and he was lost. By heaven, he had not realised he was such a weak fool!

Throughout breakfast he tried to think of a reason to cut short his visit, but none occurred to him. However, the arrival of a letter from his man of business gave him just the excuse he needed. He said nothing to his hosts but went up to his bedchamber and set Weald to work packing up his trunks.

Shortly after noon Jack went downstairs, dressed for travel in his top boots, buckskins and riding jacket, with a serviceable greatcoat over all. He found his hosts alone in the morning room, and the Duke greeted him with a look of surprise.

'Going out, Jack? Have you sent word to the stables, or do you want me to do so? I have a fine new hunter you might like to try.'

'No, no, thank you, but it is nothing like that, Garr. I have ordered my carriage. I am returning to town.' That, not unnaturally, caused a stir. Both Pru and Garrick turned to look at him as he carried on. 'The letter this morning, it was from my lawyer, Simmons. There are some matters concerning my estate that need attention.'

'Ah. Will you be going on to Lingwood then?' asked Garrick, glancing out of the window. 'It has been snowing all morning, and the weather might be worse beyond London.'

'No need for that at the present time. There is nothing at the Priory that my steward cannot resolve, once I have signed the relevant authority.' He added, forcing himself to meet the Duke's concerned gaze, 'Nothing serious, but all the same, every day it is postponed will be a worry to my tenants.'

He saw Pru cast an anxious glance out of the window and was quick to reassure her.

'It is not twenty miles to Torrington, where I shall put up for the night, and from there the roads improve immeasurably. I foresee no difficulty in travelling on to town.'

Jack was not surprised when his friends tried to persuade him to stay, but he was adamant. His cases were packed, the baggage coach was being loaded as they spoke, and half an hour later they accompanied him to the door to say a reluctant farewell.

'It is still snowing,' observed the Duchess, as a few white flakes settled on the shoulders of Jack's caped greatcoat.

'A flurry, no more, Pru. And better I leave Devon now, before travel becomes impossible.' He kissed her cheek. 'Take care, my dear, and don't worry about me. You know I am not such a frippery fellow as people think.'

He turned to the Duke, who gripped his hand. He felt a momentary qualm for not confiding the true reason for his going but quickly squashed it. They did not know of his encounter with Sabrina last night, and he could not face trying to explain it. Last night's encounter did not reflect well upon him or the lady. Best to say nothing.

He jumped into the waiting travelling chaise, raised his hand in farewell and set off, his baggage carriage trundling on behind.

The narrow lanes around Hartland prevented speedy travel, and Jack knew it would be dark by the time he reached Torrington. The snow was still falling steadily, although it was too light a covering to overly concern him. He was on his way back to town, away from Sabrina, but in his mind he could still see her, that bewitching smile, her green eyes, luminous in the candlelight. Last night she had looked more as she had done when he first met her. A modest gown, little jewellery and her hair simply dressed. Perhaps that had been the attraction.

He closed his eyes and allowed his thoughts to return to that spring evening, six years ago, when he had danced with an angel and decided he would like to become better acquainted. Her father was a gentleman of modest means, not perhaps the perfect match for the eldest son of a marquess, but Jack cared nothing for that. He courted Sabrina assiduously, even reverently. If only he had known then, she could be so easily bought.

She had listened to his compliments, her eyes glowing. He had every reason to believe she returned his regard, but within weeks she was married to a wealthy but notorious rake. There had been no apology, no explanation. She had cut him dead.

For the past six years he had tried to forget her. He had thrown himself into a whirlwind life of social events, his presence guaranteed to enliven any party. He was never out of spirits, and hostesses valued him for his charming manners and willingness to stand up with the plainest wallflower or most irascible matron. He was a confirmed bachelor, happily free of all matters of the heart and in complete control of his emotions.

Until last night, when he had given in to a passion that had lain dormant and unacknowledged for years. Jack opened his eyes and stared at the bleak snowy landscape. At least the passion was dead now. Sabrina had tried her wiles upon him once too often. Never again.

The light was fading fast. Taking out his watch, he guessed they must be only a couple of miles now from his destination. The chaise began to slow and he looked out to see the outline of a carriage resting at a drunken angle on one side of the road. There was still room to pass, but it would not do to go on without some enquiry to make sure no one was hurt. Jack gave the order to stop and jumped out, jamming his hat on his head to keep off the snow that was still falling.

Judging by the thick white coating on the upper side of the post chaise, the accident had occurred some time ago, and a quick word with the postilions confirmed this.

'We thought we might be able to get 'er as far as Torrington, but the wheel's smashed too bad for that, so we're going to take the horses on there and get someone to come out to the coach.'

'And your passengers?' asked Jack, looking about him.

'They walked on ahead, sir, when it was clear we

wasn't going to be able to carry 'em any further to-night.' The man shrugged. 'Bein' females, they neither of 'em wanted to try ridin' a carriage horse.'

'I see.' Jack looked at the broken carriage. There was nothing more he could do here. 'I will look out for them on my way.'

With a word to his driver, Jack jumped back into his chaise and set off again. The snow was beginning to settle more heavily on the roads now, which had the advantage of lightening the dusk. They had not gone far before they came upon two cloaked figures walking along the highway. As the carriage approached, the women stopped and turned, but it was only as Jack alighted from the chaise that he recognised one of them. His cheerful words of greeting were never uttered and he merely nodded.

'Lady Massyngham.'

Hell and damnation, she was the last person he wanted to meet. The look of dismay on Sabrina's face told him quite clearly that the feeling was mutual. She was accompanied by an older woman who was carrying a portmanteau. Jack thought she must be a servant or a companion, and he touched his hat to her before addressing Sabrina again.

'I saw your post chaise at the side of the road. I can take you as far as Torrington.'

It was a grudging offer and, try as he might, he

could not quite prevent betraying this in his tone, so her answer came as no surprise.

'Thank you, but we will manage.'

Her response was as chilly as the weather. Much as he would like to abandon the lady to her fate, he knew it would not do.

He said, 'It is well over a mile and the snow is getting worse. I can take you up in my chaise, and your companion can ride with Weald, my valet.'

He indicated the baggage coach, which had come to a halt behind them.

'That is very kind of you, sir,' she said, in a voice that told him she thought nothing of the sort. 'My maid and I will both ride in the baggage carriage.'

Jack curbed his temper. He wished he could leave her here to perish in the snow, but there was her companion to consider.

'Sadly, madam, there is only room in there for one passenger, besides Weald. Or do you propose that my man should ride on the box with the driver?'

She regarded him for a moment, and Jack thought she was about to say that *he* should ride in the baggage coach and leave the travelling chaise for her and the servant. Perhaps if he was a gentleman, he would suggest it himself, but Jack was in no mood to make any such concession. Let her walk if she preferred that to his company!

* * *

Sabrina observed the stony look on Jack's face and considered what to do next. It was only too clear that he was making this offer most reluctantly, and she would have liked to refuse, but what choice did she have? Beside her, Jane shifted restlessly and she realised how cold they were growing, standing in the snow. Much as it irked her, she knew she must accept.

'Very well, my lord.'

It was arranged in a trice and soon they were moving again, Sabrina sitting next to Jack and trying hard to avoid touching him as the chaise swayed on its springs.

She fumed inwardly. Of all the unfortunate encounters! When she had risen early and made her plans to leave, she had not expected that Lord John Callater would be on the road, too. She was sure the Duchess had told her he was staying for several weeks, at least until after Christmas. If she had known he was leaving so soon, she might have stayed in Devon with her parents.

The carriage journey seemed interminable, but at last they reached Torrington and pulled up outside the main coaching inn on the town square, where the landlord informed them they were very fortunate, because he still had two rooms available.

Sabrina was dismayed, but when she asked if any of the other hostelries were likely to have space, the good man shook his head.

'It being market day today, you see, ma'am,' he explained, wiping his hands on his apron. 'The inns and taverns are always full to bursting on market days. However, I do have a small sitting room I'd be happy to put at your disposal, my lord, while your man goes to see if he can find anything better?'

It was agreed. The landlord escorted them to the private parlour, while Mr Weald went off to ascertain that there was no other accommodation available in the town. Sabrina sent her maid with him, making it very clear that she would prefer to sleep in a hovel rather than spend a night under the same roof as Lord John Callater. Jane's answer to that had been short and to the point.

'You'll do no such thing, madam, so let's not hear any more of such childish nonsense!'

Sabrina remembered the words now as the landlord showed them into the private room. A small fire burned in the hearth, and she instinctively moved towards it. Jane was right, she decided as she warmed her hands, it was beneath her to behave so petulantly. That would give Jack the moral advantage and she was…she was *damned* if she would allow that!

She removed her cloak and threw it over a chair,

musing on the fact that renewing her acquaintance with Lord John Callater was causing her to find relief for her feelings in the most improper language!

'You will let me know what expenses you incur on my behalf,' she said to Jack, when they were alone.

'Of course.' He drew off his gloves and put them on the table, along with his hat and cane.

An uncomfortable silence descended upon the room, and Sabrina moved across to the window. Outside, flaring torches on the buildings around the square illuminated the darkness. The snow was still falling, and several inches now covered the ground.

'How long will it take my postilions to reach the town?' she wondered aloud.

'It could be some hours before your luggage arrives. They will need to recover the coach before they can seek you out and deliver it.'

'I am concerned for the men being out in this weather, rather than my bags,' she retorted, turning to frown at him.

His look implied he did not believe her. Not that what he thought of her mattered in the least.

'If you were concerned for the postilions, it would have been better not to travel today,' he went on. 'I suppose you were too intent upon returning to your London friends.'

'Yes, I was.'

It was not quite a lie. Sabrina had been impatient to leave Hartland, although it did not matter to her where she went, as long as it was away from Lord John Callater. What a cruel twist of fate it was that had thrown them together again.

'Devon cannot offer sufficient entertainment for one such as you, I suppose,' he said presently.

'And yourself,' she countered. 'What made *you* quit so precipitately?'

'Business.'

Sabrina waited, but he did not elaborate and they lapsed back into silence. The landlord brought them wine, which neither touched. Sabrina went back to the window and remained there, looking out into the night until she saw Jane and the valet hurrying back to the inn. She turned as they came into the room, eager to learn that they had found another inn with rooms to spare.

Sadly, any hopes of being free of Lord John's company were soon shattered. Jane announced there was not even an attic to be had in the town.

'The snow has made travel very difficult,' added Weald, shaking his head. 'Many of those who usually go home at the end of market day are looking for a bed. The two bedchambers here are all that are free. However, the landlord is amenable to putting an extra bed in each, if that will suit?'

Sabrina heard Jack's exasperated sigh. 'It will have to do.'

'And you might want to bespeak this parlour, too,' Weald advised him. 'The dining room is pretty well full already, although the landlord has set aside a table where Mrs Nidd and I can eat.'

Sabrina looked at her maid. 'Are you sure you would be comfortable in the public room, Jane?'

'Certainly, my lady,' replied her dresser calmly. 'Mr Weald and I have discussed it, and we consider it the best solution for us to take our dinner there together while you and His Lordship dine in private.'

Sabrina pressed her lips together to stop herself giving vent to her frustration.

'Is something amiss, my lady?' Jack raised his brows at her. 'I would not have thought *you* would be anxious about dining alone with a man other than your husband.'

Her eyes narrowed, misliking his tone. 'What do you mean by that?'

'Dear me, have I offended?' he drawled.

'You know very well you have!' He raised his quizzing glass but she stared back at him, refusing to be intimidated. 'Why do you insist upon teasing me?'

'I did not realise I was doing so.'

She turned her back to him, holding on to her temper by a thread, and he went on.

'You are a widow and gregarious to a fault, quite accustomed to setting the town by the ears.' She heard him move closer until his voice was at her shoulder. 'A little private dinner should be nothing to you.'

'You are mistaken,' she muttered.

'Am I?' His words were quiet, but there was no mistaking the contempt in his voice. 'I have followed your career for six years, madam. I know *everything* about you!'

'Sabrina turned at that and shot him an angry look.

'You know nothing about me,' she said, her voice low and quivering with emotion. 'You do not know me at all.'

Head up, she swept past him and towards the door, where her maid and Jack's man were standing, silent and reluctant witnesses to the scene.

'Jane, pray have the landlord send a bowl of soup up to my room, if you please.'

Jack cursed himself roundly as Sabrina hurried from the room, quickly followed by her maid. That was badly done of him. What was it about the woman that roused the worst in him?

Weald coughed as he closed the door upon them.

He said, his gaze fixed somewhere over Jack's shoulder, 'If you will forgive the impertinence, my lord, I should say you have seriously displeased the lady.'

Jack would have taken that from no other servant, but Tom Weald had known him almost from the cradle and he spoke with all the freedom of an old and valued retainer. He had taught Jack to ride, picking him up when he had fallen off his first pony, and it was Tom who had supported the anxious boy during his early schooldays. He had also been there during that halcyon spring when he courted Sabrina Kydd and during the dark, desperate months following her marriage.

Jack sighed and rubbed a hand over his eyes. 'I think you are right, Tom.'

Weald said bluntly, 'It don't reflect well upon you, sir.'

'Damn it, man, do you think I don't know that? She may be a coquette but that is no excuse for my bad manners!'

Weald considered for a moment, then he said, slowly, 'I'm thinking maybe it's because you still have some regard for the lady.'

'What?' Jack's head came up. 'That's nonsense. She is nothing to me. You know as well as I the scandals attached to her. Why, I don't even *like* the woman! Now, take yourself off and tell that rascally landlord to send in my dinner!'

* * *

A solitary meal in her room did much to settle Sabrina's nerves, although it did not lift her spirits. She had been very foolish to follow Jack to Devon, to think that she could rekindle the spark that she thought had once ignited between them. He believed the rumours that abounded, and who could blame him? She had sold herself to the devil and now she must pay the price. Perhaps after Sir Roderick's death, she should have retired to the Dower House and spent her days in lonely widowhood, but even four years of marriage had not quelled her liking for society. Was it wrong to love dancing, to want to forget the past and go out to parties, to enjoy herself?

The problem was that, although she craved company, she had no wish to find another husband. Society could not understand that any woman should want to remain single, but Sabrina had determined she would not suffer the indignity of another marriage unless she and her partner shared love and mutual respect. How foolish of her to think that she could ever find those things in Jack Callater.

She lay in her bed, listening to Jane snoring gently from the little truckle bed in the corner, and thought of what the future would hold for her. She was no longer sure that she wanted to return to her life in London, with its parties, the flirtations.

'You are merely feeling sorry for yourself,' she murmured into her pillow. 'Once this latest disappointment has faded, you will enjoy society again. And if not, well, you can always find some worthy cause to espouse. There are plenty of charitable societies who would welcome your money.'

Jack spent a restless night tossing and turning, and he was glad when Weald came in with his morning coffee. Having his man sleeping on a truckle bed in his room was not what he was accustomed to, but he could not say in truth that Weald's snores had disturbed him. No, he was honest enough to admit it was his conscience that had kept him awake half the night.

He had been less than a gentleman in his behaviour towards Sabrina. It was unworthy of him, however unworthy *she* might be.

Well, for that I can apologise, he thought as he climbed out of bed.

That is, if she was still at the inn. It was just possible that her post chaise had been recovered and repaired by this time. She might well have departed. After all, Sir Roderick had settled a very handsome sum upon his wife, and she could afford to pay for such exceptional service.

His mood darkened at the thought of Sabrina with the old rake. Not that it was any business of his if she had sold herself for a fortune. She was not the first woman to do so, but he had thought better of her. Six years ago he had been besotted enough to think her everything that was innocent and good.

He was in the act of tying his neckcloth, but he paused when he remembered the burning look of reproach Sabrina had given him last night. The way she had told him he did not know her at all. He stared unseeing into the mirror for a long time before shaking off his doubts. Confound it, she was a damned good actress, that was all. He would not fall for her tricks again.

Chapter Eight

It was shortly after nine o'clock when Jack made his way downstairs, and he had reached the half landing before he saw Sabrina. She was talking in an animated fashion with the landlord and one of the postilions in the doorway to the private parlour. They did not notice him, and he hovered on the stairs, curious despite himself to know what was happening.

He had to admit the lady presented a charming picture. A holly green pelisse with fur trim showed off her figure to advantage and enhanced the warm colour of her amber hair, which peeped out beneath a matching bonnet. He could only see her profile, but there was an added colour to her cheek as she engaged in a lively conversation with the two men.

It soon became clear that the carriage could not be repaired quickly and there was no suitable vehicle for my lady to hire.

'But that is ridiculous,' Sabrina was saying now. 'Surely there must be some way for me to travel!'

'I assure you, ma'am, there *isn't*,' said the hapless postilion, mangling his cap between his hands.

'Aye, 'tis true, my lady,' put in the landlord. 'The only thing large enough to take you and your baggage is Farmer Meddon's oxcart, and if I'm honest, 'tis so filthy it ain't fit for man nor beast!'

Jack's lips twitched. In his darker moments he would very much like to see Sabrina carried off in such an unwholesome vehicle, but he had come down this morning with every intention of redeeming himself, and he knew it behoved him now to behave like a gentleman.

He gave a little cough and said, as he descended the last of the stairs, 'Can I be of assistance?'

The two men turned to him with relief.

'Well, I hope as how you can,' said the postilion, elbowing the landlord aside. 'My lady's carriage is broke, which you will know, seeing as how you took her up last night. We managed to get the luggage carried here overnight, but the coach is still at the roadside and won't be recovered, let alone repaired, for a few days yet. So, my lady is wishful to get to South Molton and take the mail to Lunnon, only there's nothing suitable for carrying a lady and her maid. It's all on account of the weather, you see, my lord.'

'Dear me,' said Jack mildly. 'Is the snow that bad, then?'

'Well, it ain't so bad *here*,' put in the landlord. 'But we've already had word that the stage won't be coming through today, and there ain't another vehicle in Torrington to be had for love nor money. As I told Her Ladyship, the Squire has a carriage, but he's gone off in it to Barnstaple to visit his daughter and won't be back for a sennight.'

Jack had been idly swinging his quizzing glass back and forth on its ribbon while he listened, but all the time he was aware of Sabrina standing to one side of the men. She was chewing her lip and looking pensive. He knew that of all things, she really did not wish to be any more beholden to him, and his inner devil took great satisfaction from that fact. He encompassed them all in his smile.

'Well, I believe I have a solution,' he said cheerfully. 'I am on my way to London—'

Sabrina interrupted him.

'Thank you, my lord, but I would not trouble you to carry me all that way.'

'I was not going to suggest it, ma'am,' he replied, adding gently, 'That would not suit either of us, would it?'

She bristled in response, but before she could snap

back at him, he carried on in a tone of cool reason
that he knew she would dislike very much.

'I could, however, take you as far as South Molton,
from where you can continue your journey on the
mail. I believe my baggage coach will accommo-
date your maid and your trunks, ma'am, and as long
as the snow does not get worse, we should be able to
reach South Molton in what…three hours?' He met
her eyes and saw that she would dearly like to reject
his offer. He succumbed again to his inner devil and
added, 'I think you will find my travelling chaise a
little more comfortable than an oxcart.'

If they had been alone, Jack thought she might
well have thrown something at him. As it was, their
charade was played out in front of the postilion and
the landlord, who were waiting hopefully for her answer. And after an inward struggle Sabrina gave a
little nod of her head.

'Then I will accept your offer, Lord John,' she said
politely. 'Thank you.'

'Not at all,' he replied, not to be outdone in manners. 'I shall set my man to organise everything
while I break my fast. Perhaps you would care to
join me?'

'You are very kind, sir, but I have already eaten,'
she replied. 'I must go and tell Jane what is happening and fetch my cloak.'

She hurried off, and Jack could only imagine the mortification she was feeling at being even more indebted to him.

Less than an hour later, the carriages set off. Sabrina took her place beside Jack but pressed herself into the corner to avoid any contact. He had made it very plain to her yesterday how much he despised her, and his good manners today were designed merely to tease.

'I am sorry for the inconvenience I am causing you,' she said stiffly, when the silence became unbearable. 'I am well aware that you would rather not be in my company.'

'Not at all, madam. I am only too pleased to be of service.'

'No, you are not!' she retorted, nettled beyond bearing. 'You think me little better than a whore.' She saw the look of surprise upon Jack's face and was shocked by her own plain speaking. She went on more quietly, 'Perhaps you are right about that. I did not wed Sir Roderick out of affection. I married him for what he could do for my family. But I was a dutiful wife. Or at least, I tried to be.'

'You do not need to tell me this, madam.'

'Yes, I do.' She looked down at her clasped hands. Her anger towards Jack had faded with that first outburst, and there was something she needed to tell him, something that had nagged at her all these years. 'When we first met, I gave you reason to think I welcomed your attentions. I encouraged you, then I married someone else. That was wrong of me. I should have at least informed you of the fact myself, rather than leaving you to discover it from someone else. I am sorry for that and I beg your pardon.'

'Our acquaintance was very short, madam. It was of little consequence to me.'

His indifference stung, but what else had she expected?

'I am glad, then.' She nodded. 'I never meant to cause you pain.'

There. She had needed to apologise and she had done so. Now her conscience was quite clear.

Silence fell again and Sabrina turned to stare out of the window. The view was obscured by the snow, which was falling thick and fast. She had no sense of the direction they were travelling, for the narrow lanes wound their way between high banks that were topped with hedges that made it impossible to see the landscape. They had slowed to a walking pace and Sabrina knew that with the weather so bad, it would be considerably more than three hours before they reached their destination. Finally the carriage stopped completely, and she heard their coachman shouting to the driver of the baggage coach.

'Now what is amiss?' muttered Jack.

He jumped out, closing the door firmly behind him. Sabrina could only hear snatches of the conversation between the three men, but it was enough to understand that they were lost, as Jack confirmed when he climbed back into the carriage.

'We seem to have taken a wrong turn somewhere,' he said, shaking the snow off his hat before closing the door. 'This lane is too narrow for us to change direction so we must go on and hope we see a signpost, or someone to direct us. Don't worry, we cannot be very far from South Molton.'

Jack did not expect Sabrina to pay much heed to his words of reassurance. He waited, expecting her to rip up at him and blame him for this setback, but she merely nodded.

'The wind is picking up,' she pointed out, drawing her cloak more closely around her. 'If it continues to snow, then the roads could soon be impassable.'

'I cannot deny it. I am glad you recognise the severity of the situation.'

'Only a fool would not do so.'

He tried a little smile. 'And no one could think you a fool.'

'Truly?' Her voice dripped with scorn. 'Then it is the only insult you have not thrown at me!'

She hunched a shoulder and turned away to stare at the snow-covered window. Jack shrugged inwardly, leaning back against the squabs. Her apology had thrown him, but now she was back to cutting at him at every turn. He was relieved. Sabrina angry he could deal with. Sabrina contrite threatened to break through his defences as easily as a hot knife through butter.

They set off again and soon the bank and hedge on one side of the lane gave way to a neat stone wall. Jack ordered his coachman to stop. By opening the door and standing up, he could see that beyond the wall was a small, stone-built manor house, and there was the faint glimmer of lamplight coming from one of the windows. After ordering his driver to look out for the gates to the property and turn in, he moved back into the carriage.

'The weather shows no sign of letting up,' he explained to Sabrina. 'I doubt now that we will reach South Molton tonight.'

'I think you are right,' she agreed, as he resumed his seat. 'It is better for us to seek shelter than risk getting stuck in a snowdrift.'

He nodded, relieved by her calm acceptance of the situation.

They had not gone very far before the chaise turned between a pair of substantial gateposts and came to a stop before the house.

'It looks empty,' observed Sabrina, peering out of the carriage.

'No, there was a light in the window,' said Jack. 'I saw it from the road.'

The baggage coach had drawn up behind them and Weald jumped out. He hurried across to the door of the house and hammered upon it, but after several attempts he ran over to the travelling chaise.

'There is no one at home, my lord,' he said, when Jack let down the window. 'The door is bolted.'

'There must be someone in there.' Jack stared at the house. Every window was dark. Had he imagined the light? 'Look!' He pointed towards the large glazed bay to one side of the door. 'There *is* someone there. I saw a face. Go and knock again.'

'No, let me.' Sabrina put a hand on his arm. 'It may be there are only women in the house. They could well be afraid to answer the door to a stranger. Let me out, Mr Weald.'

She alighted and made her way across to the large bay window, where he had seen the face. Jack watched as she tapped on the glass.

'Please open the door for us. We need shelter.'

Her raised voice carried across the drive to the carriage, where Jack had left the window open in order to see what was happening. The hood and shoulders of her cloak were turning white now. She moved to the door and used the knocker before calling out again.

'Surely you would not leave us to perish in the snow on your doorstep.'

'No one there,' muttered Weald, who had climbed into the chaise out of the snow while they waited. 'There looks to be a stable block at the side, perhaps we could—'

'No, Tom, look. The door is opening.'

They watched as the heavy black door opened a crack, and Sabrina carried on a conversation with whoever was inside. The wind made it impossible to hear what was said, but after a moment the door opened a little more and a small figure in a pale gown could be seen.

'My lady was right,' observed Weald. 'Looks like there's no one but a serving girl in the house.'

Sabrina was now pointing towards the carriages and continuing to talk to the figure in the doorway.

'Ah, that's better,' Jack nodded. 'She is calling us over.'

'Probably best if just you go, my lord,' said Weald. 'We don't want to frighten the maid by all appearing at once.'

Jack hurried over to the door, where he was surprised to see it was not a servant at all, but a young girl. She looked to be no more than ten or twelve years old, a slight figure with a cream shawl clutched about her thin shoulders. She was dressed in a grey twill gown beneath a linen apron, which was folded over several times at the waist to stop it trailing on the ground.

'This is Miss Steadmarsh, my lord,' explained Sabrina cheerfully. 'And this is Hare Hall. Her father is from home at present, and she is quite naturally reluctant to allow anyone into the house. However, I have assured her that she need have no fears. We only wish to shelter from the snow.'

Father from home? Where was the mother, and the servants?

A host of questions flew around Jack's head, but Sabrina's look told him this was not the time to interrogate the child.

'That is quite right,' he said, taking his cue from Sabrina's friendly tone. He bowed to the girl and took out one of his calling cards, which he handed to her. 'Allow me to introduce myself, Miss Steadmarsh. I am Lord John Callater, and this is Lady Massyngham. We are on our way to South Molton, but the weather has made it impossible to go any further while it is snowing so hard. I quite understand that you may not wish to have us under your roof and we would be quite happy to take shelter overnight in the carriage house, if you would grant us permission. We have no wish to intrude upon you more than necessary.'

The girl listened, then stood looking at them for a long time, her dark eyes moving from Jack to Sabrina and back again.

'No, you may come in.' She pulled the door wider. 'I am afraid I cannot offer you any refreshments,' she said politely, 'but you are welcome to rest a while in the drawing room.'

'Thank you,' said Jack. 'May I tell my people to take the horses to the stable? I should like them to rest out of the snow, at least for a while.'

The girl nodded, and Jack went quickly back to the waiting carriages. He returned shortly, accompanied by Mrs Nidd, and they stepped into the stone-flagged hall to find Sabrina waiting for them.

'Ah, there you are.' She greeted them cheerfully and quite loud enough for her voice to carry through the open doorway to one side, where golden light was spilling out onto the stone flags. 'And you have brought Jane, sir, thank goodness! Miss Steadmarsh is lighting the candles in the drawing room for us.'

She paused, her friendly manner slipping a little when she looked at Jack.

She said quietly, 'You appear surprised, my lord, but I think it best if we put aside our differences while we are in this house. The child is worried enough. I do not want to make her even more anxious.'

He inclined his head. 'I agree, ma'am. It will not do to bicker in front of the girl.'

'Bicker! I would have said it was far more than—' She stopped, closing her lips firmly upon whatever she had been about to utter, and gave a little nod. 'Very well then, let us go in.'

Jack followed Sabrina and her maid into the drawing room, where several candles were now burning, although there was no fire in the hearth. If anything it felt colder here than in the hall but Sabrina was already declaring how good it was to be indoors. She turned to introduce her maid to the girl.

'This is Mrs Nidd, and a most useful companion in situations like these. Jane, this is Miss Mary Steadmarsh.'

Jane gave the girl a motherly smile. 'I am delighted to meet you, I am sure, miss.'

'Miss Steadmarsh was telling me that this room has not been prepared for visitors,' Sabrina went on, as if it was not blindingly obvious. 'I assured her we would be very happy to sit in the kitchen, which she tells me is considerably warmer.'

'By all means.'

Jack readily agreed, wondering what the devil was going on here. The house had the cold chill of a property not occupied for some time. Where was the girl's family? Where were the servants?

He said with a smile, 'If Miss Steadmarsh will lead the way?'

Mary nodded. She lit the candle in her chamberstick before snuffing out all the lights in the drawing room, then she led them back into the hall and through a series of stone passages to the kitchen.

As they went through the door, Jack realised that saying the kitchen was *'considerably warmer'* was an overstatement. One might not be able to see one's breath here, but the air was still cold. He had little experience of kitchens, but he thought this one looked reasonably well appointed, with an open range set into the chimneypiece at one end. A sullen fire glowed behind the bars of the grate, which was the source of the small amount of heat in the room. Sabrina moved towards it with a little exclamation of pleasure.

'Ah, how clever of you to keep the fire going, Mary.'

The girl gave a shy smile.

'It needs more coal,' she said. 'But I haven't been outside yet to get any.'

'Then we will help with that,' said Jack immediately.

He saw Sabrina's brows go up and felt a little frisson of irritation. Did she think him quite such a coxcomb that he was unable to do anything useful?

'I shall fetch some. And firewood, too,' he went on, glancing at the empty log basket.

'Excellent, my lord. And when we have stoked up the fire, Jane and I will begin preparing a meal. Mary tells me the cook-housekeeper left the larder very well stocked, before she left.' She directed another telling look at Jack. 'Two days ago.'

Two days! Not by the bat of an eyelid did Jack show his concern. Who would leave any child alone to fend for herself? Especially a gently born girl, which Mary Steadmarsh was, quite clearly.

Before going off in search of fuel for the fire, Jack made his way to the stables, where he found his valet, the coachmen and the two footmen cosily ensconced in the attic above the stables.

'The place is deserted,' explained Weald as Jack looked around him. 'Everyone seems to have left and taken the livestock with them.'

'It's the same in the house,' said Jack. 'The owner has disappeared, leaving only his daughter in residence. A child. She expects him back, but I have my doubts. The way the servants have quit Hare Hall makes me think the wages haven't been paid.'

The men looked shocked at his revelation.

'We can't leave the child here alone and that's for sure,' declared the driver of the baggage coach. 'I take it we are stopping here then, my lord?'

'We are, Dan. It is either that or take her with us.'

'Well, there's little chance of going further tonight,' said his coachman. 'We've found fodder enough for the horses, and we're snug as bugs up here. Although I can't deny that a good meal would be welcome.'

'I don't think we have any choice but to stay, the weather as it is,' added Weald.

'I agree,' said Jack. 'And as for a meal, I hope we will have something arranged very soon, but first we need fuel for the house, and since you already have a good fire here, you must know where the logs and coal are stored.' He turned to his two footmen. 'Abel, Sam, you will find the coal bucket and log basket downstairs. Pray fill them up and bring them to my lady in the kitchen, if you please, but make it clear you are returning to the stables. You had best stay here too, Tom, for the moment,' he said to his valet. 'We haven't yet suggested we should stay here overnight. Lady Massyngham is trying to win the girl's confidence, and so far we have only said we need shelter for a few hours. Once Miss Steadmarsh is more comfortable with us being in the house, I will fetch you in, but for now, bear with me.'

As soon as Jack went off in search of fuel, Sabrina and Jane made a quick inspection of the kitchen and the larder. There was no shortage of food supplies, and Jane suggested that once the fire was built up, she could set to work preparing dinner for everyone. Sabrina assured Mary that they would pay for everything, and she handed over her purse to show she was in earnest. The girl carefully counted out the coins, her eyes growing wider all the time.

'Of course, it would be extremely helpful if you would allow us to stay here for a few days,' Sabrina added. 'Once the snow has eased, we could replenish your stocks for you before we continue on our way.'

Mary looked up at her uncertainly. 'Papa would not like it. He has not allowed any guests into the house since Mama died a year ago.'

Sabrina said gently, 'That may be so, but I am sure he did not mean for you to be here all alone.'

'No.' The girl's eyes filled with tears. 'He w-went to Exeter three weeks ago to f-fetch my aunt and n-never came back…'

'Three weeks!' Jane gave a little cry of horror. 'Oh, my poor lamb. There, there, sweeting, I am here now, and I'll look after you.'

She pulled Mary into a fierce hug, crooning softly to her, much as she had done with Sabrina when she was a child.

Jack returned from the stables to find Jane Nidd in charge of the kitchen with Mary and Sabrina following her directions as they gathered together everything she required to make supper.

'Miss Steadmarsh has kindly invited us to remain at the Hall for a few days, until the snow had eased,' Sabrina told him. 'Perhaps, my lord, you would arrange for the trunks to be brought in. After you have built up the fire, of course.'

These last words were uttered innocently enough, but when Jack glanced across at Sabrina, he saw a teasing gleam in those green eyes. That made him smile. If she was able to set aside their disagreements, then he could, too.

By the time dinner was ready, the house was far more comfortable. It was agreed that all the servants would dine together in the kitchen, but they were so horrified at the idea of Lord John and Sabrina dining with them that Jack had set to work kindling a fire in the dining room. However, when he suggested Mary should dine there with them, he discovered that arrangements had already been made for her.

'The child asked if she might be allowed to eat in the kitchen with Jane,' Sabrina explained. 'I think the idea of dining alone with us, two strangers, was far too daunting.'

She looked away from him, a slight flush painting her cheeks.

'And do you find it daunting, too, the thought of dining alone with me?'

'Of course. But the situation here is difficult enough, without adding more complications. We have agreed to put aside our differences while we are here.'

She looked up briefly and he smiled.

'We have, and I am sure we can.'

Thus it was that he and Sabrina sat down together for their dinner. With the heavy curtains pulled across the window, the room was heating up nicely. The atmosphere was less chilly too, at least for the moment.

Weald took it upon himself to wait upon them, and his presence added a measure of formality to the occasion that made it easier for them to pretend there was nothing out of the ordinary in their dining alone together. Jack had found a bottle of good wine in the cellars, and this eased the situation even more, so much so that by the time they had finished their meal and they were sitting alone in the dining room, which was by now comfortably warm, they were conversing together with the ease of old friends.

'Well, thank goodness we came across this place,' he remarked. 'By the sound of that wind howling outside, it is not a night to be travelling.'

'True. And not just for our sake. Poor Mary was at her wits' end when we found her.'

'She seems to have quite taken to your maid.'

'Yes, indeed,' replied Sabrina, smiling. 'But it is not surprising. Jane was my nursemaid and she has a very motherly streak. She was only too happy to take Mary under her wing.'

'And has the child confided in her?' asked Jack, refilling their glasses. 'Do we know how she comes to be alone here?'

'Why yes.' Smiling, Sabrina took a sip of her wine. 'As soon as Jane gave Mary a hug, the girl burst into tears, and then the whole story came out! The poor child's mother died a year ago, and her father has been mad with grief ever since. Piecing together the story, it seems that wages have gone unpaid, land untended and everything was going to rack and ruin. Then, three weeks ago, Mr Steadmarsh came to his senses, if only a little, and decided he must do something to repair the damage. He went off to Exeter to fetch his sister to keep house for them and, sadly, he hasn't been seen since.'

'And it would appear the whole household pan-icked and thought he had abandoned them,' put in Jack, pouring more wine.

'Exactly.' Sabrina nodded. 'Mary says that when her father did not return to Hare Hall after a week, all the servants began to leave. Except Mrs Fitch, the housekeeper. She stayed and did what she could here until two days ago. She wanted Mary to go with her, but the girl refused to leave her home, and instead of taking what was left of the housekeeping in lieu of the wages she was owed, the good woman made sure the house was well stocked with food. Although how she expected the child to manage on her own here, I do not know!'

After this exclamation Sabrina sat back, her brow furrowed as she considered Mary's plight. Jack picked up his glass and saluted her.

'Thank you, ma'am.'

She raised her brows. 'For what?'

'For dealing so well with a difficult situation. The poor child must have been terrified to have a party of strangers turn up on her doorstep.'

'No, I did not do that much. It was all Jane. Her motherly presence put Mary at her ease and per-suaded the girl to let us stay. Not that I could have abandoned the child, even if the weather had been good enough to move on.' Her frown deepened.

'However, I wish we could know what has happened to Mr Steadmarsh. I fear, from the few snippets Mary has let drop, that he turned to drink after his wife's demise. It is possible he never made it to Exeter.'

'I had thought that, too. However, whatever has occurred, we can do nothing until the weather improves,' remarked Jack. 'Then, if Steadmarsh has not returned, we must make enquiries locally and find someone to take the child in.'

'Yes. And until then we will do our best to divert her mind from her troubles.'

Sabrina was smiling at him, as if it was the most natural thing in the world to be sitting here together, talking, and Jack could not deny that it felt very comfortable. Then he saw her expression change. The smile was still fixed on her lips but it died from her eyes. She pushed aside her empty plate and rose, saying in a matter-of-fact tone.

'I shall leave you to finish your wine, my lord. It has been a long day, so I shall say goodnight, too. No, no, do not get up. I am quite capable of opening the door for myself.'

Jack sank back onto his chair and watched her walk out of the room. The easy camaraderie had gone and she had resorted to cool civility. It was probably for the best. They could be confined together in this house for days, and he had no wish to fall under her spell again.

But Jack could not help feeling a quite irrational pang of regret. The dinner had been cobbled together, and every time Tom Weald had opened the door, he had let in a blast of icy air, but despite all that, tonight had been one of the most pleasant evenings Jack had spent in a very long time.

Chapter Nine

Daylight brought no relief from the weather. Jane came in to wake her mistress, and Sabrina stared out in dismay at the wintry scene from her bedroom window. The sky had cleared overnight but this had only caused the temperature to drop, and the snow returned with the dawn. There could be no question of travelling today, and that was worrying. Not that she should complain; they had a reasonable degree of comfort, the house was dry and they had food and servants enough to supply their needs, but the idea of being trapped at Hare Hall with Jack Callater filled Sabrina with apprehension. Last night's dinner, and the uninterrupted hour that they had spent alone together afterwards, had shown her how easy it was to fall back under the spell of his charm.

She must be on her guard now. She would never forgive his behaviour at the Hartland Ball, the way he had walked out on her after taking his pleasure. Yet her wayward heart reminded her that there had been pleasure for her, too, in those few, precious hours she had spent in his bed. He had awakened feelings in her that she had never known before. He had made her feel...*alive*! Last night she had woken in this strange bed, her body yearning so badly for Jack's touch that she wanted to go and find him, to throw herself into his arms and beg him to do it all over again.

In fact, just thinking of it was melting her bones.

'Have you learned *nothing* in your five-and-twenty years?' she berated herself inwardly as she sipped her hot chocolate. 'The man is a dangerous flirt. He has been on the town for years, his name has been linked with goodness knows how many ladies, but never a hint of marriage. If you throw yourself at him again, he will take what he wants and walk away, just as he did before!'

But the desire Jack had awoken was not so easily suppressed. She wanted him so much it was a physical pain.

Having finished her hot chocolate, she slipped out of bed and almost welcomed the chill of the boards on her bare feet. As soon as Jane had laced her stays, Sabrina sent her away. She was perfectly capable of dressing herself in one of her front-closing gowns, and goodness knew, Jane had enough to do in the kitchen, as well as looking after Mary. However, it was almost an hour later before Sabrina finally went downstairs, having scrambled into the rest of her clothes and dressed her own hair. Mary greeted her cheerfully as she walked into the kitchen.

'Good morning, my lady. Mrs Nidd has made porridge for everyone this morning.'

'Porridge!' exclaimed Sabrina, 'Do we have milk then?'

'Oh, yes,' said Mary, looking up from her own breakfast. 'We collect it from the Jessops' farm about a mile away. I told Jane about it when she took me up to bed last night, and she sent one of Lord John's men to fetch some. It is less than a mile if you walk across the fields.'

'Abel went off just before dawn,' added Jane, ladling the creamy porridge into a bowl for Sabrina. 'He brought butter and bread, too, my lady, and Mrs Jessop has agreed to supply us with milk and also a fresh loaf every day, once she learned that there was no one here to make it. I had taken the liberty of writing a note for Mrs Jessop, you see, ma'am,' she went on. 'Mary said the farmer's wife is a very respectable soul, and I thought I should give her a brief explanation of our circumstances, in case she was anxious about what might be going on here.'

Sabrina nodded her approval. 'Very sensible, Jane, I should have done the same.'

'Thank you. And I hope you don't object to eating in the kitchen, ma'am, only the dining room is mighty chill in the mornings.'

'Not at all. I would much rather be here in the warm and in company.'

'Good. And you've no need to worry about the menservants coming in. I have already sent a kettle of porridge across, and they are quite content to break their fast in their quarters above the stables. Truth be told, I think they prefer it. Abel tells me their rooms are quite snug.'

'There's honey, too, Lady Massyngham,' put in Mary, pointing to a stoneware jar on the table.

'Excellent! This is quite my favourite breakfast. And do, please call me Sabrina.'

It was heartening to see Mary so cheerful this morning, quite unlike the frightened waif they had found alone in the house last night. She chattered away happily to them, only breaking off when His Lordship's valet came into the kitchen.

'Good morning, Mr Weald.' Jane looked around from the range, where she was stirring the large kettle of porridge. 'Is the master ready for his breakfast?'

'Not quite yet, Mrs Nidd, thank you. I've come to fetch up a can of hot water.'

Sabrina kept her eyes lowered, but her lip curled in contempt as she whipped up her resentment. So,

Jack had decided to play the great lord above stairs, while everyone else rallied around doing what they could to make the house comfortable. She should have expected nothing else from him.

'His Lordship wants to make himself presentable before he comes down to break his fast,' Weald explained.

'Of course he does,' her maid agreed, much to Sabrina's annoyance. How selfish of the man, to lie abed and be waited on, when everyone else was working.

Jane chuckled and went on. 'Aye, he will want to clean himself up after chopping all those logs this morning.'

Sabrina almost dropped her spoon. She waited until Weald had withdrawn before speaking. Then she asked, as casually as she could.

'Lord John has been cutting wood?'

'Why yes, my lady. Bless him, he said he quite enjoyed wielding the axe. He brought in another bucket of coals, too, and had the fire here burning nicely by the time I came downstairs. He says it gave him something to do. Made him feel useful.'

'Oh.' Sabrina felt quite chastened. Thank goodness she had not uttered her scathing remarks aloud. 'Yes, well, we all need to help out in the circumstances.'

She went back to her breakfast and afterwards set about helping Jane with the housework. Her maid was loath to allow her to help with anything other than a little sewing, but Sabrina protested she could do more than that.

'You will remember Papa's views that every lady should know how to keep house and prepare a dinner, no matter how many servants they may have. He insisted I should spend time with the housekeeper, and in the kitchens.' She chuckled. 'I never thought I should need it, until today.'

'I don't know, Miss Sabrina…'

'Now, Jane, this is no time to stand on ceremony.' She added, with feeling, 'Lord John is not the only one who wants to feel useful!'

'Well, perhaps a little light dusting, then, my lady.'

'Is that all you can suggest? Lord, what a useless creature you think me. There must be more I can do to help.'

'Well…we could do with knowing what we have in the linen cupboards. Mary's bed needs fresh sheets, and since we have no idea how long we will be staying here, an inventory would be useful.' She lowered her voice, even though they were momentarily alone in the kitchen. 'There are signs that some of the house contents have gone missing. Only small things as far as I can tell, but I fear some of the servants helped themselves when they left. In lieu of wages.'

'Then counting the linen shall be my first task!' declared Sabrina, laughing.

Away from any room with a fire, Hare House was very cold. Draughts whistled through the passages and before sallying forth to inspect the linen cupboards, Sabrina put on her pelisse, donned an apron and then threw a thick cashmere shawl about her shoulders for added warmth. She located the cupboards in the housekeeper's room and spent a quiet hour sorting the contents and making notes.

She was on her way back to the kitchen when Jack appeared and, she could not help it, her mouth dried at the sight of him. He looked as handsome and fashionable as ever, in the well-tailored riding jacket that fitted over his broad shoulders without a crease and with his cravat neatly tied. Even his serviceable buckskins looked immaculate, disappearing into highly polished top boots. His tall, athletic frame seemed to fill the narrow servants' passage and it was impossible for Sabrina to do anything but stop as he approached.

She was still fretting over her earlier injustice to him, and this made her greet him far more warmly than she had intended. However, she could not deny it felt very right, very comfortable, to do so. When he remarked upon finding her in the passage, she told him she had been counting sheets.

'We will have to change all the bedding at some point, besides needing towels and napkins and all manner of linen, so it is best to know in advance what we have in the cupboards.' She chuckled. 'I wish I could take the credit, but it was Jane's suggestion that I make a note of everything.'

'An excellent idea. And since you are already armed with paper and pencil, perhaps you would assist me with *my* next task?' When she gave him a quizzical look, he continued. 'I am about to investigate the contents of the wine cellar, but, unlike you, I had not thought to bring anything to record my findings. And,' he went on, when she went to hand him the notebook, 'I will need to hold the lamp, so it would be much easier if I had someone to write everything down for me.'

She hesitated, but only for a moment. She had met far more dangerous men than Jack Callater, hardened libertines whose charms were legendary, but she had never yet succumbed to any of them. Common sense might suggest that she should not be alone with him, but curiosity had got the better of Sabrina. She wanted to see more of the house. At least that is what she told herself.

'Very well, if you think it would be useful?'

He nodded. 'Very useful.'

She turned and followed Jack back the way she had come.

'I should like to know that our suspicions about Mr Steadmarsh are unfounded,' she said. 'We might well be able to tell that from the state of his wine cellar.'

'Yes, that's very true.' Jack held up a large key ring. 'These are the butler's keys. Mary tells me the housekeeper had charge of them when the man left Hare Hall, so it is unlikely that the servants were able to raid the cellars. Let us go and see.'

They started at the butler's pantry, where they took one of the silver chambersticks to light their way to the basement. There they found several doors leading off a dark passage. Sabrina held the candle while Jack tried the keys. The first door opened onto a small cupboard with shelves holding a few ancient pieces of tarnished silver, but when they unlocked the second, he gave a little grunt of satisfaction.

'Aha. Success.'

Jack took the candle and led the way into the cellar. Sabrina followed. By the light of the single candle she could see it was paved with rough stone flags and had a drainage channel running down one side.

'Now why would anyone want to sit in here?' she exclaimed, spotting the table and chairs in the centre of the room. On the dusty tabletop were half a dozen upturned wine glasses.

'It is not unknown for the master of the house to entertain his friends in the cellar.'

She turned to look up at him. 'Have *you* ever done such a thing?'

'Of course.' He grinned. 'We could try it now, if you wish.'

Sabrina thought it best to ignore his suggestion and returned her attention to the cellar. Arranged around the walls were wooden racks filled with bottles and a sturdy workbench. There were also stands for barrels of varying sizes, although only a few of the smaller ones still held barrels. There were chalk marks everywhere, dates on the wine racks and notes on the barrels, which she guessed indicated when they had been last used.

'It is clear that Mr Steadmarsh took his wine very seriously,' remarked Jack. 'Or at least, his predecessors did. The supply does not look to be seriously depleted.'

'There is a candlestick on the table,' remarked Sabrina. 'If we light that, I can sit down and make notes while you inspect the cellar.'

'An excellent idea.'

Jack walked over to the table and lit the two candles fixed into the wax-encrusted holder, while Sabrina dusted one of the chairs with the corner of her apron before sitting down.

She opened the notebook. 'Very well, sir, I am ready.'

'Good. Let us start with the barrels.'

She watched him as he inspected the casks of various sizes on one side of the room. There was one he said was a drum of Madeira, and another with tapered ends that Jack told her was a small pipe of port.

'Both near-empty,' he said, rapping his knuckles against them. He moved across to the last small barrel and knocked on it. 'However, this half-anchor still holds plenty of brandy.' He held his candle close to the barrel and peered at the lettering. 'Cognac, from the Massougnes estate. I should like to try a little of that.' He glanced back at her. 'Will you join me?'

Sabrina knew he was teasing her. Ladies did not drink brandy except for medicinal purposes, but instead of saying so she laughed.

'What, at this time of the day?'

'Why not? Better to discover now that it is undrinkable than wait until dinnertime.'

'That sounds like a very reasonable argument.'

She could hardly believe she had said that, but some devilry had gripped her. She had spent years pretending to be a wicked widow, why not actually do something disreputable? Such as drinking brandy with a man in a cellar. That little devil in her head told her that was hardly disreputable at all. She picked up two of the glasses and wiped them with a clean handkerchief before carrying them over to Jack.

His look of surprise made her smile with satisfaction. He rinsed the glasses with a little of the cognac before pouring a good measure into each of them.

He held one out to her. 'You are a *connoisseuse*, perhaps?'

Sabrina did not want to admit she had never tried brandy before and gave what she hoped was a mysterious smile before taking a mouthful. The fiery liquid singed the back of her throat as she swallowed it and she fell into a fit of coughing.

Jack laughed. 'Ah, not an expert, then.'

He reached out to take the glass from her, but she resisted.

'No,' she croaked. 'I will finish this.'

'Small sips, then,' he advised, as he raised his own glass to his mouth. 'Mmm, it really is very good. What is your opinion?'

Sabrina tasted it again and managed a creditable nod of appreciation. She did not much like the taste but was determined not to be beaten, especially when Jack was looking at her with such amusement.

'It reminds me of something…hazelnuts,' she said, after another sip. 'Does all brandy taste like this?'

'Similar, but Cognac is regarded as the finest. They are not all as light and fresh as this. I shall have Tom fill a decanter and bring it to the dining room this evening.' He drained his glass. 'Shall we try something else?'

Sabrina quickly shook her head. 'No, thank you, my lord. There is work to be done.'

She was not such a simpleton. She knew better than to drink any more so early in the day. That could lead to all sorts of foolish behaviour!

Jack was well aware that he should not have suggested they drink brandy together, but somehow it was just too easy to forget the proprieties with Sabrina. Too difficult to keep a proper distance. It occurred to him now that it was the same for her. Why else would she take him up on his challenge to try the cognac, especially when it was obvious she had never drunk it before? Perhaps, like him, she enjoyed the frisson of danger that existed between them.

Now, that was an interesting thought.

'We should finish making our inventory,' she said now. 'I promised Mary we would keep a tally of everything we use and pay for it.'

'Very well, if you sit down again, I will take a look at the wine racks.'

'…and eleven bottles of Champagne on the last rack.' Jack straightened. 'Will that suffice, or do you want more details?'

'No, that is enough for our purposes,' replied Sabrina, putting down her pencil. She was glad that was done, for the brandy was having an effect. She felt a little light-headed and in no mood to concentrate. She also felt remarkably cheerful.

She smiled. 'Well done, my lord. We have achieved a very worthwhile task this morning.'

'Do you think so?' Jack pulled one of the champagne bottles from the rack and held it up. 'Worthy of a celebration, do you think?'

She really should not, but the only other thing Jane had asked her to do was to tidy the drawing room. No very onerous task. She smiled brightly.

'Yes, I think so!' She waved at the empty glasses they had used for the cognac. 'Will these do? There does not appear to be any other sort...'

'Oh, yes, I should think they will suit our purpose.'

Jack opened the bottle and poured the sparkling wine into the glasses. Sabrina picked up one and held it aloft. 'Your good health, my lord!'

Taking a sip, she could taste the remnants of the cognac in the bubbles that fizzed pleasantly on her tongue. She took another mouthful and sat back on her chair as a glow of content began to spread through her.

'You prefer this to the Massougnes, I think, my lady.'

'I do indeed.'

She smiled up at Jack, who was standing over her. She did not move when he leaned down and brushed his lips against hers. The tip of his tongue flickered all too briefly into her mouth before he straightened.

'Enough of that,' he murmured. 'Else who knows what might happen?'

Sabrina knew. She knew exactly what she wanted to happen. In fact, she was already growing hot at the thought of it. Slowly, deliberately, she pushed her shawl off her shoulders and stood up. She stepped closer to Jack and slipped her arms about his neck.

'Kiss me.'

She felt a little burst of satisfaction when she saw the fire in his eyes as she whispered the words.

He put his glass down on the table. 'I do not think that's a good idea, do you?'

In answer, she gently pulled his head down towards her, looking up at him, her lips already slightly parted in anticipation. She closed her eyes as he brought his mouth down on hers, excitement rippling through her body as he kissed her. She pressed herself against him, the heat pooling in her belly and excitement rising when she felt his hard arousal. Her blood was on fire as it coursed around her body, and she almost wept when he broke off the kiss and held her away from him.

'This is madness, Sabrina,' he muttered, frowning down at her. 'You may well regret this later.'

'No regrets, Jack.' She tugged at the apron strings and shrugged it off. 'No regrets, I promise you.'

She pulled his head down again, and this time, when his mouth met hers, the world exploded. His arms tightened around her and he kissed her thoroughly, strengthening the desire already growing inside her. Sabrina sighed as he began to cover her face with kisses and even as his mouth trailed down to her neck, she was already unbuttoning her pelisse, moving it aside so that he could continue to trail those blissful butterfly kisses along her neck. She threw her head back as his tongue flickered over the soft skin of her throat. His hands slipped inside the coat, one moving around her back and holding her firm against him while the other... She moaned softly as the other hand pushed aside the soft muslin of her bodice and caressed her breasts.

When his fingers found one hard erect nub and began to massage it, a gasp of pure pleasure escaped her. She was almost fainting with desire now and gave a little mewl of disappointment when he cupped her buttocks and lifted her up against him. In a couple of strides, he crossed to the wall, where he lowered her onto the empty workbench. He began to kiss her again, working his mouth against hers, the kisses growing deeper, hotter. She felt him push aside her skirts, then one hand smoothed over her thigh, moving slowly higher, closer to the heat. He slipped his fingers into her, stroking and caressing until she was euphoric, almost swooning. She threw back her head as ripples of excitement ran through her, building into a wave that she could not control. She gasped, cried out as the delicious torture continued, then she reached for him and was scrabbling with the buttons of his buckskins. She wanted him inside her, needing him to share this exquisite delight.

Jack almost groaned as her small hands struggled with the unfamiliar fastenings of his clothes. He breathed deep, controlling himself until she had freed him, then his pulse leapt when he felt her fingers slip around him, gently moving over his shaft, and he knew he would not be able to hold off for much longer. He pulled her closer, and she wrapped her legs about him, tilting up her hips, offering herself, and he could not resist. He entered her, exulting as she pushed back against him and in the cry of pleasure she gave as they both came to a juddering climax. Shaking, she clung to him and whimpered his name as the final spasms died away.

Eyes shut, Jack held Sabrina tight against him, her face buried in his shoulder. The faint beat of her heart echoed against his chest, and they remained still, clinging to one another for a long, long moment. Then at last he felt her stir, and with a sigh he eased himself away.

'I beg your pardon,' he began, but she interrupted him.

'There is no need. I…invited you to do that, did I not?' She slipped off the bench and began to shake out her skirts, brushing off the dust.

'I did not need much persuading.'

He reached out and pulled her into his arms again. Her lips were still red and full from their lovemaking, and he dropped a gentle kiss upon them. It went on for a long time, and when it ended she gave a shy smile before moving away.

'I cannot deny that was even better than I anticipated,' she murmured, walking back towards the table.

'There is more champagne, if you would like some?'

'No, no.' She shook her head. 'Thank you.'

'Then it will keep until dinner time.'

'Yes.' She looked distracted, ill at ease as she draped the heavy shawl about her shoulders. She scooped up the discarded apron, closed the notebook and picked it up, together with the pencil. 'I must return these to the kitchen.'

'I will come with you.'

For a moment, Jack thought she was going to say

something. Then, silently, she nodded. She waited while he snuffed out the candles on the table and picked up the chamberstick, then she walked with him to the door, and they made their way in silence upstairs to the kitchen.

He watched her walk over to the big dresser and place the notebook in one of the drawers.

'This is where Jane and I have decided we should keep it,' she told him.

He frowned a little. He did not need to know that. He did not want to talk about anything so mundane. He wanted to discuss the blinding pleasure of what they had done in the cellar. Had she been lying when she said she enjoyed it? A prickle of unease ran through him. Had he disappointed her? The stories about the wicked Lady Massyngham suggested she had enjoyed liaisons in far more outlandish locations.

'We thought the kitchen the most sensible home for it,' she went on. 'It is very conveniently placed for everyone to enter details of what has been used.' She flashed him another small smile. 'It will also be useful to have a record for Mr Steadmarsh when he returns.'

She was still talking about that damned notebook! Jack's head as well as his body was still reeling from their recent union, but he did his best to concentrate on what she was saying and answer in kind.

'Do *you* think he will return?' he asked.

Sabrina clasped her hands before her. 'I *want* to believe he will. But, having been gone for so long, is it possible, do you think?'

She turned to look up at him, her eyes concerned, and he felt an irrational flash of jealousy that she should put the concerns of Hare Hall above what they had just shared.

'I cannot say,' he said, still trying to think clearly. 'His servants evidently did not believe he would come back.'

'That is what is so worrying. I hate to think of poor Mary, left alone without anyone.'

'She will not be. We will not abandon her.'

'Well, *I* certainly have no intention of doing so.'

He stiffened. 'You think I could be so unfeeling?' He read the answer in her face, and all the old hurt surfaced. That unreasonable jealousy and his frustration with the turn of the conversation spilled over. He said acidly, 'If you remember, madam, six years ago *you* were the one who cut *me*. Once you had caught yourself a rich husband.'

'And when you walked out of the bedchamber at Hartland the other night?' she retorted, 'What was *that*, if not unfeeling?'

'Self-preservation! We enjoyed a quick romp, but

nothing more. When you tried to cozen me with your false praise, I saw through it immediately.'

'Cozen you?' She frowned. 'I never…'

He ignored her and went on savagely, 'Pray do not try to deceive me with your feigned innocence, madam! You won't catch me again with your beguiling ways. *Especially* after what we have just done!'

She was staring at him, her eyes wide. His body was still thrumming uncomfortably with desire, but all the old pain, so long contained, had welled up and found relief in anger. He mimicked her, repeating the words that had haunted him since the Hartland Ball.

'*"Oh, Jack, I have never known such happiness in a man's bed."*' His lip curled. 'You may dupe other poor fools with such lies, Sabrina, but not I!'

He saw the colour come and go in her face, first a fiery red, then the blood draining away to leave her pale as chalk. She put her palms against her cheeks as she stared at him, her eyes huge and dark against her white skin. He thought she was going to faint and took a step towards her.

'Sabrina—'

'You have said quite enough, sir!'

He stopped. The words were uttered in a steady voice that was cold and hard as the stone floor beneath their feet. She was still pale, but her eyes glittered with fury. She stood before him like a wrathful goddess.

* * *

Sabrina kept her head up, her hands clenched at her sides. Tears were not far away but she held them back by the sheer power of her will. She needed every ounce of energy she possessed to help her through this without breaking down, and she was determined he should never know how much his words had hurt her. She was an expert of disguising her true feelings. It had been a necessity, she thought bitterly. It was the way she had survived four years of marriage to a man she despised.

How ironic, then, that when she told Jack the truth, he did not believe her.

And why should he, after their coupling in the wine cellar? She could not expect him to believe her an innocent after she had thrown herself at him so wantonly for a second time. She had thought as much even before they left the cellar, as soon as she could think clearly again.

'We agreed that while we are at Hare Hall we would not quarrel.' She was reminding herself, as well as Jack. 'It is best we do not talk of anything that has gone before. If we fall out, it will make our sojourn here very uncomfortable. For everyone.'

'And what we have just done?' he demanded. 'Is that to be ignored too?'

'Of course.' She forced herself to meet his gaze,

hoping her face conveyed nothing but indifference. 'Now, if you will excuse me, I have work to do.'

She slipped past him, but when she reached the door she stopped. Despite what she had just said, she was haunted by the need to be honest with him on one point.

'I was not lying,' she said, staring at the wooden panels. 'It was true, what I told you at Hartland. I had never enjoyed a man's caresses. Until that night at Hartland, with you. And again, today.'

And with that she left him.

Chapter Ten

Jack stood in the empty kitchen and stared at the closed door, Sabrina's final words echoing in the silence that pressed upon him. Could he believe her? What man would not want to think she was telling the truth? But all the evidence was against her, all the stories, the rumours, the gossip. Even her own actions in rejecting him for a richer prize with never a word, or a hint of remorse. Perhaps she regretted that now, just as he regretted his cruel words to her at Hartland, but it was too late. He had to face up to that.

However strong the attraction, those deeds would stand between them forever, a weapon to be thrown up every time they were at odds.

'Confound it, man,' he muttered to the empty room. 'Stay civil to the widow until you can be free of this place, then forget her.'

Jack knew it would take an effort to meet with Sabrina again and act as if nothing had occurred, but it would not do to let the others think there was anything amiss. He changed into his evening coat and pantaloons for dinner and made his way to the drawing room at the appointed hour as if being snowbound with a beautiful temptress was an everyday occurrence.

He walked in to find the room warm and glowing with candlelight. Mary and Sabrina were sitting on a sofa, a branched candlestick beside them on the table. Determined to remain polite, Jack gave a little bow and even managed to greet them with a smile.

'Mrs Nidd told me I should find you both in here.'

Sabrina looked up. 'Good evening, Lord John.'

She spoke calmly enough, but Jack noticed that her eyes were wary. She waved a hand towards the tambour frame on the girl's lap.

'As you see, I am helping Mary with her embroidery.'

The little girl held up her work, and he made a show of raising his quizzing glass to inspect it.

'That is very neat. Well done, Mary.'

The girl looked inordinately pleased, and he asked her if she would be joining them at dinner. Immediately the smile disappeared and she glanced uncertainly at Sabrina.

'Mary would prefer to dine in the kitchen with Jane,' she told him. 'That is, if you have no objection, my lord?'

Yes, he objected. Jack wanted to say that he would like to have her to join them for dinner, but this mess was not of Mary's making. The poor girl had enough worries without giving her any more. So he smiled.

'Of course I have no objection.' He added cheerfully, 'This is Miss Steadmarsh's house, and she must do whatever makes her most comfortable.'

Mary gave him a grateful smile as she packed up her work, then she slipped off the sofa, and with a whispered "excuse me," she hurried away.

'I did nothing to discourage her from dining with us,' Sabrina told him, as soon as they were alone. 'Believe me, I should have very much preferred her to keep us company!'

'Pray lower those hackles and stop glaring at me, Sabrina. I am not here to pick a quarrel with you. I did not for a moment think you had tried to influence the girl. We agreed we would do nothing to discompose her, did we not? She is still a little shy of me and will be far more comfortable eating with Mrs Nidd.'

An uneasy silence fell. After a while, Sabrina rose and moved towards the side table.

'Mr Weald has already brought in some wine, if you would like a glass, my lord.'

'Not the champagne then?'

He saw her cheeks flame and cursed himself. Why had he mentioned that? It had conjured up thoughts of what had happened in the wine cellar for both of them. All at once the memory of it hovered around them in the air. Once again his body was thrumming with desire.

'We agreed,' she muttered, keeping her back to him. 'We have to forget all about this morning.'

'I know.' He took a hasty turn about the room before coming to a stand in front of her. 'Have you forgotten it? *Can* you?'

He looked down at her bowed head, and he had to stop himself from reaching out and taking her in his arms. He continued in a gentler voice.

'I do not *want* to forget it.' He thrust a hand through his hair. 'There is *something* between us, Sabrina. Some…connection that is quite out of the ordinary. I have never felt like this before. Perhaps if we could talk about it, we could get beyond quarrelling every time we meet.'

'But that is not possible,' she told him. 'Do you not see? I wounded you badly when I married Sir Roderick, and since then you have hurt me. The pain goes too deep, and it will always haunt us. It will always stand in the way of our happiness.'

He wanted to argue, to believe there was a way through this.

'Must it?' he countered. 'Can we not forgive one another?'

She looked up at him, her green eyes dark and stormy. 'I thought so once, Jack. When I danced with you at Hartland, I thought we might be able to put the past behind us, but you proved to me it was not possible. You cannot forgive me, and in truth, I cannot forgive myself for letting you down so badly.'

'If only you could tell me why you did it,' he said. 'Why you rejected me in favour of that, that *roué*.'

'If only *you* could accept that I had my reasons.' Her smile was so sad it tore at his heart. 'I am not nearly as wicked as society makes out, Jack, but we have hurt each other too much. If we were to grow closer, do you think either of us could ever forget that? Whenever we had an argument, it would be there, ready to inflict more pain. You know that as well as I.'

He did. Had he not told himself very much the same thing earlier? But the idea of them both being under the same roof for days, possibly weeks more was sheer torment. Not just for himself, he knew Sabrina felt it too. They would have to get through the days as best they could. As for the nights…best not even to think about that!

He said now, 'Then let us not argue again tonight.' She eyed him doubtfully and he smiled at her. 'Surely it cannot be that hard for us to spend a few hours together without fighting. Let me start by asking if

I may pour you a glass of whatever it is Tom had brought up for us...' He stepped across to inspect the decanter. 'Madeira?'

'No, thank you.'

'As you wish.'

Was it possible to be together without arguing? Sabrina wondered about that as Jack poured a glass of wine for himself. She wanted it to be so, desperately, but there was too much pain and resentment between them. It lurked just below the surface and however wonderful she found his kisses, however much they might both enjoy the pleasures of the bedroom, it would always be there. It they were both mild-tempered saints it would be difficult enough, but they were not. One wrong word, one tiny disagreement and it would spring up again.

The awkward silence returned. She watched Jack walk over to the hearth. There was power in every line of him, the broad shoulders and tapering waist, the muscular thighs encased in the tight-fitting pantaloons. He dropped another log on the fire, sending up a shower of sparks, then stepped back, dusting his hands. She looked at the long, tapering fingers, remembering the feel of them on her skin, the memory of his sure, gentle touch was even now turning her insides to water. Thank heaven, he was looking into the fire and not at her, or he would see how much she wanted him!

'This room looks far better than it did yesterday,' he remarked, looking around him. 'Mrs Nidd must have worked hard to fit this in with all her kitchen duties.'

Sabrina hesitated. 'Actually, I cleaned it.'

'*You* did this?'

'Yes. And I took it upon myself to tidy Mary's and my bedchambers. I would not leave it all to my maid.' She put up her chin. 'I *do* know how to keep house, even though you think me fit for nothing but dancing and gaiety!'

Sabrina wished she could take the words back. In other circumstances they might have been construed as mere teasing, but Jack could not be blamed if he saw them as provocative.

'I do not think that at all, but let us not fall out over it. We agreed it will not do for us to quarrel, did we not?'

His calm words soothed her temper. She said, 'Very true, my lord. Tell me instead what you have been doing since…this morning.'

Sabrina trailed off, flushing, and he quickly stepped into the breach.

'I took a walk to the farm. I wanted to discover something more about Steadmarsh, but it appears the man did not mix much with his neighbours. At least, not those this side of South Molton. Farmer Jessop told me they all heard that Mrs Steadmarsh had died, but he doubts any one of the neighbours knew of the family's present circumstances. It seems the Jessops only have dealings with them because they supply Hare Hall with milk and meat.'

'So we are no nearer discovering what has happened to Mary's father.'

'Sadly no. I explained the situation to Mrs Jessop, and she said she had heard nothing save that some of the servants had quit Hare Hall. The housekeeper's going was news to her, but with the weather turning so bad, people had not been out and about quite so much. She and her husband appear to be respectable folk, and she was very much shocked to think of Mary being left on her own here. She has offered to take the girl in, once the roads are clear and we can travel again.'

'How kind of her. However there is no question of our leaving yet, so we do not need to think too much about that.'

She looked up as the door opened and Weald appeared.

'Mrs Nidd says dinner is ready to be served, ma'am, my lord. If you would care to go through?'

Jack nodded. 'Yes, thank you, Tom.'

She thought Jack was about to offer her his arm, but he thought better of it and instead merely walked beside her to the dining room.

'That was very good,' said Jack, pushing away his plate and wiping his mouth on the napkin. 'Your maid is an excellent cook.'

'And your valet makes a very good butler,' Sabrina replied.

The formal rituals they had observed while dining together had done much to ease the tension between her and Jack. As well as serving the food, Weald had provided them with wine throughout the meal, and the evening had passed far more pleasantly than Sabrina had thought possible.

Jack said, 'We are fortunate to have two such accomplished people with us.'

'I would never travel anywhere without Jane,' she told him, smiling a little. 'She has been with me since I was in the nursery and is far more of a friend than a servant.'

'Weald is the same, although I never realised he was so knowledgeable about wine.'

'A man of many talents, then.'

'A treasure!' he agreed.

Their eyes met for one unguarded moment, and Sabrina felt a familiar prickle of attraction. Jack was right. There *was* a connection between them. It was so real she could almost touch it. She looked away, suddenly uncomfortable, and felt a sense of relief when Weald came in to take away the dishes. She wondered if Jack was aware of it, too, but he was busy folding up his napkin.

Weald bustled around, removing the covers before placing a decanter of cognac and glass on the table for his master. At the sight of it Sabrina's thoughts turned again to what had happened in the wine cellar. How she had kissed him, making it quite clear what she wanted of him. The pity of it was, that encounter had not lessened her desire for Jack one jot. On the contrary, she wanted him more than ever!

'Now the meal is over, do you wish to withdraw and leave me to my brandy?' asked Jack. 'I promise you I shall not tarry over it.'

He spoke lightly. She knew he was trying to make the question sound like a jest and relieve the tension between them, but Sabrina strove to find a smile in response.

'You need not hurry on my account. It has been a long day and I am going to retire.'

She rose from her chair. Quite illogically, now they had managed successfully to spend most of the evening together in civil conversation, she wanted him to suggest he should come to her room. Or perhaps he would rise now and take her in his arms, making it impossible for her to leave him.

He did neither. He merely nodded and she turned away.

'Goodnight, my lord.'

She walked to the door. One word from Jack and she would stay. She did not want to leave. Her spine tingled as she silently begged him to call her back, but he did not. She went out, closing the door behind her, and stood for a moment, listening. Hoping. At length the chill of the passage began to bite, and she made her way up to her bedchamber.

As the door closed behind Sabrina, Jack breathed out a long sigh. At last he was alone and could relax. He reached for the brandy and poured himself a large measure. He did not doubt Sabrina was exhausted. After all, she had set the drawing room to rights, had she not? Her notion of keeping house would consist of issuing orders to her servants. Cleaning and tidying Hare Hall would be a dashed sight more tiring for her than dancing around a ballroom!

Jack's hand clenched around the glass. He was being unfair and he knew it, but he did not want to think of Sabrina as anything other than a spoiled, wilful jade. The memory of their quarrel that morning haunted him. The look of horror on her face when he had mocked her and her quiet denial that she had lied. He could make no sense of it, other than to tell himself again that it was all part of her plans to heighten his desire.

He scowled into his glass.

'Well, she won't succeed,' he muttered.

Admit it, man, she already has.

His scowl deepened and he finished off the rest of his brandy.

Confound it, he should have taken dinner in his room, but that would have entailed a great deal of extra work for everyone. And more than that, what excuse could he have given, after they had agreed they would not expose their quarrel to the household? He could not, *would* not admit to a soul how much she bewitched him!

'I will fight this,' he muttered, reaching for the decanter. 'I will beat this. I must, or I am doomed.'

Another day of overcast skies and snow showers dawned. With no servants in the house, there was plenty to do to keep everyone occupied. After breakfast Sabrina carried Mary off to read with her, and Jack went outside to help the men. When there was a break in the weather, they cleared the yard of snow and threw down ash and clinker from the fires on the icy paths.

He managed to avoid Sabrina until dinner time, where they both made efforts to maintain a façade of polite civility. Conversation was desultory, all contentious subjects were avoided and, as soon as the meal was finished, Sabrina retired, pleading fatigue.

Jack closed his eyes and let out a long breath of frustration. This was even worse than last night's dinner. They had spent the evening circling around one another like a couple of wary animals, and he had never felt so exhausted.

Finishing his wine, he gathered up the empty glasses and made his way to the kitchen,where he was surprised to find Sabrina helping Tom Weald and Mrs Nidd to clean and tidy the room. She started when she saw him, as if he had caught her out in some guilty act.

'Ah.' He hesitated in the doorway, and Jane came bustling up.

'So you have brought your glasses, Lord John. Thank you,' she said, taking them from him.

'Yes. I have also put out the candles. I thought that might save you and Tom a little work.'

'Aye, it does indeed,' she replied, her shrewd dark eyes twinkling at him. 'Very thoughtful of you, my lord.'

She walked off and Jack glanced again at Sabrina, but she quickly looked away.

'Very well.' He nodded. 'I will bid you all good-night then.'

He went out, closing the door behind him. He picked up his chamberstick and made his way up the stairs. So, she preferred the company of servants to his own. Not that he blamed her. He had been doing precisely the same thing all day. What cursed bad luck to be snowbound like this, and for heaven knew how long!

It was on their fourth morning at Hare Hall that Jack awoke to find the weather had changed. It was calm and dry, and by the time he went to fetch in more logs, the sun had risen. Outside was dazzlingly bright. A clear sky overnight had left the lying snow glittering in the morning sunshine, and he breathed in the icy air as his feet scrunched across the yard to the wood store.

Abel and Sam had spent much of the previous day filling the wood baskets, chopping more logs and piling them up for use, but Jack fetched the axe to cut more. He needed to work off some of his frustration after another disturbed night. He could avoid Sabrina for most of the day, but at night she invaded his dreams. Not the starched-up ice maiden he dined with each evening, but Sabrina dancing, light as air and with her green eyes shining like stars. Sabrina teasing him, or Sabrina laughing, her face alight with merriment.

Sabrina naked, lying on the bed, her silky skin sliding against his, hair loose and flowing like honey over the white pillows...

With a growl he swung the axe. The sun glinted on the blade as it fell and sliced the first log cleanly in two. He swung it again, and again with unerring accuracy, watching in satisfaction as the logs split and fell. But all the time his mind was on Sabrina.

Six years. Six years, and still she had the power to distract him. That one swift coupling at Hartland should have been enough to convince him he was well rid of her, the way she tried to compliment him, to pretend she had never enjoyed herself so much!

She said it was the truth.

Jack savagely thrust the thought aside and brought the axe down again, this time so viciously it cleaved through the log and buried itself in the chopping block. How many lovers had she had? He wrenched the axe free. Too many to count, damn her! The blade flashed down again. And again. He grew warm with the exercise, but as the pile of logs began to mount, his anger abated.

The lady's conduct since they had been at Hare Hall was decorum personified, apart from that one, sweet moment of abandon in the wine cellar. She was more than willing to help Jane with the household chores, as well as spending a great deal of time with Mary, reading with her, dressing her hair and helping her with her sewing. Hardly the behaviour of a dissolute woman.

'It was true, what I told you at Hartland. I had never enjoyed a man's caresses.'

Jack paused, letting the axe hang by his side while he thought about that. Perhaps her wickedness was exaggerated. He had never actually heard any man declare openly that he was her lover. There were hints, of course. Sly winks and oblique comments. And there was no denying she had thrown herself into his arms. Twice. There had been no hesitation; she had been as eager as he for it to happen.

He set another log on the chopping block and lifted the axe again. He could make no sense of it. But then, who could make sense of a woman?

Jack spent the whole morning chopping and stacking the wood. The exercise settled him. It solved nothing but it soothed his mind. At last he straightened and pushed his hands into his back, easing the slight ache caused by his exertions before picking up the wood basket and carrying it to the kitchen.

Jane was pottering around, and she stopped in surprise when he came in.

'Why, my lord, what have you been up to?' She stood looking at him, her hands on her hips. 'You know there's no call for you to go bringing in the wood now, I only have to send word to the stables and the lads would do it, and very happily.'

'I know they would, Jane, but Sam and Abel are busy enough. Besides, I like to help. I need some occupation too, you know.'

'Well 'tis a pity you weren't here earlier or you could have accompanied my lady and little Mary. They have gone out for a walk, it being such a lovely day.'

'Yes, what a pity,' he replied, all the while thinking that it was a lucky escape.

Sabrina took up enough of his thoughts; he did not wish to spend any more time with her. The maid was watching him, smiling as if she could read his thoughts, and he felt a dull flush mounting his cheeks.

'Is there anything else I can do to help you, Mrs Nidd?'

'Well, perhaps, if you don't mind,' she went on, 'could you take that bucket of coals into the drawing room? It has been sitting here in my way since Abel brought it in last night.'

'Of course,' he responded with a smile. 'And I will light the fire in there, too, if you wish. The ladies will need somewhere warm to sit when they come back indoors.'

Half an hour later the drawing room fire was blazing merrily. Jack stood up and dusted his hands as he surveyed his handiwork with some satisfaction.

'Not a bad job,' he muttered to himself. 'For such a frippery fellow!'

As he turned to leave the room, a movement outside caught his eye and he went over to the bay window. Sabrina was on the lawn with Mary and he stopped to watch them for a moment. They made a pleasing picture, Mary in her red woollen cloak and Sabrina dressed in her dark green pelisse with its fur collar. Instead of her bonnet, she was wearing a jaunty little cap atop her amber curls, and there was a healthy glow to her cheeks. They were piling up the snow with their gloved hands, and although they were making little progress, they were both laughing, both clearly enjoying themselves.

Jack stood at the window, contemplating the scene, smiling a little. Then with a shrug, he turned and walked away.

Chapter Eleven

Sabrina took in another deep breath of the icy air. She and Mary had enjoyed a long walk, and Sabrina was sure they both felt the better for it. The sunshine had brought a rosy glow to the young girl's cheeks, and she had chattered away happily. They had now returned to the front lawn and Sabrina stopped to admire the view.

'Does it not look beautiful?' she exclaimed.

The old stone house was bathed in sunlight, and before it lay a thick blanket of snow, untouched and pristine. 'It is several inches deep at least, one cannot even see the drive.' She laughed. 'It is never so pretty in town, you know. The traffic on the streets soon turns any snow to slush, and it is always a very dirty grey.'

'When Mama was alive we would come outside and build snow statues,' said Mary, a wistful note in her voice.

'How wonderful,' Sabrina replied. 'We rarely did that.'

She sighed, remembering her childhood winters in London. She would spend her days indoors, reading while Mama went off to help with her charities and her father attended meetings or entertained his political friends.

'Let us make a statue now,' she said suddenly.

Mary looked at her, eyes full of surprise, and Sabrina laughed, throwing her arms wide.

'It is a shame to waste all this lovely snow. What do you say?'

They set to work with a will, dragging and patting the snow into a pile. It was a slow business, their hands struggling to add very much, but eventually their column of snow was almost the same height as Mary. Sabrina took a step back and studied it, her head on one side.

'It's not tall enough!'

She jumped as a voice called out from the direction of the house, and turned quickly. Her heart leapt when she saw Jack walking towards them. He was dressed for the cold with his coat, gloves and scarf, although his head was bare, his fair hair gleaming like ripe corn in the sunshine. He looked very cheerful, too, and Sabrina felt her own spirits rise a little more. They had agreed to be friendly, for Mary's sake, but this felt different. It was as if the constraint of the past few days had no place out here in the sunshine. She greeted him with a smile.

'Your snowman,' he said, nodding towards the figure. 'It is too short.'

'Who says we are making a snow*man*?' she countered playfully.

'Are you not?' He came up to them, grinning. 'Mary, what do you think it is?'

'I thought we were making a man,' she replied. 'But you are right, my lord. It is not tall enough.'

Sabrina laughed. 'Traitor! Very well, sir, it is up to you to make it taller if you can.'

'I will. Watch me.'

He began to gather up snow into a ball, rolling it around to make it bigger while Sabrina and Mary continued to build up their pillar of snow, all of them laughing and working together. At last Jack declared himself satisfied with the body and lifted the round head into place.

Mary clapped her hands. 'Excellent! Thank you, my lord.'

'Ho!' cried Sabrina in mock outrage, 'You would give him all the credit, when we did most of the work?'

'No, Mary is quite right,' said Jack, settling the

head more firmly on the body. 'You needed my genius to complete this masterpiece.'

'Your—'

Sabrina gasped at his audacity. She scooped up a large handful of snow, squeezed it into a ball and hurled it at his broad back. It landed with a satisfying thump squarely between his shoulders. Mary gave a squeal and clapped her hands to her mouth as Jack turned slowly around.

'What was that for?' he demanded.

'Your arrogance,' she retorted. She had acted without thinking, but she was not prepared to apologise.

'Very well, then!'

As soon as she saw that he was going to retaliate, Sabrina reacted, but even as she scooped up more snow Jack's snowball landed on her shoulder. She shrieked as icy shards flew off onto her cheek.

It was an unequal fight. Jack's aim was far better, and Sabrina found herself being pelted with the soft missiles. She called to Mary to aid her, but the girl was giggling so much she was of little help. Sabrina fired back snowballs as quickly as she could, but most of her efforts missed their mark. Jack was coming closer and that was to her advantage. She tossed a hastily formed ball towards him and by chance it caught him on the chin.

'So we are aiming for the face now, are we?'

He wiped off the snow and advanced quickly, a fresh white ball balanced menacingly in one hand. Uttering something between a laugh and a scream Sabrina turned and fled, but she had not gone far when Jack made a grab for her arm. In her efforts to pull away, she lost her balance and stumbled, tripping Jack, who was close behind her. They both fell headlong into the snow and lay there, laughing too much to get up.

Jack raised himself on one arm and looked down at her, his eyes dancing with merriment. 'Are you hurt?'

'Only my pride,' she answered cheerfully. 'Nothing serious.'

He was so close Sabrina could see the laughter lines around his mouth, and she detected the sweet scent of freshly cut wood on his clothes.

'Good.' He jumped up and held out his hand. 'Let me help you up.'

Sabrina allowed him to pull her to her feet. She was smiling, totally at ease. The blood was still fizzing through her veins, and she had not felt so happy and carefree for years. She quite forgot all the harsh words they had exchanged and was quite unconscious of the fact that she was standing with one hand clasped in Jack's. The other was resting lightly on his chest, and she could feel the beat of his heart against her gloved palm.

Their eyes were locked together, unspoken messages passing between them. Jack's gaze became more intense as his fingers tightened around her hand, and she caught her breath, gazing up at him. The intervening years fell away as if they had never existed. Sabrina remembered feeling like this when she had first met Lord John Callater. Happy, excited, a little breathless. In love for the first time in her life. The only time.

I still love him. I have always loved him.

'Oh, my goodness!' cried Mary, running up to them. 'You are both *covered* in snow!'

The glow in Jack's eyes faded into a rueful gleam, and Sabrina knew the moment was broken. Who knows what they might have said, might have done, if Mary had not been there?

Stifling a sigh, she dragged her eyes away from Jack and addressed the girl.

'Yes, how careless of us. We should go in.'

'Not just yet,' said Jack. 'We must finish the snowman first. Mary, perhaps you would run inside and ask Mrs Nidd to spare a carrot for his nose and two small lumps of coal for his eyes. Tell her I sent you.'

Sabrina watched the girl run off, then turned back to Jack. He was still looking at her.

He said, 'I owe you an apology.'

'That is quite unnecessary, I tripped—'

'No, not that. For not believing you had been a faithful wife.'

'You had good reason.' She gently freed herself from his grasp and stepped away from him. 'I have made no effort to defend myself from the gossips and rumours. How could you be expected to believe it, when the whole world thinks differently?' She looked away, gazing off into the distance, trying to find the courage for what must be said. 'When I met you, all those years ago, I *did* like you. Very much. I think I knew you were about to make me an offer only... Sir Roderick made his proposal first.' She exhaled, a long sigh carrying with it years of remorse. 'It was wrong of me to let you hear of it from others. I should have told you, but I did not know what to say. I am sorry if I caused you pain.'

'But why?' His voice was loaded with hurt and confusion. 'Why take Massyngham rather than me? He was rich as Croesus, to be sure, but I am no pauper. Was my fortune not enough for you?'

More than enough. If it had been up to me, I would have taken you with nothing!

Tears stung her eyes and she fought back the urge to weep, trying to block out all the heartbreak and the memories.

'It was your father's doing!' He ground out the words.

Her eyes flew to his face. He nodded at her, no longer smiling.

'For all your father's protestations of liberalism, he sold you to the highest bidder.'

'No! It was not like that.'

'What then? What induced you to marry that old libertine?'

Sabrina bit her lip. She wanted so much to tell him, but there was so much she could not say, even now.

He said quietly, 'Will you not tell me?'

'I… I cannot do so.'

'Why?' He was frowning at her now. 'What is it that you cannot say to me? Confound it, Sabrina, I need to know. I need to *understand*.'

She shook her head. 'Massyngham is dead. That part of my life is over. Is that not enough?' She tore her gaze away and looked past him. 'Mary is coming back. Pray, Jack, let's not spoil her day.'

He stared at her in silence for a moment, then he nodded. 'Very well. I shall not ask you again, neither will I waste my time in idle conjecture. For me, the matter is closed.'

He turned away to meet Mary, and as the girl ran up, Sabrina saw his charming smile reappear, but it was not for her. Her spirits, so recently in alt, were now as low as could be.

He said, 'Ah, there you are Mary, and you have a carrot. Well done.'

'Yes!' The girl held out her hands. 'And coal, too.'

'That is excellent. Now, let us give our man a face.'

He walked off with the little girl and Sabrina hung back to shake out her skirts and regain some measure of composure. The playful interlude was a bittersweet reminder of what might have been, and the conversation between her and Jack had shown it could never be brought back. There were circumstances she was not at liberty to share with him. Things she had sworn she would never tell anyone. Jack would never forgive her for rejecting him in favour of Rogue Massyngham, and that was the price she must pay for her secrets.

They spent a few moments together admiring the snowman before Sabrina suggested they should go indoors. They entered through the garden door, leaving a trail of snowy footprints melting on the flags.

'Goodness me, look at the state of you!' declared Jane Nidd when they all trooped into the kitchen. She turned back to the range, where several pots and pans were resting on or near the glowing coals. 'You'd best sit down and take off your boots before you go up to change out of your wet clothes. You too, Lord John,' she added, addressing Jack with what Sabrina considered a deplorable lack of formality. 'There's a boot jack in the corner.'

'My dear Mrs Nidd, I cannot possibly use that on my Hessians,' replied Jack, seemingly aghast at the notion. 'Weald would never forgive me.'

'Then you had best call him down to help you,' came the sharp retort. 'It looks to me like they're in a fair way to being ruined as it is, and I don't want the extra work of having to clean the stairs of your dirt if you wear them up to your room.'

Mary giggled at the exchange, but Sabrina silently sat down to unlace her own boots. Jack had clearly worked his charm on her maid, who now treated him as if he was a favourite member of the family.

She frowned as she tugged off a boot. How dare they all be so cheerful when her own spirits were so low!

'Off you go, Miss Mary,' said Jane, shooing the girl out of the kitchen. 'I will come up to you as soon as I have finished here.'

'You already have a great deal to do, Jane,' declared Sabrina. 'Mary and I can dress each other, and then I will come down and help you to prepare dinner.'

But this Jane would not allow.

'No need for that, my lady,' she said. 'It's all done and just needs to simmer until it's ready. And I have closed the curtains in the drawing room, too, so it will be lovely and warm in there for you and my lord to sit and enjoy a glass of wine before your dinner.'

'Jane, you are an angel,' declared Jack.

He was grinning at the maid, and Sabrina felt something twist inside her. Her earlier good mood had evaporated, and now she felt tired and dispirited. She did not wish to spend another evening alone with Jack Callater, pretending a civility neither of them felt.

'Perhaps Mary would like to join us tonight,' she suggested.

'No need for that, my lady. She'll do well enough eating here in the kitchen with me and Mr Weald before we serve dinner to you and His Lordship in the dining room, as is proper.' Sabrina wanted to argue more, but Jane waved her away. 'If you two have removed your shoes, then off you go, out of my kitchen. You are very much in the way!'

'There, that's telling you,' murmured Jack.

He winked at Sabrina, who looked away, her heart leaping like a salmon and her cheeks flaming. Was he...could he be *flirting* with her? Surely he would not do that, not after what he had said this afternoon. And yet he had definitely winked at her. Perhaps he could not help himself. Yes, that would be it. The man's nature was to flirt with every woman who came within his orbit.

Jack picked up his boots and departed but Sabrina hung back.

'I think it would do Mary good to sit down to dinner with us, Jane. She is quite old enough to join the adults at table.'

'Another night, perhaps, but the poor child has been out in the fresh air all day and will be ready for her bed in an hour or so.'

'Actually, it has been a tiring day,' agreed Sabrina, clutching at straws. 'Perhaps I will just take a little supper in my room…'

'Oh, no, you will not, Miss Sabrina! You need a good meal, and that is best served in the dining room rather than me traipsing up and down stairs with trays! You will dine with His Lordship, as agreed, and there's an end to it.' The maid stopped stirring the pot and waved the ladle at her. 'Now off you go and change before you catch your death of cold in those wet skirts.'

Sabrina knew that when her maid resorted to calling her *Miss Sabrina* any further argument was futile. She withdrew, but she had an unsettling feeling that her maid was attempting to matchmake. And yet, by the time she had reached her bedroom, her disquiet was fading. She could not forget that wink. There was no doubt Jack Callater could be an entertaining companion, and if he could forget their differences that easily, then why should she not do so, too?

Jack ran quickly up to his bedchamber, feeling remarkably cheerful, his happy mood brought on by the sunshine and that impromptu snowball fight. It had lifted his spirits. There was no doubt he and Sabrina could get on very well, as long as they did not talk about the past. In fact, he thought as he stripped off his wet clothes, it was very easy for them to fall into an easy camaraderie, so why not relax and enjoy their time together at Hare Hall?

He threw the clean shirt over his head. Nothing had been resolved; she still would not tell him the real reason she had married Massyngham. If her father had not pressured her to accept the man, then the only explanation was that she had been dazzled by his wealth. Jack did not want to believe that, but it was most likely the truth, and something that Sabrina would not want to admit.

It gnawed at him that she should be so mercenary. He had thought better of her, but he would not let it worry him while they were stuck at Hare Hall. Once they returned to London, they could go their separate ways and never meet again, but while they were snowbound here, why not enjoy it? He knew Sabrina's smiles were no more than a masquerade for the child's sake. True, he would have to guard his heart, but Sabrina was a beautiful and intelligent woman, and as long as he was careful, there was no reason why he should not enjoy her company.

It was only when he moved to the mirror to tie his fresh neckcloth that he realised he was smiling.

Chapter Twelve

Jack entered the drawing room in time to see Sabrina adding logs to the fire. He frowned.

'I could have done that.'

'No need, I am perfectly capable of tending a fire.'

'I am well aware of that.' She glanced up at him, her gaze a mixture of surprise and suspicion. He went on, 'You are a very capable lady, Sabrina. And yes, before you ask, I am paying you a compliment. I should like to save you the trouble, that is all.'

The shadow of doubt fled from her green eyes, and she even gave him a little smile before turning back to look down at her handiwork. The flames were already beginning to lick around the fresh logs. When she spoke again, her tone was considerably warmer, and Jack was encouraged to think she too was determined to make the best of their situation.

'There is something very satisfying in keeping a blaze going, is there not? You should come and sit close to the fire, my lord, or you will not feel the benefit.' She indicated the fine woollen shawl she had thrown around her shoulders. 'You see that I came prepared for the chill!'

Her friendly tone augured well for the rest of the evening, and he replied in a similar vein.

'Very well, but first can I bring you a glass of wine, ma'am?' He walked over to the side table where a decanter and glasses had been placed in readiness.

Sabrina assented, and he filled two glasses and carried them over to where she was sitting, in one of the two armchairs pulled close to the hearth. She seemed distracted as she took the glass. He watched her take a sip.

'Is anything amiss?' he enquired. 'Are you not enjoying your drink?'

'No, no, there is nothing wrong with the wine,' she assured him. 'It is very good.'

'Then why are you frowning?'

'I am concerned at how much of Mr Steadmarsh's fuel we are using. Are we perhaps being a little profligate? This room, for instance. We could not but make use of it this evening, after Jane and Mr Weald went to such a lot of trouble to ensure it was warm enough. However, I think I should tell them to let the fire go out in here. It seems very wasteful to keep this room heated as well as the dining room.'

'But a lady must have somewhere comfortable where she may withdraw while the gentleman drinks his brandy at the end of a meal.' His quip did not bring a smile, as he had hoped, and he prompted her. 'Is that not so?'

Her gaze shifted from his face, and she studied the glass she was holding between her hands.

'I thought,' she said slowly, 'I thought I might remain in the dining room with you tonight.'

Jack stilled. 'Do you think that would be prudent?'

One hand fluttered. 'It is a little late for that, I think.'

She peeped up at him through her lashes, a shy glance, half hopeful, and he smiled.

'I should like that.'

They spoke little over dinner, but Jack thought it was a more comfortable meal than they had enjoyed together yet. Sabrina was far more at ease, and when the meal was over, he poured brandy for himself and Madeira for Sabrina.

'Unless we have more snow overnight, I shall send one of the men out tomorrow to ascertain if the roads are passable,'

'We seem to be deep in the country here,' she replied. 'The lanes could be blocked for miles.'

'Possibly, but I learned from Farmer Jessop that the

stage passes not a quarter of a mile from the gates of Hare Hall, which will ensure efforts are made to clear that road. All we have to do then is get along the lane. We would have arrived by that route, if we had not missed our way coming here.'

'I am not sure we should put too much faith in a countryman's estimation of a quarter of a mile,' she cautioned him, smiling a little.

'True, but let us hope the estimate is not wildly inaccurate, and we can reach the road without too much trouble.'

'I am sure you must be anxious to get back to town, my lord.'

Was he? Jack considered the matter and was surprised to find that part of him would like to stay at Hare Hall forever, locked away from the world in this little bubble. But he had things to attend to. He needed to see his lawyer, and the sooner the better, to sign the final papers that would secure everything and put his tenants' minds at rest. Until that business was settled, he would be kicking his heels in London, where he would revert to his bachelor ways, visiting his clubs, taking fencing lessons and sparring at the boxing academy. As well as attending parties given by hostesses who would never dream of including the Wicked Widow in their invitation list. As for Sabrina, she must be missing her hectic social round, dancing until dawn and flirting outrageously.

He looked up to find she was regarding him, waiting for his reply.

'Yes, I want to get back.' He toyed with the idea of telling her about the business that required his attention, but thought better of it. Such mundane matters as rents and poverty had no place in her lively, sparkling world.

She nodded. 'Being snowbound is a nuisance, although it has not been quite so bad as I expected. My main concern is young Mary. I will not quit Hare Hall and leave her alone. We may have to take up Mrs Jessop on her offer to take her in, until her father returns.'

'Very possibly.'

'The alternative is that I remain here and look after her.'

'You would do that?'

'Of course. You can return to town. Indeed, you should, but I am not needed there. Jane and I would easily stay here until the weather clears and enquiries can be set in motion to discover what has happened to Mr Steadmarsh and, if necessary, to seek out relatives who could care for the child.'

'And you would take that task upon yourself?'

Jack's question, and the tone of surprise he inadvertently used, put an end to the good accord that had existed between them during dinner. Sabrina flushed and her chin came up.

'I am not quite so flighty as you imagine, my lord.'

'I never meant to imply you were,' he said quickly. 'It is just that...'

'Perhaps you mean I am not a fit and proper person to look after Mary,' she said, sitting very still.

'No! Not at all. You wilfully misunderstand me, madam.'

She glared at him, then the stormy look faded. 'Perhaps I do misunderstand you, because I expect you to find fault with me.'

He sighed. 'It doesn't work, does it? I thought I could ignore everything that stands between us, but it is not possible. It is there, all the time, waiting for one or other of us to let down our guard.'

'Yes.' Sabrina gave a little shrug and rose to her feet. 'It grows late and I am very tired. I will bid you goodnight, my lord.'

She moved towards the door, but as she passed his chair, Jack's hand came out to grasp her wrist.

'I do not think you unfit to look after the girl, Sabrina, however difficult that is for you to believe. But for the past six years I have heard nothing but the rumours concerning you. Surely you can see why I *might* think that?'

'Things are not always as they seem, my lord,' she said coldly, tearing herself free.

Before she could reach the door, he was out of his seat and standing in her way.

'Then tell me,' he demanded. 'Stop this prevaricating and *tell me* why you have allowed yourself to be perceived in such a scandalous light.'

She waved one imperious hand. 'What does it matter to you?'

'Because it prevents us being at ease together, Sabrina! Every time we begin to relax together, something is said and we begin to fight again.' He caught her shoulders. 'I want to be friends with you, but until we can be honest and open with one another that cannot happen.' She looked away from him, her mouth drooping, but he would not stop now. He wanted the truth. He wanted to put to flight his doubts about her once and for all. He said, 'Tell me that you did not play hostess at your husband's debauched dinners. Tell me it is all lies, the stories of his cronies playing at cards or dice to win the right to take you to bed!'

A little shudder ran through her, and she closed her eyes. 'I hosted the dinners, yes, but nothing more.'

'Hah!'

'It is true.' She raised her head and glared at him. 'If I had not agreed to it, Roderick would have put some, some *doxy* in my place. But I insisted on leaving once dinner was over. I retired to my room and left them all to carouse as they wished. I was never unfaithful to my husband.'

'Did you love him?'

'No.'

'Yet you married the man, even though his reputation was well known. In heaven's name, *why*?'

She waved away his question. 'That is not important now. What is important is that I kept to my marriage vows. I was faithful to Sir Roderick, faithful unto death. And beyond.'

'Of course you were.' He gave a savage laugh and released her. 'How can you say that, when I have seen the men drooling over you in town?'

'I cannot stop them looking at me.'

He huffed out a sigh and began to pace back and forth, finally coming back to stand in front of her.

'Your husband was a libertine. He surrounded himself with all the most debauched of his kind, and you entertained them!'

'What else would you expect of me, in my husband's house?' she retorted, spots of angry colour staining her cheeks. 'It would be pointless for me to deny the rumours now. Let society think and say what it wishes of me, but I have told you the truth, Jack. I never took a lover while my husband was alive, and

I have never been any man's mistress. I may flirt, but it goes no further than a kiss on the hand.'

'And you expect me to believe that?'

'Yes, I do!' Sabrina threw the words at him, her eyes darting fire.

Her breast was heaving as she fought to control her breath, and Jack stared at her, trying to make sense of her words.

'I don't understand.'

'Is it not plain enough?' She spread her hands. 'Sir Roderick managed to consummate our marriage, which made it binding, but not long after that he returned to his mistresses for his…pleasures. I was little more than a trophy. Something to boast of to his acquaintances. I agreed to live with him, and I allowed him and his friends to say whatever they wished. Idle boasts to enhance their conceit. Most of them were so riddled with the pox I doubt they could have *performed* even if they had wished to! But I never slept in any man's bed except my husband's. Until I fell into yours!'

On that parting shot she was gone, hurrying out of the room and shutting the door with a snap behind her. Jack raked one hand through his hair and walked slowly back to the table. With a sigh he sat down to finish his brandy. He wanted to believe her, but if it was true, then it made his own behaviour at Hartland even more deplorable.

He was just draining his glass when he heard a soft knock at the door. He looked up to see Jane Nidd peeping into the room.

'Oh, I am sorry, my lord. I heard someone on the stairs and thought you had gone up to bed.'

'Not quite, but come in, Mrs Nidd. I am about to retire.'

As he pushed himself to his feet, she came further into the room.

'Then I will save you the trouble of fetching the glasses to the kitchen,' she said. 'I hope you and my lady had a pleasant evening?'

'Yes…although I fear she is at odds with me again.'

'Oh? And why might that be, my lord?' she prompted him gently.

'We were discussing what will happen when the roads become passable. If Steadmarsh is not returned, then she planned to ask Mrs Jessop to take Mary in.'

'Aye, that is correct,' Jane Nidd replied, coming up to the table. 'And to my mind it's a very sensible idea.'

'Yes. But Lady Massyngham is now considering staying here to look after the girl until her relatives can be contacted. That is quite an undertaking,' he said, watching her closely. 'It would be very generous.'

'My lady *is* very generous.'

'But to remain at Hare Hall, so remote. To give up her friends, the balls, the theatre…' *the parties, the flirtations* '…she will be bored beyond bearing.'

The maid pursed her lips, as if debating whether to speak. Then, 'You have a very poor opinion of my mistress, do you not, sir?' She smiled. 'I have known Miss Sabrina since she was a babe. She loves to dance, it is true, but she could no more abandon that poor child than she could cut off her own hand. I can see you are not convinced, my lord, but I fear you take too much heed of the stories concerning my lady.'

'Are none of them true, then?' he asked bluntly.

The maid looked at him for a moment, considering her answer.

'She has had a great deal to bear.'

'Oh?'

'It's not my place to say any more, but my lady has been much maligned.'

'Then I fear I have been guilty of jumping to conclusions about your mistress,' he said ruefully. 'Will you tell her I am very sorry for it?'

'No, my lord. I think you should tell her that yourself.'

Jack sighed. 'I do not think she would believe me. We cannot meet without coming to blows.' He added, deciding to confide a little more, 'I have not been… kind to her.'

Jane was looking very solemn now, and he wondered if Sabrina's loyal maid was going to ring a peal over him. Instead she replied slowly, choosing her words with care.

'Marrying Sir Roderick was…difficult for my lady. She never said anything to me, but I think it broke her heart.'

'Then why the devil did she do it?'

'Tush now, I have said far more than I should!' She picked up the glasses and turned away from him. 'I will bid you goodnight, my lord, and finish setting the kitchen to rights, ready for the morning.'

Jack followed Mrs Nidd from the room and made his way to his bedchamber. Going over everything she had said, he was confused about how to think of Sabrina. It was possible Jane was merely trying to elicit his sympathy for her mistress, but he thought not. He could no longer believe Sabrina was quite as bad as rumours painted her, but she had jilted him cruelly, and in the past six years all the hurt and anger had burned deep. Could he forget it all now? More importantly, could Sabrina forgive him for his subsequent treatment of her?

Sabrina sat at the dressing table and brushed out her hair, but her thoughts were very far away. When she had first met Jack Callater, she had been an innocent. In the past six years she had become inured to the gossip and sly innuendo; she had built a shell around her, to prevent anyone seeing the individual behind the glittering pretence that was her life. She had thought herself happy enough, content with her world of parties and entertainment, of falling exhausted into bed after dancing until dawn. Meeting Jack again had shown her what a shallow existence it was. His disapproval had cut through her defences.

How she wished now she had not travelled to Hartland. How she regretted succumbing to the attraction she had felt for Jack. She could not deny she had enjoyed lying with him, exploring his body, giving herself up to him so completely, but how could she now expect him to think her anything other than wanton? Four years of marriage had shown her that men like her husband despised the women who went so easily to their beds, but she had thought Jack different. Honourable, caring.

That was why she had shared with him more information about herself and her marriage than she had told anyone before, but there was still so much she could *not* say. He thought she had married for money, and how could she deny that? How could she deny the assertion that she was fast when she had thrown herself into his arms almost as soon as meeting him again?

At Hartland she had begged him to take her to his bed and here…her behaviour in the wine cellar had been quite abandoned. She stopped brushing and stared into the looking glass, seeing the honey-coloured hair cascading over her shoulders and the delicate features that men called beautiful. What would happen when the golden tresses lost their sheen and her countenance was ravaged with age? Would Jack still want her then? Or would he move on, and she would be left to endure a loneliness even worse than she had known during her marriage.

A soft knock on the door interrupted these dismal thoughts, and she resumed her brushing, forcing a lightness to her voice as she bade Jane come in.

'It is not your maid, but I would like a few words, if I may?'

Jack was standing in the open doorway. Sabrina jumped to her feet. She should order him to leave. *Could* she do so? Would he go, after the intimacy they had shared? She did not know the etiquette prevailing in such situations.

'I saw the light under your door,' he said, before she had decided upon a reply. 'Will you talk with me?'

He stepped into the room, closing the door behind

him, and she said quickly, 'It is very late. And there is no fire in this room.'

He spread his arms. 'I am still fully dressed, as you see, and you could wrap up in a blanket. It will not take long, I promise you.'

Sabrina had no defence against the hesitant smile or the coaxing voice. She walked over to the bed and pulled off the coverlet to wrap around herself.

'Very well.' She went back to the dressing stool and waved one hand towards the only chair in the room, near the empty hearth. 'Perhaps you would like to sit down.'

He shook his head and stood for a moment, frowning at the floor, then began to pace back and forth, as if trying to find the right words. Sabrina waited patiently. She was not afraid of him, even though her heart was hammering against her ribs. Finally he spoke.

'There is an old proverb, or a line from the Bible, that you should not let the sun go down upon your anger.' He stopped walking and stood, looking down at her. 'I wanted to tell you that I am—*was*—angry. My pride was hurt at the way you married Massyngham without a word of explanation. How you ignored me, avoided me. I accept now that you had your reasons, even though you will not share them with me. It was wrong of me to believe everything I heard of you, and very foolish of me not to see that Pru would never have invited you to the Hartland Ball if you are as wicked as gossip makes out.'

'The Duchess has always been most kind to me,' murmured Sabrina, 'but she believes the best of everyone.'

'Aye, and she is generally right! If she had believed a half of the things that were being said about Garrick when they met, it would have turned out very differently for them.' He shook his head. 'I should have listened to her, but I *wanted* to believe the lies, you see. I wanted to think you a mercenary woman, living only for your own pleasure.

'Confound it, Sabrina, I acted like a rogue, ripping up at you, taking you to my bed and then walking out on you. I was jealous. Jealous of Massyngham for marrying you, and jealous of all those supposed lovers! The more I have come to know you, the more I am convinced that I was wrong. You are kind, Sabrina, and generous, but can you find it in your heart to forgive me for being such a fool, for thinking so badly of you?'

Sabrina stared at him, noting the worried frown, the contrition in his eyes. Of all things, she had not expected this!

'Of course I can forgive you,' she said quietly. 'I *do.*'

The tension eased from his shoulders. He crossed the room and reached down to take her hands.

'Then can we start again?' he asked, drawing her to her feet. 'There will be no more arguments or recriminations about the past. You have my word.'

'You think we could be friends?'

'More than that, Sabrina. I want you to be my wife. I believe we could deal very well together.'

He was smiling down at her, his blue eyes full of warmth that set her heart pitter-pattering so hard it was difficult to breathe. She wanted to believe him, but the ghosts of her past hovered in the shadows.

The coverlet had fallen from her shoulders, but it was not the chill air that made her shiver suddenly. It was the thought of the scandal if it was announced she was to marry Lord John Callater. Every salacious snippet, every old rumour would be brought out and dusted off. She had accepted it, lived with it for years, but it would be different if she married Jack. His reputation, his character would be tarnished. She could imagine now the sly looks, the sniggers. His family would be outraged. His friends would laugh up their sleeves; they might even expect her to share her favours with them, as it was believed she had done with Massyngham's cronies.

'Well?' Jack pulled her into his arms. 'What do you say? Will you marry me?'

* * *

Sabrina knew what she must do. She had learned early on in her marriage how to reject a man's advances without causing him to lose face. In this instance it should be easy, because there was no disgust and revulsion to be concealed this time. Only her own heartbreak.

She gently disengaged herself from his arms, saying, 'How kind you are, Jack. And how generous of you to honour me with such a proposal.' She turned away to scoop up the coverlet and throw it back around her shoulders. 'I am flattered, and tempted, too, but I do not think it would work, my dear friend. I really am not the marrying kind.'

'I do not believe that.'

'Perhaps you should.' She smiled at him. 'I was faithful to my last husband, but seeing how easily I fell into your arms, how can we be sure I shall not be tempted again by the charms of some other man, once we are married?'

'I would make damned certain you are not!'

'Oh, Jack, how would you do that?' She laughed up at him, raising a hand to touch his cheek. 'Would you keep me in an ivory tower? We both love company far too much for that. Even at Lingwood Priory there would always be house parties and assemblies, not to mention the London Season with all its balls, breakfasts and routs.'

She saw surprise and confusion dawning in his eyes and stepped back a little, keeping her smile in place, but all the time she was wondering how much longer she could continue with this superlative performance.

'I don't understand,' he said slowly. 'You are *refusing* me?'

'I am, my friend, I must. For your sake as much as mine. I enjoyed our little dalliance, very much. You introduced me to such delights as I never knew with Massyngham. I shall treasure those memories always, and I hope you will think fondly of them, too. There.' She held out her hand to him, not by the flicker of an eye betraying how difficult this was for her. 'I am glad we have cleared the air. Now in future we will be able to meet as friends, will we not?'

She kept her head up and an assured smile curving her mouth so that he could be in no doubt she was dismissing him.

'Of course.' He took her hand and bowed over it, his lips brushing her fingers like a butterfly's wing. 'Thank you for your time. I shall bid you goodnight, ma'am.'

He turned and went out, closing the door behind

him with a quiet, very final click. Sabrina listened to his receding footsteps while her heart splintered into myriad shards, each one piercing her very soul.

Chapter Thirteen

'Good morning, my lord.'

Jack opened his eyes to see Tom Weald bringing in his morning coffee. He had slept badly, going over and over that last conversation with Sabrina. She had rejected him. She had told him they would meet in future as friends.

Friends! How the devil could he be friends with a woman whose presence sent him out of his wits with desire?

He sat up, cursing under his breath.

'Why did you not wake me, man?'

'Because there was no need, sir.'

'Of course there is a need,' he retorted. 'I wanted to cut more logs before breakfast.'

'That has been done, my lord. The coach drivers being unable to go anywhere, and having seen to the horses, they set to the task with a will. Everything that needs doing has been done. And my lady is helping Mrs Nidd prepare the breakfast, which she said to tell you would be another hour.' He handed Jack his cup. 'So you see there really is no need for you to get up, my lord.'

'Damn you, do you think I can lie abed when everyone else is working so hard?' He scowled. 'Her Ladyship must indeed think me a lazy good-for-nothing!'

'Oh, I doubt that.'

The valet chuckled as he searched one of the trunks for a clean shirt, and Jack scowled. If Tom only knew how contemptible she thought him. Fit only for flirtations and building snowmen! He had offered her his hand and she had refused him.

Bah! What does it matter what she thinks of me? I have put myself beyond the pale as far as she is concerned. I might as well stop trying.

When Jack eventually went downstairs to the kitchen, he found everyone gathered for breakfast. The room was pleasantly warm and filled with cheerful chatter. His eyes immediately sought out Sabrina, and the breath caught in his throat at the sight of her. Confound it, knowing she was now beyond his reach he wanted her even more! She was busy helping Jane with the cooking, a large apron fastened over her gown, and that glorious honey-gold hair scraped back into a knot. Her cheeks were flushed with heat from the fire and she was laughing. Not the polite smile she used for her society acquaintances, but genuine laughter. Her face was alight with it, eyes twinkling.

She looked up as he came in, and Jack noted how her smile slipped. There was a heartbeat's hesitation before she wished him a cool good morning and he took a crumb of comfort from that as he greeted her with a smile of his own and a small bow. She was not quite as unaffected by last night's events as he had feared.

Jane was much more welcoming.

'Ah, my Lord John.' She saluted him merrily with her spoon. 'Will you not join us at the table? Farmer Jessop gave Sam a flitch of bacon, so we breakfast like kings today.'

The men gathered about the table had all risen, but Jack quickly waved them back down again. It was clear no one was standing on ceremony this morning.

'I'll join you and gladly,' he replied, 'unless there is anything I can do to earn my keep?'

Much shaking of heads and murmurs of denial greeted his offer, and he sat down beside Mary. He engaged the girl in conversation until a plate piled with bacon and eggs appeared before him, and he uttered his thanks before setting to work to break his fast. The babble in the kitchen continued around him, and he felt his spirits lift when a glance towards Sabrina showed that she had also regained her happy smile as she toiled alongside Jane at the range.

A few moments later she turned and surveyed the room, nodding in satisfaction.

'There,' she declared. 'I believe we have made a pretty good job of that, Jane!'

A chorus of agreement ran around the table from the men, most of whom had already cleared their plates.

'I take it you and Mrs Nidd have already eaten?' Jack asked her.

'No, but we will join you now,' she replied. 'We insisted everyone should go on and eat. It would not do to let good food grow cold.'

Her smile encompassed them all, and glancing around the table, Jack knew everyone sitting there was now her slave. Without exception, he realised, looking into his own heart.

It was then that Jack knew he truly loved Sabrina. He had never stopped loving her. What a damned fool he had been not to tell her so when he went to her room last night. She had spent years fending off the attentions of men who wanted her merely for what she could give them, and last night he must have appeared no better than any one of them. No wonder she had rejected him. True, she had turned him off with kind words and the assurance that they could always be friends, but he knew the truth now. With a startling clarity, he realised that he did not want to be merely friends. He wanted her whole heart.

And yet, as he sat at the kitchen table, listening to everyone chatter away, he decided that he would settle for friendship if that was all she would give him. It was small comfort, but better than losing her altogether.

The blazing sun encouraged Jack to think that perhaps the roads might soon be clear enough to travel. The two coachmen, eager for something to do, went out to investigate and came back to report that, although there was no sign of any traffic having yet passed along the main road, they had met a local farm labourer, who opined that the stage would be through before the end of the day.

Jack went off to tell Sabrina the news and found her in the dining room, tidying up from last night's meal. When he walked in, she was on her knees by the dining table, and he was surprised into a laugh.

'What *are* you doing, Sabrina?'

'Sweeping under the table,' she told him, holding up the brush and crumb tray.

'Is that really necessary.'

'But of course! When Mary's father returns, I do not want him to think we have ill-treated his property. This is one of those tasks that can only be done satisfactorily in daylight, and Jane has no time, so I thought I should do it.'

She dropped the tray and its contents into the empty pail beside her before climbing to her feet.

'There. At least we will not be treading crumbs into the carpet tonight,' she said, dusting her hands. 'I shall have much greater respect for my housemaids in future. For all the servants, in fact. I did not realise how much there was to do in keeping house!'

'Well, I hope you will not have to be doing it yourself for much longer,' he told her. 'It is possible we may be able to leave here tomorrow.'

It was a moment before she reacted to his words, then she said, 'Well that is good news.'

'Yes. I thought perhaps I could walk to the Jessops Farm today and arrange for Mary to go to them in the morning. From what Sam and Able have learned, it is unlikely a vehicle will be able to get along the lane for some days yet, but we could take Mary across the fields to the farm in the morning, and her luggage could follow on once it can be collected by cart—'

She put up one hand to stop him. 'It is by no means decided that Mary will go to the Jessops. Oh, I know they are kindly people and have agreed they will take her, but we have not yet broached the idea to Mary and she will need a little time to grow accustomed.'

'Then we can delay our departure—'

'Oh, I see no need for you to inconvenience yourself further, my lord. Jane and I can make our own arrangements once we are ready to quit Hare Hall.'

She spoke lightly enough, but Jack was not deceived. Disappointment rose, bitter as gall in his stomach.

'You do not *want* to travel with me.'

'I think Jane and I can be useful here a little longer,' she replied. 'Mary's bags need to be packed up and the house will have to be put in order.'

'Then we should all stay and help.'

'That is not necessary. Although perhaps you might leave one of your footmen here—'

'What you mean is you do not want *me* here. So much for the *friendship* you talked of last night!'

She looked away from him. 'I do not wish to inconvenience you further.'

'I find you on your knees sweeping the floor and you talk of sending away what little help you have here! You know it is not sensible, Sabrina.' He waited. 'Well, is it?'

'Now you are being ridiculous,' she retorted, eyeing him resentfully. 'I must get on—'

She went to turn away from him, but he caught her arm.

'You have every right to be angry with me, Sabrina. I have treated you abominably, and I am very sorry for it.'

She flushed, 'I told you last night that I do not hold that against you. It is all forgotten.'

'Then allow me to be of some use to you now, when you need it. Let me help you.'

'You can help me best by leaving Hare Hall,' she said quietly, although she made no attempt to shake him off.

'Dash it, woman, there are barely enough of us here now to keep the place running comfortably! Tell me how it would help you if I leave.' Jack moved closer. She was still facing away from him, but she had bowed her head a little. His eyes were drawn to the back of her neck, where a few wispy golden curls had escaped from the severe topknot. It took all his willpower not to drop a kiss on the exposed skin. He dragged in a ragged breath. 'Do you hate me that much?'

'No!' She turned then, although she would not look up at him. 'I have never hated you, Jack.'

'Never?' A little flame of hope deep inside him flickered into life. 'Do you mean, in spite of all I have done to hurt you?'

He heard her sigh. She said quietly, 'I have hurt you, too.'

The little flame grew stronger.

He said, 'That is what happens, when people allow themselves to care…and I believe we do care for one another.' He reached out and put a finger beneath her chin, gently coaxed her to look up. 'Is that not so?'

Sabrina's throat dried at the warm glow in his blue eyes. It set her heart thudding in her breast, and as their gazes locked, she felt again the tug of desire deep in her belly. She had spent a sleepless night wondering if she had been right to reject Jack's proposal. In the cold dark reaches of the night it was easy to believe all the difficulties between them could be swept away, but with the daylight came the certainty that it was best to end this now, before the doubts and recriminations tore them apart. And yet, standing here so close to Jack, she wanted him so badly that she could barely think at all.

The air felt thick with expectation. It was coiled around her, thrilling, frightening, holding her captive, and all the while desire spiralled inside until her body was positively aching with it. It would be so easy to give in and throw herself into his arms. To agree to anything…

She swallowed, unable to look away from his intense gaze. All her attention was fixed on Jack, and she barely noticed the soft rumble of voices coming from the hall. She wanted to lean into him, to rest her head on his breast and feel the solid beat of his heart against her cheek. She was ready to count the world well lost.

'Well, Sabrina Fair?'

His use of that familiar term and the twisted smile he gave put to flight the last shreds of hesitation. She was opening her mouth to reply when the door burst open.

'Sabrina, Lord John,' cried Mary, running into the room. 'Papa is here. He has come home!'

Chapter Fourteen

Jack saw Sabrina flinch as the childish voice shattered the moment. He took a step away from her. Happiness had been within his grasp, but the moment was gone now, and it took a supreme effort of will to turn and face whoever had come into the room.

Mary of course, her young face wreathed in smiles. Holding her hand was a tall, very thin man with grey hair and a face lined by care. Jack gave him a little bow.

'Ah, Mr Steadmarsh, at last.'

'I'll give you at last, sirrah! What the devil do you mean by appropriating my house?'

Before Jack could form a reply, Sabrina stepped forward, looking calm and very much more in command of herself.

'It is hardly an appropriation, sir,' she said mildly. 'We were snowbound and took shelter here. When we discovered your daughter was quite alone and had no one to look after her, we saw it as our duty to stay.'

'And who might you be, madam?' demanded Mr Steadmarsh, not a whit appeased by her explanation.

'I *told* you, Papa.' Mary piped up. 'This is Lady Massyngham. She and Mrs Nidd, her maid, have been very kind to me. And Lord John, too. He has been helping Abel and Sam with chopping wood and keeping the fires burning.'

Mr Steadmarsh was beginning to look a little confused by all the names. It was then that a small woman dressed all in black stepped out from behind him and spoke for the first time.

'I am Mrs Luckarty, Mr Steadmarsh's sister, come to keep house for him. It seems to me there's a great deal to be explained here,' she said crisply. 'Perhaps we should all sit down.'

'Yes indeed,' agreed Sabrina. 'There is a good fire already burning in the drawing room, and I am sure we would all be more comfortable there.' She turned a coaxing smile towards Mr Steadmarsh. 'I know it is not my place to order things in your house, sir, but you have only this minute come in, and perhaps, just this once, you will allow me to fetch in refreshments for you all?'

'No need for that, my lady,' replied Mrs Luckarty. 'I know fine well where the kitchen is.'

Sabrina beamed at her, refusing to take offence at the lady's abrupt tone. 'Of course you do, ma'am. You will find Mrs Nidd there, and I am sure she will be very delighted to see you.'

Mrs Luckarty went out in a rustle of bombazine skirts and Sabrina led the others off to the drawing room. Jack held the door and she glanced up at him as she passed, but he could read nothing from her look.

Sabrina ushered everyone into the drawing room, knowing she must put aside all thoughts except how to deal with this new situation. The arrival of Mr Steadmarsh and his sister had turned everything on its head. The first thing to do was to explain to the anxious father just what had occurred at Hare Hall since he left. With Mary's help, they pieced together the story, and Mr Steadmarsh listened closely, shaking his head occasionally and interspersing the odd question.

'I am beholden to you, Lady Massyngham, and to you, Lord John,' he said, when at length they were finished. 'I never thought, when I set off for Exeter, that I should be away for such a time, or that my servants would behave so reprehensibly. But the fault is mine, most assuredly, and I alone must take the blame.'

He broke off as Mrs Luckarty and Jane Nidd came

in. They both carried trays bearing tea and coffee pots, saucers and cups. Sabrina was about to suggest the gentleman might prefer a glass of wine when she recalled her suspicion that grief had driven Mr Steadmarsh to drink. The man was already frowning direfully, as if struggling now with great troubles.

'It is only right that I give you all an explanation,' he said heavily, when everyone was supplied with a hot drink.

Sabrina put up a hand to detain her maid, who was about to leave the room.

'Perhaps you would like Jane to take Mary to the kitchen, sir,' suggested Sabrina. 'They might read together there...'

Mr Steadmarsh shook his head. 'No, no, my daughter deserves to hear the truth about her father, however distressing.'

Receiving a nod from Sabrina, Jane silently withdrew.

Jack said gently, 'Sir, Lady Massyngham and I have no need for explanations, if you would rather not. We are only too happy that you have returned safely.'

'No, no, let me tell you everything.' He glanced towards his sister. 'They say confession is good for the soul.

'I had been finding life...difficult since my dear

wife's death. I was neglecting my duties, thinking only of my own grief. Mrs Fitch, my housekeeper, could see that things were not going well, and she urged me to seek help, impressing upon me the need to find someone who could act as a mother to Mary. Thus it was that I decided I would go to Exeter, to seek out my sister Luckarty and ask her to come to Hare Hall and help us for a while. If I had realised quite how parlous things had become here, I would never have gone! At the very least, I should have taken Mary with me. I see that now. My journey south was beset by problems…'

His words trailed away and he bowed his head. Mrs Luckarty, who was sitting beside him, leaned forward and patted his knee.

'Now, Brother, you were steeped in grief and not thinking clearly. No one blames you for that.'

'Perhaps not, but I blame myself,' he declared, looking up. 'I saw only my own selfish concerns, so mired in self-pity that I succumbed to drink on the journey. For several days after I reached Exeter, I was quite unable to go on. As it was, when I finally arrived at Mrs Luckarty's house, I was barely able to make myself understood.' He turned his head to look at his sister. 'I shall be eternally grateful that you did not turn me away at first sight, Ada! Instead you took me in and tended me until I was in my right mind again. For that I shall always be in your debt.'

'Hush now, Brother!' Mrs Luckarty shifted on her chair. She said gruffly, 'It is what anyone would do for family. You were in the Slough of Despond and 'twas my duty as a Christian to help you out of it.'

'It was far more than I deserved, Ada, and I would not have blamed you for shutting your door upon me. For my Mary's sake, I thank you.' He dragged out a handkerchief and blew his nose before continuing. 'Of course, I had no notion that things had reached such a pass here.'

'The servants thought you were never coming back, Papa,' said Mary, who was sitting beside him on the sofa. 'Even Mrs Fitch thought it, although she stayed as long as she could after everyone else had left.' She took his hand and smiled up at him. 'But I always knew you would come, once the snow had cleared.'

'And you were right, my maid,' declared Mrs Luckarty. 'Your papa would never abandon you. And as for the servants, well, we shall find more, and better ones, too. I'm here now and I mean to stay just as long as I am needed!'

It was undoubtedly a relief to have Mary's family with her, but Jack soon realised that although Mrs

Luckarty was a very practical woman, her brother was quite the opposite. He had been accustomed all his life to being waited upon and was happy to sit by the fire in the drawing room while everyone else kept the house running as smoothly as was possible without the help of any housemaids or indoor servants.

'We must be thankful his sister has come with him to take charge,' said Sabrina, when Jack remarked upon it shortly before dinner.

They were momentarily alone in the dining room, where she was setting the table while he prepared the fire.

'It is no wonder things came to such a pretty pass,' he said, adding a log to the pile of kindling he had coaxed into a blaze. 'At least the fellow has given up drinking anything stronger than small beer.'

'I think the poor man has had a salutary lesson,' she said, leaning over to tweak a knife a little straighter. 'I have no doubt Mrs Luckarty will soon have him facing up to his responsibilities. She has already set him to spend an hour each day reading with Mary.' She stepped back, critically surveying her handiwork. 'There. I think that will do.'

'It looks very good to me.' He came to stand beside her. 'If anyone complains I shall take them to task! You have been exceptionally busy since we came here.'

'Thank you, but what else *could* we do? At least I have been spared the very worst household tasks, which Jane and the others have tackled.' She added, with a touch of restraint, 'You, too, have worked hard and without any complaint, my lord.'

'Aye, I have,' he agreed, glancing down at his work-roughened hands. 'I shall be obliged to wear chicken-skin gloves for weeks when we get back to town, like the veriest fop!'

He grinned at her, and when she smiled back at him, he was emboldened to say what had been on his mind since their conversation had been interrupted.

'There is no reason now why you should not return to town with me.'

Immediately the smile disappeared. He started to reach out for her, then stopped.

'I beg your pardon,' he said ruefully. 'My hands are not only rough but dirty from the fire!'

'Do not apologise for your honest toil, my lord.'

Her response encouraged him to try again.

'Sabrina, whatever you think of me, pray allow me to escort you to London. It is a long journey back to the capital from here, at least two nights on the road, and it will be made more hazardous by the uncertain weather. I shall not rest until I know you are safely back in Brook Street with your own servants to look after you.'

'It is already decided that we will spend two more days here, helping Steadmarsh and Mrs Luckarty to settle,' she replied after a moment. 'My own carriage may be mended by then. Perhaps you would allow one of your servants to attempt to take a message to my own postilions at Torrington. If the roads are clear, they can come here and carry me back to town.'

'Of course. I will send Sam out first thing in the morning.'

'Thank you. You are very good.'

'However, I would advise you against being too hopeful, Sabrina. The Jessops have had reports that many of the roads are still blocked with snow. If Sam cannot get through to Torrington, will you then consent to travel with me?' He could see she was minded to refuse, and he went on quickly. 'You do not need to give me your answer now. We will not be travelling until Saturday, and I will do my best before that to show you that I am a gentleman.'

Her green eyes were dark and troubled, and he knew she doubted his ability to keep his distance. Jack thought of the attraction that sparked between them at every meeting, the heat that flooded him whenever their eyes met. He wanted her with every fibre of his being, and it put him on edge whenever they were together. It clouded his thinking.

And yet there had been companionable moments,

times when they had been comfortable in each other's company. Talking together at dinner, sharing a glass of wine. They had even built a snowman and frolicked on the lawn, until playfulness had been routed by desire. They both felt it, he was sure of that now. He had seen it in her eyes, the warmth, the longing. It was always there, hovering around them, ready to strike at unwary moments.

And now she was afraid to be alone with him.

What do you expect? You took her to your bed and then abandoned her. That is hardly the conduct of a gentleman!

He closed his eyes.

'I can act as I should,' he declared. 'I *will*.'

When he looked at Sabrina again, she was still regarding him doubtfully.

He said, 'Trust me to deliver you safely back to the capital, Sabrina. After that, you have my word I shall not trouble you again. What do you say?'

Sabrina saw the sober, anxious look on his face and knew he was in earnest. It would be far more sensible to let him take her to London. Jane would berate her soundly if she insisted on travelling separately in a hired carriage, which had been her intention. It would not be half so comfortable as Lord John's well-appointed vehicle. Not only that, she would have to explain to her maid just why she refused to be in Jack's company and how was she to do that? How was she to confess that she was too weak to resist the temptation of her own body, the desire that flowed through and around her whenever Jack Callater was near.

She said at last, 'If my own vehicle cannot get through, I will consider it. Providing we can behave like civilised acquaintances until we depart.'

'We can,' he assured her. 'Thank you.'

Jack made her a little bow before picking up the coal bucket and walking out of the room. He would not let her down. He would strain every sinew to behave like a gentleman. Even if it meant rolling naked in what was left of the snowdrifts at regular intervals to cool himself!

For the rest of that day and the next two, Jack exerted himself as never before. His behaviour to the others did not change, but he was on his guard not to single out Sabrina. It helped that there were more people in the house. They were never alone together and there was plenty to keep them occupied, but still he found it exhausting. He was obliged to ignore it if, in an unguarded moment, Sabrina smiled at him or if their hands should brush and set his skin tingling with the shock of it. Never once did he let his eyes follow her as she moved across a room, or dwell too long on her face when they were sitting down together.

His reward came at dinner on the eve of their departure, when Mr Steadmarsh brought up the subject of their forthcoming journey.

'I recall you said your own carriage was being repaired in Torrington, Lady Massyngham. Have you had word of it?'

'Alas, Mr Steadmarsh, the roads in that direction are still impassable,' she replied. 'Lord John's man could not get through. But I left my people instructions to make their way back to Brook Street, if they do not hear from me.'

'The snow causes such havoc in this part of the country,' remarked Mrs Luckarty, shaking her head. 'It can come on so suddenly, with great drifts blocking the lanes for weeks on end. You are fortunate that you will be able to complete your journey with Lord John.'

Jack kept his eyes fixed upon his plate. He had not pressed Sabrina for an answer and he waited now with bated breath for her reply.

'Yes,' she said. 'I am very grateful for Lord John's offer to escort me to London.'

'And his travelling chaise is a luxurious equipage,' enthused Mr Steadmarsh. 'I took a look at it when I went out to the carriage house this morning. Everything looks to be of the finest quality, the well-padded seats, the springs…even the sheepskin foot rug to add to your comfort.'

Don't look up, man. Don't reveal how relieved you are that she has agreed to come with you.

But of course he did look up. Sabrina was watching him and he wanted to smile at her across the table. To convey in some way how pleased he was that she had agreed to come with him, but he was afraid she might still change her mind. Instead he addressed Mr Steadmarsh.

'Why, thank you, sir. The chaise is a recent purchase, don't you know, and to the very latest design…'

Sabrina listened to the two men discussing the finer points of the chaise and from there they soon moved on to carriage horses. Jack had shown neither excessive pleasure or surprise at her decision to accept his offer. She should be reassured by that, since he was keeping to his word not to discompose her, but it left her feeling sadly flat. She gave a little inward sigh. What a contrary piece she was, to insist a man keep his distance and then be disappointed when he did just that!

Chapter Fifteen

They left Hare Hall at dawn on Saturday morning, Sabrina and Jack in the luxurious chaise with Jane and Tom Weald following in the baggage coach, which was almost as well equipped. At first they drove along roads that still showed signs of the recent snows, with the fields on either side white and gleaming in the fitful sunshine. However, as they drew nearer to London the snow disappeared and the landscape was all dull browns and greens beneath an overcast sky.

Inside the travelling chaise the atmosphere was strained. Sabrina and Jack were unfailingly polite to one another, but Sabrina could not help a creeping feeling of depression. She had spent years honing her acting skills, first in her marriage, where she hosted balls and parties with every semblance of enjoyment, then when she returned to Society, pretending to be the Wicked Widow everyone thought her, surrounded by admirers but keeping them all at a distance.

Only once had she allowed a man past her defences, and he was now sitting beside her in this sumptuous carriage, treating her with a deference that irked her almost beyond bearing. There was a constraint between them. When they stopped to change horses, and she found the obsequious behaviour of the landlord amusing, the laughing glance she threw at Jack was met with only a cool, distant smile. And when he helped her down from the coach at each stop, he released her so quickly it was almost as if he could not bear to touch her.

It did no good for Sabrina to tell herself this was what she had wanted. That it was she who had insisted on this level of propriety. It was difficult not to share a joke with him, to keep their conversation to the merest commonplace. It irked her almost beyond bearing to keep her hand from seeking his when a sad thought occurred to her, and not to ask him for his thoughts when he was sombrely gazing out of the window. She missed the unguarded glances, the warm smiles. She even missed their arguments. At least she had felt alive then. Now she felt bereft. She loved him too much to be his friend, but this unnatural politeness was almost unbearable. Not only did she find it depressing, it shredded her nerves.

The distance between them was only inches, but it might as well have been a mile.

It was growing dark when they reached the Punch Bowl, the final posting inn on what seemed to Jack to have been an interminable journey. He jumped down and spoke to the landlord before turning back to hand Sabrina out of the chaise.

'I have ascertained that they have sufficient rooms available. We will stop here tonight and travel on to London tomorrow. If we make an early start, you will be back at your own house by noon.'

She looked up at him, surprised.

'But it cannot be more than two hours journey from here,' she objected 'I would by far rather continue tonight.'

'*You* might, madam, but my servants and horses need to rest before we cross the Heath. I will not risk driving over that lonely stretch of road exhausted and hungry, and in the dark, too. We shall finish our journey in the morning.'

He was tempted to add that it was not his choice. He, too, would by far prefer to travel on and put an end to this miserable journey, but he refrained. They had both maintained a reasonable level of civility so far, and he would not spoil it now.

The inn yard was well lit by torches that made it

as bright as day. The landlord had secured them a private dining room, and Sabrina and her maid were escorted to their bedchambers, where they might rest until dinner was served. Jack remained in the yard to have a few words with the ostler and assure himself that his carriages would have the best horses available in the morning for the final leg of their journey, then he followed a servant into the inn.

As they stepped into the entrance, he heard a blast of noisy laughter from the taproom on one side.

'They seem to be enjoying themselves,' he remarked to the servant.

'Aye, sir. We've had a group of gentlemen dining here tonight, and one of 'em's been sporting his blunt very freely.'

Jack followed the man's glance into the taproom as they passed and saw a stocky, crop-haired gentleman calling for more drinks. The crowd, which included a large number of soldiers in their colourful uniforms, was loudly cheering this open-handed behaviour. It was not unusual for fashionable rakes and Corinthians to drink in local taverns and gin houses but Jack did not recognise the man as anyone he knew, although the fellow was respectably dressed and clearly no local farmhand. By the sound of the raucous laughter already issuing from the room, Jack guessed there would be some sore heads in the morning, but at that moment he wished he might change places with one of the revellers. Anything rather than spend another awkward dinner with Sabrina.

Sabrina was shown to a bedchamber off the first-floor gallery. It was comfortable enough, but she already had a headache coming on and decided she would prefer to have supper sent up to her rather than struggle to sit through another meal with Jack. She did not like the restraint that had sprung up between them. It felt as if they had already said their goodbyes and were now merely strangers.

No, worse than strangers. There was an awkwardness now in his company that was far too painful.

A knock at the door interrupted her thoughts, but it was not Jane, returned with her supper on a tray.

'I met Mrs Nidd on the stairs.' Jack's frame blocked the doorway. 'She tells me you are minded to dine alone.'

'Yes. That is correct.' She stood her ground, determined not to invite him in.

He nodded. 'When we arrived here, I thought I should prefer that, too, but then I realised that after tomorrow we will not see one another.'

'It is what we agreed—'

'I know.' He rubbed his jaw. 'I would like us to enjoy our last night together.'

'No!' Her response was immediate, uttered in panic, and he went on quickly.

'Pray listen to me, Sabrina. I am suggesting nothing more than dinner. A dinner for friends, not the stilted polite acquaintances we have been recently. It feels as if, once Mary's father returned, everything changed between us. All our energies went into packing up and leaving Hare Hall. We have barely spoken to one another since then, save out of necessity.'

Sabrina sighed. 'What does it matter, when tomorrow we shall go our separate ways?'

'I don't want it to end like this. I want to sit and talk with you. Laugh with you. To raise a glass to your future happiness and have you do the same for mine. One final happy memory of our time together before we take our leave of one another tomorrow.'

She shook her head. 'I do not think that would be wise...'

'Since when have we ever been wise, Sabrina?'

She was not proof against his rueful smile. She had no illusions. She knew where it could lead if she agreed to this. If she let down her guard in his company. The attraction that was never far away would break through her weakened defences. It was there now, drawing her in, filling her senses with the scent of him. She wanted to reach out and rest her palm against his chest, feel his heart beating in time with hers.

'I give you my word we will do nothing but eat and talk,' he said, as if reading her mind. 'Nothing will happen unless it is what we both want. He leaned a little closer. 'Dine with me, Sabrina. This is our last night together. Let us enjoy it.'

Would she come?

Jack paced the floor of the dining parlour. She was right. It was not wise. It was not sensible. It could only postpone the inevitable, the time when he would not see her again, save from a distance. Yet the thought of dining alone while she supped in her room, the both of them unhappy, was not to be borne.

'I hope I am not late?'

He turned, already smiling in relief at the melodious sound of her voice. She was here. That was the first hurdle over. Now to see if they could actually spend a pleasant evening together.

Dinner went well. Jack exerted himself to please Sabrina, while she was determined to be pleased. Nothing occurred to mar their enjoyment of the meal; they found plenty to discuss without touching on delicate subjects. When he had poured the last of the wine into their glasses, she raised hers to salute him.

'Thank you. This augurs well for the future,' she

said, smiling. 'Should we by chance encounter one another in town, it need not be awkward.'

'No.' He touched his glass against hers. 'We have proved it is possible to meet as friends.'

Who are you trying to fool, man? You want her as much as ever. If she was to turn from saint to seductress again, you would be lost!

Sabrina met Jack's eyes across the wine glasses. She was outwardly calm while her conscience pricked uncomfortably. Her smiles had been genuine, as had her enjoyment of his company, but for her, the evening had not been an unalloyed success. She had been constantly aware of a small, insistent tug of desire. She had been determined to ignore the temptation, but she was not strong enough to banish it completely.

'I should retire,' She finished her wine and carefully put the glass down on the table.

'If that is what you wish.'

'It is.'

It is not at all what you wish! You want him to persuade you to stay.

They both rose from the table, and he walked across to pick up the cashmere shawl she had brought with her.

'You had best wear this. There is a chill in the night air.'

'Thank you.'

Sabrina stood, silent, while he arranged the woollen shawl around her, trying not to think of the way her spine tingled to know he was so close. His hands lingered on her shoulders for a moment, and she held her breath. Would he kiss her? She closed her eyes, imagining him turning her about and pulling her close, lowering his head so that their lips could meet. She wanted it so much that her body burned with longing.

'I will escort you to your room.'

As he spoke, he moved away from her, and the sudden chill of loneliness was almost too much to bear.

He walked to the door and Sabrina could only follow. It was the right thing to do. The sensible choice and she must comply, even though inside she was screaming for something else entirely.

Silently they went up the stairs to the gallery. After opening her door for her, Jack stood aside for her to enter. Once she was over the threshold, Sabrina turned back to look at him. Even in the shadows she could feel the heat of his gaze upon her before he looked away, muttering under his breath.

'What is it?' she asked him. 'What is wrong?'

He looked up at the starry sky, his breath escaping in a hiss. 'I should have been stronger. I should never have allowed things to go so far between us.'

'Do…do you regret it then?' Something twisted around her heart, squeezing it hard.

'No. No, but I should have taken more care.' His eyes came back to her. 'Sabrina, there is something we have not discussed, and I am not so irresponsible that I can ignore it. What if.' He stopped, took another breath. 'What if you are with child after, after what we have done?'

She shook her head. 'I am not.'

'You cannot be sure about that.'

'Yes, I can.'

She clutched her shawl about her a little tighter, but she knew the chill was deep in her core, rather than outside.

'I am barren,' she said bleakly. 'My husband brought in his doctor to examine me, a few months after we were married. He wanted an heir, you see, and he was…disappointed when I did not conceive.'

'I am so sorry.'

Her head came up and she said, with a hint of defiance, 'I am not. Sir Roderick's passion for his new bride waned very rapidly. I was too…innocent for him, and after the first night he bedded me only for an heir. Once he knew I could not give him one, he left me alone.' She gave a little laugh. 'So you see, Jack, you should be pleased I did not accept your proposal. As Massyngham told me, a wife is worthless if she cannot fill the nursery with *brats*.'

Her voice cracked on the last words, and she did not protest as Jack stepped over the threshold and folded her in his arms.

She blinked back the threatening tears as he held her, his cheek resting against her hair. She drew immense comfort from him, but only for a moment, then she pushed him gently away. He released her immediately and she dashed her hand across her cheeks.

'You should go now.' She marvelled at the steadiness of her voice. He put out a hand and she quickly backed away. He was very kind, but she must not mistake that for anything stronger. 'Goodnight, Lord John.'

Jack hesitated. Sabrina's evident distress caught at his heart. He desperately wanted to comfort her, but how could he remain when she had dismissed him so finally? Silently he turned and made his way to his own bedchamber.

The morning brought no relief to Sabrina's low spirits. The idea of returning to Brook Street and her old life held no appeal, but what else could she do? She did not want to go back to the Dower House.

The new baronet was trying hard to emulate Sir Roderick's dissolute ways, and she had no wish to live in the vicinity. If her parents did not live so close to Jack's best friend, she might be tempted to buy a house nearby, but she knew that would not do. She needed to get away completely from Lord John Callater. At least until she had conquered this passion she had for a man who no longer loved her.

Had he ever truly loved her? She wondered. He had been but five-and-twenty when they first met, and they had known each other for only a few months. Long enough for her to form a lasting attachment, but perhaps it had been different for a man of the world, like Jack.

Sabrina took breakfast in her room and then instructed Jane to inform His Lordship that she was ready to depart and would wait for him downstairs. She put on her bonnet, fastened her cloak and stepped outside onto the gallery. Below her the yard was bustling with activity as coaches and horses were being prepared for imminent departure.

The sun was rising in a clear sky, and she stopped for a moment to take in a deep breath of the crisp air. It was impossible to remain melancholy on such a bright day. She had much to be thankful for, and many years ahead. She was determined she would not repine. Not that she thought there was any possibility of her and Jack becoming reconciled, but she was still young. There was time yet for her to live a full and satisfying life. She would give up London and the round of balls and gaiety. She might even travel. A grand tour, perhaps. She had always wanted to visit Italy. Perhaps she might go to Paris, too...

A sudden altercation in the yard below caught her attention. She glanced down to see a group of ragged urchins who had been begging at the yard entrance being driven away by a groom brandishing a riding crop. Sabrina watched them, frowning a little. The biggest was a girl, probably only a little older than Mary Steadmarsh. She was ushering the younger ones away, keeping herself between them and the angry groom.

Those children should be in school, she decided. Or perhaps the older ones should be found gainful employment.

Perhaps she could put her energies into helping such poor wretches. That would certainly fill her days! Papa had been involved in politics; she could be more useful, too. It was not unknown for ladies to engage in worthy causes. She was rich, and not without friends...

'Miss Kydd?' The enquiring voice at her elbow

made her start. Sabrina turned to find a stocky gentleman standing beside her.

'It *is* you, Miss Kydd,' he said, smiling broadly. 'Or, more rightly, Lady Massyngham these days, is it not?'

'Why Dr Watson!' she exclaimed. 'How do you do, sir?'

She greeted him happily, her recent thoughts of Papa making her very glad to meet his old friend.

'I am very well, ma'am, very well. And your parents, how are they? You are travelling with them, perhaps.'

'No, no, but I am just returned from a visit to them. In Devonshire.'

'Ah, yes. I hope they are in good health?' He exhaled and shook his head. 'How I miss those conversations with your father, my lady. We had such lively meetings at your house, did we not? Such a good friend as he was to us all.'

Knowing Papa had cut all ties with his London friends, Sabrina thought it best not to respond to this. Instead she said, 'And your son, James, how is he?'

'Oh, never better, ma'am, never better. Full of plans and energy for the cause, you know.'

Sabrina smiled but once again, she did not reply. Mention of "the cause" reminded her of why Papa had been obliged to retire from public life. She had

had no contact with any of his more radical acquaintances since her marriage, but she had seen their names in the newspapers occasionally. Of course, the reports were biased against any anti-government protest, but she was very much afraid the men with whom Papa had met and discussed political reform were now dangerously impatient for change.

'You should come along to our next meeting.' Dr Watson interrupted her thoughts. 'You might renew your acquaintance with old friends. Something to tell your father when you see him next, eh?'

Sabrina said nothing. From all she had read, she was sure Papa's old friends were no longer satisfied with the peaceful protests and petitions he had advocated. It would be unwise to mention anything of this to her father.

'Henry Hunt is going to be there,' Dr Watson went on. 'I am sure he would be pleased to see you, my lady, and to hear news of your father. He is to speak for us. We are trying to persuade the Prince Regent to receive our petition for Parliamentary reform. In fact, you might be able to help with that, Lady Massyngham. I am sure you have the ear of any number of influential men, eh?'

Sabrina did not like the sly look that accompanied these words, and she found herself resorting to the polite smiles that she had employed so many times to hide her true feelings without giving offence.

She said, 'My husband moved in influential circles, it is true, but I have no dealings with that society now. I shall not be able to attend your meeting, Dr Watson, but I pray you will remember me to your son.' She decided to bring their conversation to an end and held out her hand. 'Give my regards to Mr Hunt, too. Please tell him I wish him well in his endeavours, as long as they are peaceful.'

The doctor's smile slipped a little, but he recovered and said, as he bowed over her hand, 'Well, well, we shall be assembling at Spa Fields, opposite Merlin's Cave Public House on Monday next, if you change your mind, my lady.'

She tucked her hand back into her muff as he walked away from her. There was no doubt Dr Watson and his son were very passionate in their belief that political reform was needed to help those struggling to survive. Perhaps there was something she could do to help such people. Papa would approve.

'Who the devil was that?'

She turned and saw Jack standing in the doorway of his chamber.

'What is that to you?'

'He is not the sort of man with whom you should be associating.'

A spurt of irritation flashed through Sabrina. How dare Jack look down upon anyone who was not of his own station! She did not doubt he would order the very best of everything for himself and ignore the plight of those less fortunate.

'He is Dr James Watson,' she replied coldly. 'An old friend of my father's. Not that it is any business of yours!' With that she swept past him and hurried away to the travelling chaise waiting in the yard.

Jack did not follow her immediately. He had recognised Dr Watson as the fellow carousing in the taproom last night and thought him a strange companion for such a mild-mannered man as Sir Anthony Kydd. But Sabrina was right, it was none of his business. With a shrug, he set off down the stairs.

A chill breeze had sprung up, and as he stepped into the yard a piece of paper blew across and settled on the toe of one of his highly polished Hessians. He bent and scooped it up, idly glancing at the print, It was a handbill.

'"A meeting in Spa Fields",' he read aloud, '"Petition to the Prince Regent…the present state of Great Britain…arrogance, folly…crimes…dread Crisis…"' Frowning, he let his eyes go back to the headline, which was a quote from Lord Nelson. '"England Expects every Man to do his Duty".'

Fighting talk, if ever he had heard it. Jack glanced back towards the taproom, narrowing his eyes as he tried to summon up a picture of just what he had seen last night. Watson had been calling on the tap boy to bring drinks for everyone, but Jack recalled now the sheaf of papers the fellow had been holding in one hand. It might have been a supply of these printed handbills, inviting the poor and oppressed to join a meeting. Jack gave a low whistle. If his suspicions were correct, Dr Watson was a very dangerous man. He screwed up the paper, and as he walked on, he tossed it to a waiting ostler, suggesting the lad throw it on the fire.

Shortly after noon the elegant travelling chaise bowled along Brook Street and pulled up outside the smart town house that Sabrina had hired. Jack opened the door and jumped out.

'Well, madam, we have come to the end of our journey.'

He turned back and held out his hand to Sabrina. She took it and stepped down to join him on the pavement.

'Thank you, my lord. I am excessively grateful to you.'

He said irritably, 'Let us be done with this false

civility, madam. I have delivered you safely to town and now you are free of me.'

She lifted her head. 'We are free of one another, Lord John. Which is what we both want.'

No. He wanted to drag her into his arms and kiss her. To undress her slowly, pulling loose the ribbon garters and kissing every inch of skin as he rolled down her silk stockings. He wanted to take her to his bed, to kiss and caress her until she was moaning with the sheer pleasure of it.

He firmly stamped down the disquieting thoughts.

'Well then, "Since there is no help…"'

He saw her eyes widen at his quotation. She knew the next line of Drayton's sonnet as well as he. His lips curved into a smile of self-derision.

'Don't worry, Sabrina Fair, I shall not ask you to kiss and part from me. Instead I will show you what a gentleman I can be. I bid you *adieu*, ma'am, and wish you nothing but happiness.'

He realised he was still holding her hand and would have released her, but her fingers suddenly tightened.

'Jack, I am sorry. I wish this might have ended differently.'

He looked at her, taking in the lovely face, the sea green eyes shadowed now with remorse, the full red lips that he still wanted to kiss, even though he knew she could never love him. Then he shrugged.

'So too am I, madam.'

With that, he freed his hand, shouted a word to his driver and jumped back into the chaise. As the coach rattled away, more lines of the sonnet ran through his head.

...you get no more of me/And I am glad, yea glad with all my heart/That thus so cleanly I myself can free.

There was still a hint of her perfume in the carriage, and with something between a groan and growl, he threw himself back into the corner.

'If only it was that easy to be free of her!'

Chapter Sixteen

'There.' Jack signed his name with a flourish and handed the paper back to his lawyer.

'Send that off immediately, Mr Simmons, and my steward can implement the changes. It should reassure my tenants that I have no wish to force them out of their homes.'

'And this, sir?' Simmons held up another signed paper. 'It's a bad time to be selling your bonds, Lord John.'

'I can do without the interest they bring in, but my people cannot live without more help.'

'Well, 'tis very generous of you, sir, but I fear it may not go down well with the other landowners in the area.'

'Perhaps not, but I am concerned that those on my estates should not suffer unduly from these high prices. It will do me little good in the long run if they get into debt.'

'A pity everyone is not as liberal-spirited as you, my lord,' remarked the lawyer, carefully folding the documents. 'Then we might not have such unrest in the country. There's some as want to use the grievances to stir up the people.'

'There always will be such people,' replied Jack, rising. 'It never takes much to rouse the mob.'

'Aye, and they are having some success in this present time, my lord. Only two weeks ago there was a meeting held in Clerkenwell. Vast crowds turned up, around ten thousand I am told. Quite an event it was, and peaceful in the main. Although I heard Lord Castlereagh's windows were broken.'

'Well, I have done what I can for my people,' Jack said curtly. 'Others must look to their own conscience.'

Jack took his leave. He had not meant to be so abrupt with his lawyer, but his head was still full of Sabrina. Confound it, since he had left her in Brook Street yesterday, she was never out of his thoughts. Simmons mentioning rabble-rousers reminded him of that fellow at the Punch Bowl she had been talking with. Dr Watson. Unless he was very much mistaken, that was someone she should avoid.

'None of your business,' he told himself, as he set off back to Albany. 'She told you as much, so forget the matter!'

Yet he could not forget it. Something was nagging at his mind as his coach rattled through the streets. And when he returned to his rooms he went directly to his sitting room and looked through the invitations wedged into the frame of the looking glass above the mantelshelf.

It did not take him long to find what he was looking for, and a few hours later, washed and dressed in his finest evening clothes, Lord John Callater strolled into the ballroom of Deanham House, where he was greeted rapturously by the host.

'Jack, you old rogue, where the devil have you been hiding?' demanded Lord Deanham. 'We had quite given up hope of seeing you.'

'I was snowbound, Jerry,' he replied, his eyes wandering over the assembled crowd. 'Tedious business, but there it is.'

'Aye, dashed nuisance that. But you are here now, and ready to dance, I hope? My wife will not forgive me if I let you go straight off to play cards.'

'Of course.' Jack made an elegant bow. 'Always ready to oblige.'

It was some time and several dances later that Jack was able to slip off to the card room, where he joined a group of young bucks standing in one corner. He exchanged greetings and spent some time conversing with them before he turned to the business that had brought him here.

'I have a fancy to go to Brooks's,' he remarked, taking a glass of wine from the tray of a passing waiter. 'Is anyone here a member?'

'Devil a bit, Callater,' cried Hugh Claverham, a black-haired individual in a nip-waisted coat. 'Watier's is the place to go now, don't you know!'

Jack smiled. 'Indulge me.'

'Oldroyd is a member, I think,' drawled another of the group. 'Bertie, you still go to Brooks's, don't you?'

Mr Oldroyd pulled a face. 'Rarely.'

'But you could introduce me?' Jack persisted.

'I could, if that is really what you want?'

Jack gave the dandy his most charming smile. 'It is!'

Sabrina put down her embroidery and looked at the clock. It was almost time to change for dinner, thank heavens. She had been back in London two full days now, and time had never dragged so slowly. She had kept herself busy all day, spending an hour that morning discussing menus with her housekeeper before penning a letter to Mary Steadmarsh. She had also practised at the pianoforte and read several chapters of *Glenarvon*, but even Lady Caroline Lamb's salacious portraits of Society's leaders could not distract her for very long.

There were numerous invitations on the mantelshelf, and she toyed with the idea of going out. It was not too late; she could still go out to one of the many parties, if she so wished, but she did not. She was determined not to go back to that old life, providing fodder for the gossip mongers. She would find something more to do with her life.

She went up to her room, where she found her maid laying out her gown for the evening.

'Jane, what would you say if I said I was going abroad?'

'I'd say that's very sudden, ma'am.'

'Yes, well, I am bored with town,' said Sabrina, stepping out of her day gown.

'Are you now?'

She averted her eyes from the shrewd gaze of her maid.

'I thought we might go to Europe. Now the war is truly over, I believe many people are travelling again.'

'Aye, well, I suppose you might as well dance until dawn in Paris as in London.'

Sabrina gave an uncertain laugh. 'Oh, Jane, do you think me such a sad, frivolous creature?'

'No, my lady, I think you might be running away.'

Jane was deftly fastening the buttons on the back

of her gown, and Sabrina was glad she did not have to hide her consternation. She swallowed.

'R-running away?' she asked, trying to sound incredulous. 'From what?'

'From the chance of happiness with a good man, Miss Sabrina. Lord John is clearly head over heels for you. Or he would be, if you would let him.'

'I cannot do that.' Sabrina twisted her hands together. 'He does not know everything.'

'Then tell him.'

'No. I cannot. Papa—'

'I don't think Lord John is one to blab, Miss Sabrina, and if he did, there is no proof now of any wrongdoing. Besides, it's an old story. I doubt anyone would give it a thought.'

'I would. And Mama, too,' replied Sabrina. 'And Lord John Callater would be obliged to think about it, if he allied himself with my family. The truth would be bound to come out, and he would share in the disgrace.'

'Well, you should let His Lordship make his own mind up about that,' replied, Jane, draping a Norwich shawl around Sabrina's shoulders. 'Now, you go on down to your dinner and think over what I have said.'

A solitary meal gave Sabrina plenty of time to consider her maid's words. She refuted the accusation of running away. It was nothing of the sort. She was protecting Jack from making a mistake and saving them both a great deal of heartache. He might think he wanted to marry her, but how could they ever be happy if he knew the truth?

She had sold herself to save her father from a prison sentence. Papa wanted to reform the political system, to protect the poor from rich noblemen like Lord John Callater, heir to the Marquess of Doune. How could they ever be reconciled? Kind as he was, Jack would never understand that she, too, had sympathy with those who wanted change. Then there was her reputation. That was so tainted it would undoubtedly tarnish him, too, and she could not even redeem herself by giving him an heir.

The same arguments went round and round in her head until she went up to bed some hours later.

No, she thought miserably. It was best they went their separate ways.

A blustery, chill December day did not encourage Sabrina to leave the house the following morning, and she was engaged in writing a letter when Lord John Callater was announced. Her pen spluttered, and she was obliged to dry the blots before she could give her attention to her visitor.

'Good morning, Lady Massyngham.'

She eyed him warily. 'Why are you here?'

His brows went up. 'Is that how you greet your visitors?'

'We agreed that when we returned to London, we would be done with one another.'

'I do not think that is possible. At least,' he added quickly, 'not yet.'

'Oh?'

She tensed, wondering how best she might escape. Then she reminded herself sternly that she was not some timid creature, ready to flee at the slighted threat. This was her house and she would not be intimidated.

Her chin came up and she gave him a chilly look.

'I do not believe we have anything more to say to one another.'

'Now, that is where I disagree with you, Sabrina. I think we have a great deal to discuss.'

He took a step closer and her aloof manner disappeared. 'Please, Jack, let us not go over this again. We cannot meet without pulling caps.'

'That is not quite true. We have enjoyed some *very* pleasant encounters. Have you forgotten?'

The teasing glint in his eye brought a flush to Sabrina's cheeks. She turned away and walked over to the window.

'Oh, why are you making this so difficult?' she muttered, staring out at the street below.

'Because I do not *see* any difficulty. Nothing that we cannot resolve.'

A bitter little laugh escaped her.

'There are things about me that I cannot tell you. About my marriage. My family.'

'Cannot tell me, or will not?'

Jane's words came back to Sabrina. She had gone over the arguments for hours last night, but every time she came to the same conclusion. She bowed her head.

'You must forget me, Jack. I am not worthy of you.'

Staring at Sabrina's back, Jack could see the dejection in every line of her body, and his heart went out to her. He moved closer.

'I think that should be my decision, don't you?

'But you do not know—'

'I think I have guessed most of it.' He put his hands on her shoulders and turned her to face him. 'I know you did not marry Massyngham for his wealth. He had some hold over your father, did he not?'

Sabrina's troubled countenance told Jack he was right.

'I thought at first it might be gambling debts, so I went to Brooks's. I spent quite some time there, as a matter of fact. I met several of its members who were well acquainted with your father, and I have now discounted that. It was something else.'

She moved away, lifting one hand as if to silence him. But he would not stop now, he would chance everything on a last throw of the dice.

'It must have been something very serious to make you sacrifice yourself so wholly. I did not speak much with Sir Anthony at Hartland, but it was clear he still holds his liberal views. They might even be called dangerously revolutionary.'

'No! Papa believes, believed in reform, but he was never a radical.'

'You told me Dr Watson was a friend of your father's, as was Henry Hunt.' Her eyes flew to his face and he allowed himself a slight smile. 'I heard you asking Watson to give Hunt your regards. I imagine Sir Anthony is also acquainted with Cobbett, who is a renowned advocate of parliamentary reform. Is that not so?'

'Papa no longer corresponds with any of them.'

She was watching him carefully. She reminded him of a wild animal, ready to bolt. Jack strolled across the room to place himself between Sabrina and the door. He was determined to get to the bottom of this. Confound it, his happiness and Sabrina's rested on the outcome!

He went on, keeping his tone, calm, conversational.

'I saw Dr Watson on the night we arrived at the Punch Bowl. He was giving out handbills for the forthcoming meeting and I made a few enquiries. His son James is a well-known firebrand. I also heard that when your father was in London, he was not averse to entertaining the Watsons and their ilk at Russell Square. That is, until your parents moved so suddenly to Devonshire, very soon after your marriage.' He paused, watching her. 'It is well known that Massyngham's settlement upon your marriage was very generous. Talking with those members of Brooks's who remember Sir Anthony, some of them believe he gave up his radical views to please his powerful new son-in-law. One or two think *you* persuaded him to do it, in order to secure a rich husband.'

'No! I would never—'

She stopped herself and Jack said quietly, 'If you do not want me to speculate, you should tell me the truth, Sabrina.'

She regarded him for a moment, biting her lip, then she sighed. 'I suppose it cannot matter now, save in your opinion of me.'

One side of his mouth quirked up. 'I doubt anything will change that very much, now. But you are looking very pale,' he said, looking closely at her. 'Perhaps it would be best if we sit down for this.'

She did not protest as he guided her to the sofa and

gently pulled her down beside him. He turned slightly so that he could keep his eyes on her face.

'Now, my dear, tell me everything. In your own time.'

Then he sat back and waited.

Sabrina was silent for a long while, then she began to speak, choosing her words with care.

'You may remember, when we met, that Papa held a minor post in Government. He was much moved by the plight of the poor and thought this way he might do some good for those less fortunate than ourselves. The smaller landowners, for example, and farm labourers. For some time he had been corresponding with William Cobbett, pledging his support for his efforts to increase wages and reduce taxes. Papa wanted only peaceful protests, petitions and the like, but in some of his letters he mentioned those who visited our house in Russell Square. Men who advocated the use of force.'

'James Watson, for example?'

'Yes, amongst others. Poor Papa had never considered the risks of hosting such meetings, even though the government were meting out severe penalties to those they considered revolutionaries. He merely thought he could do some *good*.'

She paused, staring down at her hands clasped tightly in her lap.

'What happened?' He prompted her gently.

'That year…' Her eyes flickered briefly on his face. 'The year I met you, Mama had decided that, despite the expense, I should enjoy a full Season. I was nearing one-and-twenty, and Mama thought if we waited until Papa had risen higher in government it would be too late to find me a suitable husband. She wanted me to make a *good match*.'

Jack smiled a little. 'What mother does not want that for their child? So, you had your Season. Is that when you met Sir Roderick?'

'Yes. We danced a few times, but I never thought… I did not give him any encouragement. Quite the reverse!'

She looked up then, her green eyes pleading with him to understand.

'I believe you,' said Jack gently. 'That would not deter a man like Massyngham.'

'No, it did not. Cobbett had just been arrested for seditious libel, and somehow, Sir Roderick obtained several of the letters Papa had written to him. He threatened to hand the letters over and expose my father as a dangerous revolutionary. If he had done so, not only would Papa have lost his position, he would have been imprisoned. Unlike Cobbett, he did not have the funds to pay for comfortable quarters in Newgate. I did not realise how much he and Mama had spent upon my come-out. We would have been penniless.' She clasped her hands together and stared out across the room. 'I struck a…a bargain with Sir Roderick. I agreed to marry him, in return for his silence. Do you understand now why I did not see you again? Once the betrothal was announced, I was too ashamed to speak with you.'

'You preferred me, and everyone else, to think you had married Sir Roderick for his wealth.'

'At the time I had no choice. I could not tell anyone the truth, but you… I would not have been able to lie to you.' She bowed her head. 'I am sorry, Jack.'

'So too am I.' He thought of the anger he had felt, and six wasted years. 'What happened to the letters?'

'Sir Roderick kept them, to ensure my…my compliance. I did not get them back until he died, then I burned them. I told Papa what I had done, but by then they had been in Devon for four years and he had promised Mama that he would not get involved in anything like that again.'

'And is that everything?'

Is it not enough?

Sabrina wanted to scream the words at him. Their worlds were too different. They could never be reconciled.

'Yes.' She rose, not looking at Jack. 'You see, really, it changes nothing.'

'Massyngham forced you into marriage. I understand that. But it does not explain your actions once he was dead.'

She schooled her face into a semblance of indifference.

'He left me a handsome fortune. I decided to enjoy it. I became a wicked widow.'

Heavens, how coolly she could speak, even though inside, her heart was hammering as if it was trying to beat its way out through her ribs.

Muttering an oath, Jack jumped to his feet. 'That does not make sense! What you told me, that there had been no lovers, that no one but Massyngham had taken you to bed before me…are you saying that was all lies?'

Her eyes slid away from his angry glance, and she pretended to study her reflection in the mirror about the fireplace.

'I thought it might increase your desire for me. That is all.'

'And it did, damn you!' He sucked in a breath, trying to contain his anger. 'By heaven, madam, you deserve your reputation.'

'I am surprised you ever doubted it.' She pushed a stray curl back into place. 'There, you have heard everything. I would like you to leave now.'

Jack was looking at her, frowning. Sabrina turned back to face him, pinning on a smile, concealing her true thoughts as she had done many times over the years. She could do this! All that was left was to dismiss him, as she had dismissed men so often in the past.

The difference this time was that she knew, beyond doubt, that if Jack reached out for her, if he challenged her to say she did not love him, then her defences would come crashing down.

Sabrina held out her hand, uttering a cool 'Good day to you.'

She waited, wondering how long she could keep her fingers from shaking. Then it was all over. He ignored her outstretched hand, gave a stiff little bow and left the room without another word.

Chapter Seventeen

Jack walked the half-mile back to Albany, a storm of fury and regret raging inside him. Sabrina had never loved him; she had only desired him, and to that end she had lied, time and again. Perhaps marriage to Sir Roderick Massyngham had scarred her far more than he knew. Or perhaps she had cared for the old rogue after all. He did not like the idea, but whatever the truth, it was clear she did not want him. Heaven knows he had tried his best to win her, but he had gambled enough to know when it was time to stop. So be it. He had wasted long enough trying to win the Wicked Widow and, knowing what he did now, he should be thankful to be free of her. It was time to move on.

He began that very evening, joining a party of friends for dinner before attending a musical soirée, then accompanying Hebden and Oldroyd to a ball, which he left just as the first streaks of dawn were lighting the sky. He strolled back to Albany, slightly befuddled, where he fell into a mercifully sound and dreamless sleep.

Determined to continue with this round of pleasure that gave him little time to dwell on the past, the next morning Jack embarked upon a full day of social engagements that went on well into the early hours of Sunday. And thus it was that the morning coffee Tom Weald left at his bedside remained untouched until the valet returned some hours later with a fresh cup.

'Damn you, Tom, what do you want now?'

'It is nearly two o'clock, my lord. You are engaged to ride out with Mr Claverham in an hour.'

Jack groaned and buried his head under the pillow. He was about to consign Tom to the devil, but he knew it would not do. Appointments must be kept at all costs, and if he stayed in bed he would only spend the time thinking of Sabrina. Confound it, he missed her so much it was like an open wound!

'Very well.' He sat up and reached for the coffee. 'I will need to wash.'

'I have already taken the liberty of ordering hot water to be fetched up, sir. It will be here directly.'

'Wait a moment.' Jack turned a bleary eye towards his man. 'It is Sunday, is it not? I thought I had given you the day off.'

'You did, sir. I shall be away as soon as I have you dressed and fit to be seen.'

Jack grunted. 'What would I do without you, Tom?'

'I dread to think, my lord. I will go and fetch your clean linen.'

The fresh air of Hyde Park and the company of Hugh Claverham and his friends did much to restore Jack's spirits, but he could not ignore the growing restlessness. Perhaps he would retire to Lingwood and throw himself into country pursuits. With the current unrest sweeping the land it might be reassuring to his neighbours and his tenants to have him spend more time at the Priory. His recent trip to Hartland had reminded him of the pleasures of a rural life. Whole days spent out of doors, walking or riding across the land. The satisfaction of helping one's tenants improve their farms with new methods and equipment. Evenings spent talking over your day with the woman you love.

Jack quickly stifled that last idea. He was done with women.

'What say you, Callater? We are all going back to mine for a snug little dinner. Will you join us?' Hugh Claverham's cheerful voice interrupted his thoughts. 'No need to change your clothes, we won't be inviting any females to join us. Just an evening of good food, wine and perhaps a game or two of cards. What do you think of that?'

'I say that is just what I need,' he replied at once.

'Capital!' cried Hugh. 'The light is already fading, let's waste no more time. We'll stable the horses and get to the wine!'

Sabrina returned from the Sunday service and, once she had divested herself of her gloves, bonnet and pelisse, she made her way to the drawing room. A good fire blazed in the hearth and she walked across to warm her hands, but the chill remained in her heart. An unhappy dissatisfaction with her life was never far away these days. She had not been comfortable at church that morning. Oh, she had smiled and greeted her acquaintances, engaging in small talk and idle chatter that had no real importance, but she had not enjoyed herself. It was all so, so *false*! She had been back in town less than a sennight, and already she was sick of it.

'Bless me, my lady, but you haven't touched the cake I brought in for you!'

She looked up to see her maid had come in and was regarding her, hands on her hips.

'I am sorry, Jane. I was not hungry.'

'Now, that ain't like you, ma'am. Are you sure you aren't...sickening for anything?'

Sabrina pressed her lips together. Jane meant was she pining for Jack Callater, which she wasn't. Not at all! That was over. She had made very sure of it now. She moved away from the fire.

'No, no, it is merely a fit of the megrims,' she said, walking to the window. 'I cannot help noticing how much poverty there is in town. It was not only the beggars, who I see now on every corner, but there are so many ragged children, waiting to earn a penny by running an errand or holding a gentleman's horse.' She crossed her arms and hugged herself as she gazed down at the traffic passing below her window. 'Not to mention the street sweepers, surviving on the coins they receive from pampered creatures like myself who want to keep their shoes free of the detritus on the cobbles!'

'Now, Miss Sabrina, you know they have always been there, and they always will. It is not as if you do not make generous donations to any number of good causes.'

'I know, Jane, but the hardship seems so much worse now. Is it any wonder people are growing restless with the injustice of it all? Do you remember Mr Hunt? He used to call upon Papa, when we lived in Russell Square. He is speaking at a rally tomorrow, about this very subject. Although I doubt it will do any good. Society is wilfully blind. It only sees the poor as an inconvenience.'

'Come now, ma'am, not everyone thinks like that,' said Jane, bending to pick up the teacup and plate. 'Lord John for example—'

The mention of his name touched a nerve in Sabrina.

She said bitterly, 'Jack Callater is amongst the worst of them, I am sure. Why, he could not wait to get back to town and all its pleasures. Business, he called it. It was nothing of the sort. He merely wanted to see his friends and go to his club!'

'For your information, madam, the *business* that brought Master Jack back to town was the reorganising of his finances, in order that his tenants and farmers need not worry about their rents during these hard times!'

'How on earth can you know that?'

'I happened to hear it from Mr Weald, and he is not one to make up these things just to puff off his master.'

To Sabrina's amazement, a dull flush appeared in her maid's thin cheeks.

'Yes, well, that's as may be, Jane,' she went on in a quieter tone. 'I really would not know.'

'No, Miss Sabrina,' said Jane, turning for the door. 'I think anyone can be wilfully blind if it suits them!'

* * *

Sabrina watched her departure in surprised silence. Jane was usually very level-headed, but she had clearly fallen under the spell of Jack Callater's charm. In other circumstances Sabrina might have found it amusing, but in her current mood she could not laugh at it. Even worse, thinking of Jack doing some good for his people pricked at her conscience. Dancing until dawn with partners she cared nothing for was a worthless pursuit. She needed to find another outlet for her energies. Something worthwhile. If Mr Hunt was talking at the meeting tomorrow, then perhaps she would go and listen to him. He was a splendid speaker, and she knew he advocated peaceful change. As an old friend of her father's, she had no doubt he would agree to talk with her and discuss what she might do to help his cause.

It was nearing midnight when Jack returned to Albany. He had left the others drinking ever more outrageous toasts to one another, but somehow the evening had fallen sadly flat for him. The walk home through the dark streets had only added to his sombre mood. This life of idleness was doing him no good at all, he thought as he climbed the stairs to his set of rooms. He needed something more.

When he entered his parlour, he was surprised to find the lamps and fire still burning.

'Tom, you still up?' He blinked across the room at his man, then frowned. 'I gave you the day off. Didn't expect to see you until the morning.'

'I know, sir, but I needed to speak with you.'

Jack shook his head. 'Not now, old friend. Not quite sober, you know.'

'I gathered that, my lord, but I have the kettle near the boil, and I could easily prepare a jug of coffee for you?'

Jack wanted nothing but his bed, but there was something about his man's demeanour that gave him pause.

'Is this important?'

'I believe so, sir.'

'Very well then. A tankard of small beer, if you please. And bring something for yourself!'

Five minutes later they were both sitting beside the fire.

'Now,' said Jack, having refreshed himself with a long draught of ale, 'what is it that is so important you need talk to me this minute?'

He leaned forward, his eyes on Tom as the man wrapped both hands about his tankard and stared down into it.

'It concerns Lady Massyngham.' Jack recoiled,

shaking his head, and Tom went on quickly, 'I think she may be heading into trouble, my lord.'

'She is no concern of mine now.'

'I don't believe that, sir. The thing is—'

'Damn you, Tom, how dare you contradict me! I have dismissed men for lesser offences!'

Jack found his man's eyes fixed on him with a disconcertingly clear gaze, and he sighed. They both knew he could never turn away such a faithful servant.

He said, grudgingly, 'Very well, since you have me here, you had best say what is on your mind.'

'Thank you, my lord. I was speaking with Mrs Nidd today, you see, and—'

'Wait. Lady Massyngham's maid? Where the devil did you bump into her?'

Tom shifted in his chair. 'I didn't exactly *bump into her*, my lord. Jane—Mrs Nidd, that is—is very fond of oysters so I escorted her to Mrs Robbins' dining rooms.'

The small beer was clearing Jack's head, and he narrowed his eyes at his man. 'Am I to understand that Mrs Nidd had been given the day off, too?'

'Yes, my lord. That's not unusual, on a Sunday.'

Even in the lamplight, he could see a ruddy stain had coloured his man's cheeks.

'And…is Lady Massyngham aware that you two are…?'

'Mrs Nidd and I are not anything, my lord!' retorted Tom, affronted. 'It's just that we got to know one another while we was in Devonshire and thought we might…keep in touch.'

Jack hid a smile, unwilling to add to his man's discomfiture. Instead he bade him to go on.

'Mrs Nidd is worried, my lord. Her mistress has declared she wants to do something for the poor.'

'Charity work? Good for her.'

'No, my lord. She intends to go and see Mr Henry Hunt.'

'Now, why the devil should she do that?' exclaimed Jack.

'It seems Mr Hunt was a great friend of her father's. He used to visit the family when Sir Anthony lived in London. They held some of their meetings there. And there were other, more radical visitors, too. Jane says Miss Sabrina met them all.'

'But that was years ago.'

'Aye, sir, it was, but Mrs Nidd fears that her mistress hasn't forgotten them and…'

'And what?'

'Since she's returned to town, Lady Massyngham has been different, my lord. Twitchy, Jane called it, and now she declares she must have something to do!'

'That does not mean she is going to campaign for political change,' argued Jack. 'More likely she is going to find some sort of charitable work.'

'Aye, sir. I told Jane that's the sort of thing ladies take up, when they want to do something useful. But she thinks that her mistress picked up some dangerous ideas from those early meetings, and even though Sir Anthony has cut all ties with the radicals now, she is determined to meet up with Mr Hunt.'

Jack thought about it and shook his head. 'No. Sabrina is far too sensible to do that.'

'Then why is she set upon going to the meeting at Spa Fields tomorrow, my lord?'

'The devil she is!' cried Jack, sitting up very straight.

Tom Weald nodded. 'Mrs Nidd is certain of it. And what worries her more is that when she protested that it was too dangerous, her mistress declared she will go alone, and now she has forbidden Jane to go with her!'

Jack frowned. 'And why are you telling me all this?'

'Because we wondered if you would have a word with my lady. She thinks a great deal of you—'

'Now that is where you are wrong,' said Jack bitterly. 'A word from me is likely to send her flying in quite the opposite direction!'

'But Mrs Nidd is that worried, sir. And I admit, I am too. After talking with her, I made a few enquiries of my own and there's a small group of firebrands amongst the organisers who are bent on causing trouble.'

'There will always be some like that in any gathering, Tom.' Jack sat back and closed his eyes. 'Lady Massyngham is old enough to make decisions for herself. I cannot believe she would be so foolish as to attend such a meeting if she thinks it at all dangerous.' He pushed himself out of his chair. 'I am going to bed, and I suggest you do the same.'

'But, sir—'

'No, Tom. I can do nothing to help, and there's an end to it!'

'But there's no knowing what a body will do when they're desperately in love.'

Jack stopped. '*What* did you say?'

'Not I, my lord. Mrs Nidd. She says she knows the signs. Her mistress is not herself.' Tom looked down at the carpet, adding casually, 'She thinks my lady has lost her heart to you.'

'Ha! The woman doesn't *have* a heart. She is a strumpet!'

'That's not what Jane tells me. Miss Sabrina was obliged to marry that old lecher and—'

Jack interrupted him, saying roughly, 'I have no wish to listen to servants' gossip, Tom.'

'Well, this ain't gossip, Master Jack. Lady Massyngham has spent the past six years avoiding all the lures thrown out to her. Not that it was easy, having to host her husband's parties and mix with the very worst sort of people.' Tom snorted. 'Quality, they call themselves, but you and I know many of 'em ain't fit to lick my boots!'

'I know perfectly well the circles she moved in!' Jack growled.

'Aye, and you should know by now that the lady ain't like that at all,' retorted his henchman. 'Jane tells me she never looked at another man until you came along. Proper shook her up it did, meeting you again. And now the poor lady is grieving so hard it's clear she's nursing a broken heart.' Tom paused to scratch his head. 'And it's my belief she's not the only one.'

Jack's scowl deepened and he clenched his jaw against the angry words he wanted to utter. Instead he strode out of the room and slammed the door behind him.

'Blasted interfering servants!' he muttered as he shrugged off his clothes and climbed into bed.

Confounded women. He was damned if he would bother himself about any of them!

Chapter Eighteen

After declaring yesterday that she would not take Jane with her and coming as close as she ever had to falling out with her maid, Sabrina was determined not to change her mind. Her maid's disapproval at attending the meeting at Spa Fields might undermine her resolve to seek out Henry Hunt. And whatever Jane might say, she had no need of a chaperone. She was travelling in her own carriage right to the door of the inn where Mr Hunt was to speak. After that, depending on how their meeting went, she would either remain at the inn or listen to him from the privacy of her carriage. There could be no harm in that.

Sabrina did, however, decide she must dress sensibly for this outing. She chose a plain, chestnut brown pelisse, from which she had removed a frivolous fur collar, and she put on a matching bonnet that not only covered her hair but had the advantage of a wide brim to shield her face from curious eyes.

'There,' she said, regarding herself in the glass. 'I look sober enough, do I not?'

'Oh, Miss Sabrina, let me go with you!'

'No, you had much better stay here. In fact,' she added, after a look at her maid's countenance made her suspect she might set out to follow her, 'I order you to remain in the house today. Do you understand me, Jane?'

Having elicited a promise from her maid, Sabrina set off from Brook Street. It was not yet eleven o'clock, and she planned to speak to Mr Hunt as soon as he arrived at Merlin's Cave, the public house from where he was to make his speech. However, as they approached Clerkenwell the roads became ever more crowded with people moving towards Spa Fields.

After trying several roundabout routes, her coachman came to a halt.

'It's no good, my lady, I can't get no further.'

'Very well, I shall walk,' declared Sabrina, opening the door.

'Do you think that's wise, ma'am?'

'Of course,' she said, pausing on the step to look about her. Everyone she could see was dressed respectably, and it was well known that Henry Hunt was a powerful advocate of peaceful meetings. However, perhaps she would not stay once she had spoken to him 'Wait here, if you please. I shall not be very long.'

* * *

She set off along the street and soon found herself surrounded by several dozen others, all heading in the same direction. As they approached Merlin's Cave, the numbers swelled until everyone was being jostled along. Sabrina began to feel the first stirring of alarm. It was impossible to decide just where they were going, but a question to a woman close by elicited the information that they were all on their way to Coldbath Fields, from where Mr Hunt and his party were expected to make their entrance.

Sabrina considered turning back, but one look at the hordes behind convinced her that it would be more difficult to withdraw than to go on with the throng. She was fairly close to the front of the crowds and she decided that when Mr Hunt did arrive, she would be able to push her way through and attract his attention.

An outbreak of cheering made her look up. Over the assembled heads she could see two flags made of red, white and blue cloth bobbing towards them. There was also a banner bearing the legend, "The Brave Soldiers are our Brothers, treat them kindly."

The words sent a sudden chill down her back. Why would anyone want to brandish such an inscription, unless they were expecting trouble?

Everyone suddenly surged forward. As she was

carried with them, she saw that a waggon had been drawn across the road and two men climbed up onto it. One was Dr Watson and the other man Sabrina recognised as his son, although she had not seen him for several years. She listened to the doctor address the crowd in stirring accents. Her unease increased when James Watson junior took over. It was impossible to make out every word because of the noise around her, but she heard enough to feel concerned.

'The whole country is waiting for a signal from London, my friends!' cried James. 'Then they will fly to arms…there must be no tythes or enclosures… Bishops are no more than useless lumber. Free the prisoners… Storm the Bank of England! Make our demands. No rise in bread. No Regent, no Castlereagh…off with their heads!'

Sabrina was now seriously alarmed. The crowd were already baying for blood as she turned and began to push her way back through the crowd. No one paid any heed to her, but neither did they move out of her way. If she could just reach the buildings at the side of the road…

'Sabrina!' It sounded like Jack's voice, but it couldn't be. 'Sabrina!'

And there he was, beside her. Dizzy with irrational relief, she clutched at his hand. He put an arm about her and began to force a path for them through the crowd until they reached the relatively safety of the pavement. He had pulled her up the steps and into the shelter of a doorway before she found her voice.

'What are you doing here?'

'I came to find you.'

'To find me? B-but why, how?'

'Never mind that now.' He was looking over her head, his eyes darting everywhere. 'We must get out of here.'

Aware of the dangers posed by the baying mob, Jack tried to pull Sabrina closer but she held him off.

'No, I cannot leave yet. I am here to see Henry Hunt.' She turned to stare out over the crowd. 'He must be here by now!'

Jack saw that the younger of the two speakers had jumped down from the waggon and seized one of the flags. He was exhorting everyone to come with him to Threadneedle Street.

'That man is Dr Watson's son, James,' said Sabrina, twisting out of his grasp. 'I know him. I can ask him what has happened to Mr Hunt.'

'Sabrina, no!' Jack followed her down the steps and caught her arm. 'Come out of the way. This is no time to be asking questions.'

The flag was heading in their direction, the mob parting to let the man through and then closing in again behind him, howling and crying like pack animals. But even as Jack was urging Sabrina back into the doorway, Watson spotted them. He turned and moved across towards them.

'Well, well. Miss Kydd. Or should I call you Lady Massyngham now? Come to support us, have you? In lieu of your cowardly father? He's gone off to the country, out of the way!'

Sabrina shook her head at him. 'He had no choice about that, James.'

'Then come and join us, madam.'

The man held out his hand and Jack stepped in front of her.

'No! On your way, sir. She'll not come with you.'

'Ho, is this your latest beau, Sabrina? You want to fight with me, eh, my fine fellow?'

Those closest to Watson picked up on his animosity and immediately launched themselves at Jack. He had neither the time nor the room to draw his sword stick before he found his arms pinned to his sides. He was pulled into the road and several heavy fists pummelled him. As he fell to his knees, he heard Sabrina shout out above the baying mob and his own grunts of pain.

'Stop that! James, tell them to stop. Leave him, get *away* from him!'

'He's agin us!' cried one man, as Sabrina pushed herself between Jack and his assailants.

'No, he is not,' she cried, shielding him from the mob. 'This man is a friend to the people.'

'He's rich,' screeched a voice. 'A damned land-owner hammering his people into the ground!'

They surged forward, but Sabrina stood her ground, raising her voice so that it carried loud and clear as a bell over the crowd.

'*No!* Lord John has *cut* the rents for his tenants and is using his own money to sustain them. He has promised there will be no evictions and he is a man of his word!'

Jack struggled to his feet and Sabrina took his arm to support him. She had lost her bonnet in the fray and some of her dark golden curls had come loose and tumbled over her shoulders. Despite the danger, he felt his heart swell with pride for her as she stood tall and unafraid at his side. The mob had quietened a little and she called across to Watson.

'Call off your men, James. Go on your way, if you must, but leave us be.' She said, earnestly, 'Please, James. For the friendship you and I once shared. For the sake of the fellowship my father showed yours.'

Jack kept silent. Addressing Watson had had an effect. The baying had died to a dull muttering now, but the air around them was still full of anger, and he knew it could very easily turn into violence. He gathered his strength, trying to work out where it hurt most and how best he could protect Sabrina if the mob turned on them again. Watson was wavering, glaring at them. Then, as the crowd around him began to grow restless, he suddenly lifted the flag and waved it.

'Follow me, my friends. We march to Threadneedle Street!'

'And Newgate,' someone yelled. 'To the Bastille!'

Watson moved off and Jack pulled Sabrina against him as the mob surged after their leader. They managed to keep their feet and finally force their way to the side of the road. He placed her against the wall and stood close, his back protecting her from the seething mass of bodies who were still streaming past them. When the noise and the crowd had abated a little, she leaned against him, her head on his shoulder.

'Oh, why did you have to come?' she asked him, her voice breaking. 'Why did you risk yourself for me?'

He gave a ragged laugh. 'Do you really need to ask?'

She looked up at him, dawning wonder in her eyes, and he knew she understood him at last.

'Foolish, foolish man!' Half laughing, half weeping, she buried her face in his coat.

Jack hugged her close, the agony of his bruised ribs as nothing compared to the need to ask another question. 'Why did you protect *me*?'

She went very still, and he held his breath, waiting for her answer.

At last she said, shyly, 'For the same reason, I hope?'

He let out his breath in a long, relieved sigh as she looked up at him. He smiled down at her, ignoring the pain in his bruised cheek.

'I love you, Sabrina Fair.'

With a sob she threw her arms around his neck and kissed him. 'Oh, you foolish, headstrong, *wonderful* man!'

Sabrina gave herself up to the kiss, revelling in the feel of Jack's arms about her, exulting in the fact that he loved her. But such feelings only lasted a few moments. She had not intended to give herself away like that, and she was already regretting her impulsive actions when the noise from the crowded street reminded her that the danger might not yet be over. She put her hands against his chest and, reluctantly, he raised his head.

'What is it, love?'

Instead of answering him, Sabrina looked over his shoulder. She was relieved to see that the mob following James Watson had moved away and were no longer a threat. Then a shout went up from the remaining crowd; someone had spotted a carriage approaching from the other direction.

'Mr Hunt has arrived,' she said.

'Do you wish to stay?'

Jack's question surprised her, but it pleased her, too. He was giving her a choice, allowing her to decide for herself, despite the dangers. However, she knew he would not leave without her.

'Not today,' she told him. 'You took a beating and need to rest. Let us move away from here.'

Jack took her arm. He said nothing but he was glad she had decided to come away. Hundreds of people were still surging into the fields to listen to Henry Hunt, and they had to fight their way through them, against the flow. Jack's ribs were aching badly, every step was painful as they wove their way between the groups of people moving towards Merlin's Cave.

At last the crowds grew thinner and Sabrina pointed down the street.

'There is my coach,' she told him. 'Where is yours?'

'I sent mine away,' Jack replied. 'The traffic was at a stand as I approached Islington. But that is no matter, I will go and find a cab.'

'That would be foolish when my carriage is at hand

and you are in such pain. Do not deny it,' she said quickly, anticipating his reply. 'I can tell from your breathing that your ribs are injured.'

'Bruised, I think, certainly on the left, but nothing broken.'

'Let us hope so.'

Jack put his hand against his side as he drew in another breath. There was no escaping the fact that some of the punches had found their mark. He would be bruised and sore for a few days yet.

He said, when they reached the coach, 'You had best take me to Brook Street. I told Tom Weald to meet me there.'

'Why would you do that?' She looked up at him in surprise.

He said, casually, 'I thought he and Mrs Nidd could support one another until our return.'

His innocent reply drew a smouldering look from Sabrina, but she gave her orders to the driver before climbing into the carriage.

'I suppose it was Mr Weald who told you I was coming here today,' she said, as they began to move.

'Yes. He had it from Mrs Nidd. I hope you will not be angry with her. She is very worried about you, you know.'

'She has no need to be.'

'No? She told Tom that since returning from Hartland you have not been happy.'

'How dare they discuss my concerns!'

'No, it was very wrong of her to tell him, was it not? Just as it was wrong of Tom to inform *her* that I had lowered the rents for my tenants.' He paused. 'That is how you knew about it, I suppose?

'Yes.' A touch of colour stole into her cheeks.

'Dear, dear,' he said mildly. 'Gossiping servants. What should we do, turn them off?'

The stormy look in her eyes faded, and after a moment she laughed. 'You know we cannot do that.'

'Well, we are going to have to do *something*, since they are clearly very taken with one another.' He hesitated, then. 'We could turn one of the attics at Lingwood into their own private quarters for them, I suppose. If you would like to live there, that is, after we are married.'

She flushed. 'We are not going to be married, my lord.'

'I think we must now, don't you?' He took her hand. 'I do love you, you know.'

She looked at him, her eyes troubled. 'Oh, Jack, you don't know me!'

'I know enough, my darling, and the rest makes no odds to me. Although,' he added, teasing her, 'given your reputation as a wicked widow, I am hoping we will both enjoy our nights together...'

Her response surprised him. He thought she might laugh, or be outraged, but he did not expect her to burst into tears. She was sitting on his right, so he was able to put his arm about her without too much discomfort. He drew her close, and she cried into his shoulder while he crooned soothingly.

'Oh, my darling, forgive me. I did not mean to insult you.'

'I know that,' she muttered, hunting for her handkerchief. 'But you do not understand. I have lived a lie for so long. *That* is my true wickedness.' She eased herself out of his hold and sat up very straight. 'I c-cannot marry you unless you know everything about me.'

'Very well, although I doubt anything you say will shock me.'

She gave a little nod, wiped her eyes and sat with the handkerchief scrunched between her hands.

'But I must tell you all of it, then you can judge me for yourself.'

Jack realised it would be useless to tell her he had already made up his mind about her. He sat back again and motioned to her to continue. 'Go on.'

'Sir Roderick promised to return the letters to me, as soon as we were married.' Her head dropped a little lower. 'That is, as soon as the marriage had been c-consummated. But as I told you, he kept them and held the threat over my head for the four years of our marriage. My mother had already persuaded Papa to leave London and Sir Roderick's settlement was generous enough to cover the cost of buying the property in Hartland immediately. The subsequent sale of the house in Russell Square allowed them to live quite comfortably and out of the public eye, but while the threat remained, Papa could not be safe, and I dare not defy my husband.'

Sabrina was silent for a moment, pulling the handkerchief back and forth through her fingers while she searched for the right words. This part was by far the most difficult, for these were her own secrets. Things she had not disclosed to anyone.

'It became clear to me soon after our marriage that Sir Roderick's health was failing. Years of drinking and wenching were catching up with him, but he wanted everyone to believe he was still a great lover. I was part of his pretence, even when I no longer shared his bed. It amused him to have me play hostess for him, but I refused to join in his sordid games.'

She turned her head to look at Jack.

'I said I could never lie to you, but I did. I lied when I told you I had made up all those things I told you of my innocence in order to rouse your desire. I thought… I thought it would give you such a disgust of me that you would never want to see me again.'

'You were right,' he said grimly. 'It did. Almost. But why? Why did you allow the world to think you were as licentious as Rogue Massyngham?'

'To begin with it mattered not to me what anyone thought. And besides, what else could I do? Only when Sir Roderick was dead and I had destroyed the letters could I be free. Until then I kept up a pretence. I remained faithful to my husband but I managed to keep his debauched friends at bay. It was not hard, most of them were already impotent, although I was content to let them boast of their triumph with me.'

'But afterwards, when you became a widow,' said Jack. 'You had a choice, then.'

'Yes.' She went back to tugging at her handkerchief. 'I could retire into pious seclusion or I could go back out into the world. I was four-and-twenty and I craved company. I knew everyone thought me a wicked, decadent woman but I did not care for that. I liked dancing and card parties and attending the theatre. I was very happy to accept a man's escort. It could be very convenient. But, contrary to the rumours, I never took any one of them as a lover, and I allowed no man to call me his mistress.'

'Wait!' He put up his hand, frowning. 'Are you

telling me that in all the years of your marriage, and to this day, you never lost your heart to any man?'

'Yes, I am.' She looked up and met his eyes. 'Because I had already lost it to you, Jack Callater.'

She looked away again quickly.

'I do not expect you to believe me,' she went on. 'I have no doubt you will despise me even more, knowing how much I deceived you.'

'No,' he said, gathering her into his arms. 'I think you have been incredibly noble, and brave. And do not forget that I deceived you, too, when I pretended not to care. But we can put it all behind us now. Let us make a pact. There will be no more lies between us. We will always be honest with one another, as a man and wife should be.'

'There will be gossip.' She held him off. 'My reputation will not be quickly forgotten.'

'If I do not care a jot for that, then neither should you.'

'It is not only that.' She hesitated. 'Do not forget, I cannot give you children.'

'Oh, my dearest heart, that is very sad, but we will overcome that together. We will have each other.'

'But you will be Marquess of Doune one day. You will need an heir.'

'I have brothers, one of them is already married with a hopeful family. The line will not die out.'

'You say that now, but you might change your mind.' She stared at his neckcloth. 'You might fall out of love with me.'

With a laugh he pulled her closer. 'I have not fallen out of love with you in the past six years, despite everything I heard about you. And believe me, I did try to forget you. I tried very hard to do so.'

'I thought you hated me,' she whispered, burying her face in his shoulder.

'No, no, I could never hate you, although I was angry. And hurt, but I never stopped loving you.'

'Oh, Jack!' She threw her arms about him as tears welled up again, but this time they were tears of happiness.

Jack put his hand beneath her chin and tilted her face up towards him.

'It is you that I want,' he told her. 'I cannot live without you. I know there must always be a sadness if we do not have a child of our own, but since it cannot be helped, then we will make the best of it. There will be plenty to do at Lingwood, improving the estate, looking after the farms and the tenants. And we will have visits to London, too. We need not shut ourselves away entirely from the entertainments of the capital. And no doubt you wish to take up some charitable work. You might even wish to do something to support Hunt's political reforms.'

Her eyes widened at that. 'You would allow me to do that?'

'Of course. You are your own woman, my darling, I would not wish to change that.' He shifted his position and winced a little. 'You will have to excuse me if I do not get down on my knees, love, but my ribs are already complaining! So, what do you say, Sabrina Fair? Will you make me the happiest man on earth and marry me?'

His face had grown misty and she blinked hard to clear her vision. 'Yes. Of course I will marry you!'

With a huge sigh of relief he kissed her, exulting in the way she responded to him, forgetting the bruises on his face and body, forgetting everything except the fact that Sabrina loved him.

'Oh, Jack, my darling, Jack,' she sighed, when at last he raised his head. 'I think I must be the most fortunate woman alive!'

'Then I am the luckiest man,' he murmured, smiling down at her. 'I know there is much injustice in our world, Sabrina. I am only too aware of the plight of the poor, and I will be very happy to work with you to remedy that, but not in this way, my love. Not with violence and riots. We will be reformers rather than revolutionaries. There are good men and women in this land who are striving for a peaceful change. We will help them. We will work with them to achieve a vote for every man.'

'Every man?' she murmured, her eyes glinting with mischief. 'Not every woman, too?'

He grinned and pulled her back into his arms. 'One step at a time, my love.'

Epilogue

Norfolk, 1817

'Lingwood Priory is always at its best in the spring,' remarked Jack as the new and luxurious travelling carriage swept through the gates.

Sitting beside him, Sabrina looked eagerly out of the window. She could not see the house yet, but the drive wound its way through a small park dotted with mature trees, and the green grass was brightened by golden swathes of daffodils, nodding in the April sunshine.

'It is quite beautiful.' She turned back to him. 'I love my new home already!'

Her heart soared when she saw how much her remarks pleased him. He took her hand and lifted it to his lips. 'Do you think you can be happy here?'

She answered with a beaming smile. 'If you are with me, my love.'

'Always.'

He pulled her into his arms and kissed her, driving everything else from her mind save the pleasure of loving and being loved by this man. Even after nearly four months of marriage she still could not quite believe her good fortune.

'Look,' he said, when at last he released her. 'You can see the Priory from here… What do you think of it?'

Sabrina sat up and turned to look at the house, its mellow creamy stone walls gleaming in the spring sunshine.

'It is not so large as Massyngham,' Jack went on. 'The original buildings were mostly destroyed during the Reformation and the refectory remodelled into a house. My godfather did a great deal of work on it before he died, so I hope you will find it comfortable enough for the present. There was no time for me to make any major improvements to Lingwood before I brought you here, but in any event, I should like you to be involved in any changes we make. This is your home now, Sabrina.'

'It looks beautiful,' she assured him. 'I cannot wait to show Mama and Papa.' She turned to him and took his hands, feeling her happiness spilling out. 'They were so delighted when we married, Jack. It has done Papa so much good to think I am now comfortably established. Pru wrote to tell me that he and Mama are now involved with all her charities in Hartland and proving themselves a great help.'

'I am very glad to hear it,' said Jack. 'They have promised to visit us in the summer, and we shall entertain them most royally, never fear.'

Sabrina kissed him then turned again to gaze out at the rolling parkland.

'Oh! Is that a real ruin over there?'

She pointed across to a small area of tumbled stone and ragged walls that rose out of the grass.

'Yes.' He laughed. 'We have no need to build romantic follies at Lingwood! That is the remains of the cloisters. Not much, but enough to provide our local poets with inspiration!'

'I shall look forward to exploring.'

'Aye, but not now,' he told her as the carriage slowed. 'First you must meet everyone.'

The array of servants gathered on the drive was a little daunting, and she was thankful to see it was Tom Weald who ran forward to open the door as the carriage drew up.

'How good of you to come on ahead and prepare everything for us,' she greeted him, once Jack had handed her down. 'I hope you and Jane are happy with your new quarters?'

Tom grinned. 'Thank you, ma'am, We are more

than happy. And very grateful that you could do without us for the past two weeks.'

'Pho, it is not as if we could not cope for a few days and allow you to have a honeymoon,' she replied, smiling at him.

Jack saw the dull flush darkening his man's cheeks, and he laughed.

'Enough, madam, you are putting Tom to the blush! Come along and meet everyone.'

The formality of the new mistress's arrival was somewhat eased when Jane came running forward to envelop her mistress in a warm hug, but once the maid was assured that Her Ladyship had survived the journey perfectly well, Jack was able to lead her past the long line of servants.

He smiled to himself as she greeted them all warmly, repeating their names and taking time to exchange a few words with every one of them. Making them all love her, he thought, just as she had done at Hare Hall. His heart swelled with pride for his new wife.

At last he could take her into the drawing room, where he begged her to sit down.

'It has been a long journey, you must be tired.'

'I am far too excited to be tired,' she told him, looking around the room. She removed her gloves and bonnet and cast them onto a chair. 'I cannot wait to see the rest of the house.'

'Well, you must,' he insisted, helping her out of her pelisse. 'You will sit down and take wine with me, and a little cake, before I allow you to move again.'

'Tyrant!'

Sabrina twinkled up at him, and he kissed her swiftly before drawing her down beside him on the sofa. He kept his arm about her and she leaned into him.

Even when the servants brought in the refreshments, he continued to hold her, and as soon as they were alone again, Sabrina reproached him, saying they were acting like newlyweds.

'Which is just what we are,' he reasoned.

That made her laugh. 'No, no, we have been married nearly four months now. It is Jane and Tom Weald who are most recently married.'

'So they are.' Jack got up to pour two glasses of wine and bring them over. 'Such a lot has happened since we were snowbound in Devon.'

It had indeed, thought Sabrina, sipping her wine. Their wedding had taken place on Christmas Day and garnered much public attention. Sir Anthony and Lady Kydd travelled from Devonshire especially for the ceremony, but Sabrina had been concerned that her reputation would overshadow the event. However, she need not have worried. The Marquess and Marchioness of Doune had made the journey to London for the marriage of their eldest son, and the presence of such eminent figures as the Duke and Duchess of Hartland and Lord and Lady Tarleton guaranteed the day's success. Not one of the invitations had been declined.

'Will your neighbours approve of me?' she asked suddenly. 'I am sure some, if not all of them, will have heard of my reputation. And there are your tenants, too…'

'They will all love you,' he told her. 'Especially since it means we will spend most of our time at the Priory. The recent war, followed by the year without a summer, has caused great hardship. It will take us all some time to recover. It is much better for Lingwood if I am here, where they can see that I am working to improve matters and I can explain any changes to them.'

'I should like to help you with that,' she murmured. 'If I may?'

He grinned at her. 'I shall insist upon it! My only concern is that you might grow bored with this rustication.'

'Not I.' She finished her wine and went over to the window, staring out across the park. 'How could one ever be tired of this view?'

He came across to stand beside her. 'I agree with you, it has much to recommend it.'

'And as you say, there will be much to do here.'

'You must not overtire yourself!'

'No, no, but I cannot bear to be idle. There will be the necessary bride visits, of course, and I have my charitable work for the poor and destitute, but when everything settles down, I shall set to work on the house and garden.'

'I think you can be sure you will find plenty to occupy you here, Sabrina.'

'And I cannot wait to explore Lingwood,' she told him. 'The last part of the journey here was so delightful, the primroses growing at the roadsides and then driving through woods carpeted with bluebells. And it was so wonderful to see all the hedgerows, burgeoning with new life!'

'And it is not only the hedgerows that have new life in them,' he murmured, slipping his arms around her.

His hands rested on her stomach and she put her own over them.

'Yes. Our own baby, Jack.'

He bent to kiss her neck. 'I could hardly believe it when you told me.'

'Nor I, but I can easily understand it. The doctor at Massyngham was too afraid of losing his rich patient to tell Sir Roderick that *he* was the problem, and not

I.' She chuckled. 'The poor man would have looked no-how if I had taken a lover and he had been obliged to explain away a child. The very experienced physician I visited in London told me there is no reason why I shouldn't bear you *dozens* of children!'

'No reason at all,' he said, turning her round to face him.

'We shall be the most admirable parents.' She went on, slipping her hands around his neck. 'They will learn to mind us very well. You will be kind, but firm and I...' She gazed up at him, her lips quivering with mischief. 'I shall not have one bad thought. I will be positively saintly!'

His eyes glinted and he pulled her closer. 'Not too saintly, I hope.'

And with that he kissed her, which filled her head with very wicked thoughts indeed.

* * * * *

COMING SOON!

We really hope you enjoyed reading this book.
If you're looking for more romance
be sure to head to the shops when
new books are available on

Thursday 21st
December

To see which titles are coming soon, please visit
millsandboon.co.uk/nextmonth

MILLS & BOON

MILLS & BOON®

Coming next month

A MARQUIS TO PROTECT THE GOVERNESS
Parker J. Cole

'You said you trusted me.'

'I do, André.'

'Then what is this all about?'

He pulled the letter from a hidden pocket of his waistcoat and handed it over to her.

'The letter,' she breathed.

'So you did know about it?'

'Only after Jacqueline told me that I'd received one. I did not know who it was from until you told me.'

Deciding to take her word at face value, he said, 'It's from the king's mistress, as I said.'

An odd look appeared on her face, surprise mixed with unease. He thought for a moment that she would take her leave of him, but instead, she stood there as she opened the letter, reading it in the dim light. When she finished, she placed it back into the envelope and stared out into the darkness.

After a moment, he asked, 'What does it say, Isadora?'

Turning back to him, she said, 'It says that my employer is to escort me to the palace in four days' time.'

His mouth opened and closed. 'Why?'

There was enough light to reveal the changing dynamics

of her face. The uncertainty making the corners of her mouth turn down. The slight melancholy in her eyes before her eyelids drifted downward, shielding them from his gaze. 'I can't say. It's a secret too dangerous to tell.'

'So you won't tell me what a woman I despise is writing to you about,' André countered.

'There's too much at stake, André. My secret is such that, if discovered by the wrong people, it could put the crown in jeopardy.'

It was a very serious claim to make, giving André pause. He mulled over the idea in his mind before he asked, 'Are you a spy?'

Isadora pressed her lips together. 'I cannot say,' she answered finally. 'You will find out everything soon enough.'

Continue reading
A MARQUIS TO PROTECT THE GOVERNESS
Parker J. Cole

Available next month
www.millsandboon.co.uk